## Praise for Anna Castle *Match*

"Sherlock Holmes fans will find *Moriarty Meets His Match* exquisitely well-done: true to the nature and characters of both men, but adding extra dimensions to Professor Moriarty's character that greatly enhance the entire Holmes scenario. Very highly recommended as a 'must' for Sherlock enthusiasts and anyone who relishes a good whodunit mystery." — D. Donovan, Senior Reviewer, Midwest Book Review

"Fans of both Sherlock Holmes and the man he dubbed the 'Napoleon of Crime' will absolutely love Castle's fidelity to the details and atmosphere of the canon, and newcomers who have never read Arthur Conan Doyle (or, for that matter, John Gardner's great Moriarty novels) will also find themselves eagerly reading along, thanks to Castle's great skill as a storyteller. Enthusiastically recommended." — Steve Donoghue, Historical Novel Society Reviews

## Praise for Anna Castle's *Murder by Misrule*

*Murder by Misrule* was selected as one of Kirkus Review's Best Indie Books of 2014.

"Castle's characters brim with zest and real feeling... Though the plot keeps the pages turning, the characters, major and minor, and the well-wrought historical details will make readers want to linger in the 16th century. A laugh-out loud mystery that will delight fans of the genre." — Kirkus, starred review

"*Murder by Misrule* is a delightful debut with characters that leap off the page, especially the brilliant if unwilling detective Francis Bacon and his street smart man Tom Clarady. Elizabeth Tudor rules, but Anna Castle triumphs." — Karen Harper, NY Times best-selling author of *The Queen's Governess*

"Well-researched... *Murder by Misrule* is also enormously entertaining; a mystery shot through with a series of misadventures, misunderstandings, and mendacity worthy of a Shakespearian comedy." — M. Louisa Locke, author of the Victorian San Francisco Mystery Series

"Castle's period research is thorough but unobtrusive, and her delight in the clashing personalities of her crime-fighting duo is palpable: this is the winning fictional odd couple of the year, with Bacon's near-omniscience being effectively grounded by Clarady's street smarts. An extremely promising debut." — Steve Donoghue, Historical Novel Society

"Historical mystery readers take note: *Murder by Misrule* is a wonderful example of Elizabethan times brought to life...a blend of Sherlock Holmes and history." — D. Donovan, eBook Reviewer, Midwest Book Review

"Anna Castle combines humor with a complicated mystery to deliver a fun, satisfying read." — Starting Fresh

"I love when I love a book! *Murder by Misrule* by Anna Castle was a fantastic read. Overall, I really liked this story and highly recommend it." — Book Nerds

## Praise for Anna Castle's *Death by Disputation*

*Death by Disputation* won the 2015 Chaucer Awards First In Category Award for the Elizabethan/Tudor period.

"Castle's style shines ... as she weaves a complex web of scenarios and firmly centers them in Elizabethan culture and times." — D. Donovan, eBook Reviewer, Midwest Book Review

" I would recommend *Death by Disputation* to any fan of historical mysteries, or to anyone interested in what went on in Elizabethan England outside the royal court." — E. Stephenson, Historical Novel Society

"Accurate historical details, page turning plot, bodacious, lovable and believable characters, gorgeous depictions and bewitching use of language will transfer you through time and space back to Elizabethan England." — Edi's Book Lighthouse

"This second book in the Francis Bacon mystery series is as strong as the first. At times bawdy and rowdy, at times thought-provoking ... Castle weaves religious-political intrigue, murder mystery, and Tom's colorful friendships and love life into a tightly-paced plot." — Amber Foxx, Indies Who Publish Everywhere

## Praise for Anna Castle's *The Widows Guild*

*The Widows Guild* was longlisted for the 2017 Historical Novel Society's Indie Award.

"[Castle] brings the Elizabethan world wonderfully to life, and if Francis Bacon seems overshadowed at times in this novel, it's because the great, fun creation of the Widow's Guild steals the spotlight. Strongly Recommended."— Editor's Choice, Historical Novel Society.

# Also by Anna Castle

## The Francis Bacon Mystery Series
Murder by Misrule
Death by Disputation
The Widow's Guild

## The Professor & Mrs. Moriarty Mystery Series
Moriarty Meets His Match
Moriarty Takes His Medicine

## The Lost Hat, Texas Mystery Series
Black & White & Dead All Over
Flash Memory

A Professor & Mrs. Moriarty Mystery — #2

# Moriarty Takes His Medicine

*Anna Castle*

Moriarty Takes His Medicine
A Professor & Mrs. Moriarty Mystery

Print Edition | January 2017
Discover more works by Anna Castle at www.annacastle.com

ISBN-10: 1-945382-06-6
ISBN-13: 978-1-945382-06-2
Produced in the United States of America

*To my brother Jay*

# Chapter One

*London, 1885*

James Moriarty was an unhappy man, at least from eight in the morning until eight at night. For the other half of the twenty-four hour span, he counted himself among the most fortunate of his kind. He loved his wife as passionately as he had on the day he'd married her three months ago. He just didn't know if he could live with her.

Not in this house, at any rate. At Angelina's insistence, they'd taken a lease on a four-story terrace in Kensington, a fashionable neighborhood south of Hyde Park. She dove into the monumental task of furnishing and staffing the overlarge abode with gusto. She spent hours away from home, haunting auctions and furniture warehouses. Copies of *Exchange & Mart* scribbled in red pencil littered the house. Even when she paused to drink a cup of tea or nibble a bite of lunch, wallpaper sample books and Cassell's *Household Guide* commanded her full attention.

Natural enough. The home was a woman's proper sphere of action, after all. It surprised Moriarty that his extraordinary wife had taken so well to that traditional role, but what he knew about women wouldn't fill a teacup.

He didn't begrudge her the occupation, but he couldn't share it with her. In fact, she'd banned him from participation after he suggested they paint all the walls the same color — a soothing bluish gray — to save the mental strain of devising a fresh scheme for each floor. He had no contribution to make, other than to shower her project with funds. This too would be natural enough — except that he had no other sphere.

*Sphere? Bah!* He couldn't find so much as a quiet corner in which to read his newspapers in the morning with a third cup of tea.

He'd just been evicted from the kitchen by a beetle-browed cook who had scolded him up the stairs with a torrent of agitated French. Moriarty had only identified the testy individual as their cook by his puffy white hat. He had never seen the man before.

Juggling teacup and papers, Moriarty emerged from the staircase into the hall, crossing to enter the back sitting room or morning room. Its designation changed on a daily basis. He hoped it might become a library — possibly even his library. It had one empty bookcase and a nice nook beneath the rear windows where a man might read or write letters. Alas, it still had not yet been supplied with chairs, just crates and odd shapes covered with sheets.

The room at the front of the ground floor was the dining room, easily identified by the large octagonal table that had come with the house. The shape pleased Moriarty. He liked the symmetry of it. He kept that opinion to himself, however. If she knew, she'd probably throw it out. That hadn't happened yet, and the table had its own chairs. He could read his paper there.

He peeked through the door to find the spirit of the house pacing around the table, studying a stupefying array of fabric swatches and wallpaper samples. What kind of deranged society required so many different kinds of wallpaper?

Apparently the choice of paper and drapes was a critical one, capable of determining their entire future lives. Success and failure were invisibly coded in each pattern, most of which Moriarty could barely distinguish. He failed to understand the importance of such decisions. His inability to see the imaginary future in place of the actual present was a source of continual frustration for his wife.

Angelina spotted him in the doorway and her eyes flashed a warning. "Not in here, James!" Her voice held an edge. Moriarty's spirits sank. These days her humor depended on whether this green matched that yellow, not on his presence or absence or state of mind.

She would never admit it. They'd argued the housing question at length after returning to London from their extended honeymoon. She'd wanted Mayfair or Belgravia; he'd put his foot down at the expense. He'd suggested Ealing or Bedford Park, respectable new suburbs on the western fringe of the metropolis. She'd crossed her arms and refused to speak to him for a full day.

This end terrace on Bellenden Crescent represented a compromise. Moriarty had not failed to notice that the house was a short walk from Belgravia and a long drive from Bedford Park — typical of their compromises.

"There's nowhere else to sit." Moriarty's heart skipped a beat, as it always did when his gaze lit on her oval face, her russet hair, and her amber-colored eyes. She wore a striped dress of some shiny material, dark blue with a frivolous bow on one hip, accentuating her trim figure. "There are workmen upstairs. They've covered everything with sheets. And that fellow in the kitchen chased me off as if I were a recipe thief."

"Antoine Leclercq," she snapped. "Our cook. I told you about him."

"Did you? I forget which is who. There are different people in here every day." He began edging around the zone of fabrics toward the chairs by the front windows.

She blocked his path. "You can't lounge around in here this morning. The drapery men will be down to measure as soon as they finish upstairs."

"They can work around me. I won't put them off by more than six feet and that only vertically." He chuckled at his wit.

She was not amused. "Really, James. Do try to cooperate, at least until the worst is done."

"I only want a place to read my newspaper. Is that too much to ask? You keep telling me I'm a gentleman of leisure. Well, isn't that what we do? And isn't a seat by the window in the dining room the logical place to do it?"

She clucked her tongue at him. "Logic has nothing to do with life, as you perfectly well know. Can't you read the papers at your club?"

Moriarty belonged to the Pythagoras Club, a haven for mathematicians and scientists. He'd never been there during the day. He didn't even know when they opened the doors. And what would the other men think if they saw him idling about at this hour?

"There are other clubs," Angelina said, reading his mind as she did so often and so easily. Yet after four months, her interior workings remained as mysterious to him as ever. "White's, for example."

"Are we short of money already?"

She shot him a sour look.

White's was the most exclusive club in London and notorious for gambling. The Moriartys were funding their lavish new life with money he'd won during their honeymoon touring the spas and casinos of Europe. He had never gambled before, but, as a mathematician with a special interest in probability theory, he'd caught on quickly. Simple, really, especially card games. It also helped to have a naturally stoic countenance.

"Surely there's something interesting going on at the Royal Society." Angelina spoke in the chipper tone of a mother coaxing a sulky child out-of-doors. That tone always put his back up and he'd been hearing it a lot since they moved into this house.

He hated that tone, but he hated his own futility even more. How many hours could a man spend reading in the libraries at Burlington House? No talks were given in the morning; real scientists worked during the day. Besides, Moriarty had received a chilly welcome at the first meeting he'd attended after they returned to London. The other members remembered all too vividly the turmoil he'd caused last May.

He could go down to the London Athletic Club and take another row on the Thames, but he'd spent three hours doing that yesterday and didn't feel up to it yet. A man's body could only tolerate so much exercise.

"I'll go up and sit in the bedroom," he growled, despising the churlishness in his voice.

"Fine. But don't leave that dirty cup among your clean linens."

The clocks began to chime the quarter hour. There were four smaller clocks, one on each mantelpiece, and a grandfather clock in the hall on the first floor. They kept slightly different times, and their unsynchronized chimes echoed throughout the house. The first chime, a tinny *ting-ting-ting*, started each round from the back half of the upstairs drawing room, followed by this clanking one in the dining room. Then the grandfather clock issued its sonorant bongs. The other two small clocks straggled behind in their distinctive voices. The cacophony lasted a full minute and a half. Moriarty had timed it with his pocket watch.

He'd complained about them, but Angelina had dug in her heels. "I love them," she'd claimed. "They're like little bells tinkling in the wind." He'd given up. Marriage, he was learning, meant choosing your battles.

5

Her attention had already turned back to her samples. Without looking up, she said, "I'm going out in a minute. I'll have lunch near the shops. Antoine will fix something for you. You can eat in the kitchen just this once. And don't forget we have guests for dinner tonight." She swept out of the room, trailing the scent of gardenia in her wake.

That scent aroused him, as always, but now it also made him a little sad. Did all marriages suffer such rocky starts? He doubted it. The fault lay on his shoulders. She had her proper occupation well in hand. He was the one out of place.

Moriarty crept up the stairs, clutching his rumpled papers to his chest. How had he come to this? He had once been a respected professor of mathematics at Durham University, engaged in the life of the mind, training up young scholars and corresponding with colleagues around the world. He'd been cast out of that life through no fault of his own and managed to re-establish himself in London with a decent, often interesting job at the Patent Office. He'd lived the simple, well-ordered life of a bachelor with two rooms in a quiet house and meals delivered by his landlady on an undeviating schedule. He'd expected to remain in that life for many years to come, if not forever.

Then he'd met Angelina and his world turned upside down. He courted her in his awkward way and, after a few exciting weeks, succeeded in bringing her to the altar. The honeymoon had been pure heaven and profitable as well. They'd been so busy enjoying themselves and discovering one another he hadn't given a thought to the future. Now he had plenty of time to consider his options and was forced to recognize that he hadn't any.

He had amassed too great a fortune to sit in a stuffy office for thirty hours a week or to burden himself with pimply undergraduates, even if there were an institution willing to employ him. The scandal of last May clung to him like a factory reek. He could embark on a course of private study of some kind — if he had a place to sit and work, which he did not.

He'd become superfluous to his own life.

He reached the bedroom at the front of the second floor and flopped into the armchair opposite the unmade bed. The sight of the rumpled covers soothed his temper somewhat, reminding him of those nocturnal hours of happiness, without which he could no longer live. He set his cup on the small table, took a sip of cold tea, and opened *The Times*.

He'd barely read one paragraph when the new housemaids scurried in to make the bed. These were two sisters, brown-haired and rosy-cheeked, fresh from the country, and ignorant as mice. Angelina had rescued them from the household of a lecherous master, a man Moriarty also despised. At least he and his wife had the same enemies. Moriarty applauded her motive in giving these girls a safe harbor and they seemed to be good enough at their jobs. Unfortunately, they were terrified of him despite his best efforts to appear unthreatening.

Now they spotted him lurking behind his newspaper and squealed in unison, clutching their dust cloths to their bosoms.

"Don't worry," he said, rising. "I'll go. I'll go — somewhere."

They backed away from him with eyes wide, as fearful and uncomprehending as if he'd leapt up and cursed at them in Chinese.

They blocked his direct path to the hall, so he sidled past the bed to the interior door, which led into a second bedroom now being used as a dressing room for Angelina. Her wardrobe had expanded by an order of magnitude during the three weeks they'd spent in Paris.

"Lookin' for me?" Peg Barwick, Angelina's Cockney lady's maid, stood in a lake of silks and satins, a measuring tape around her plump shoulders.

Moriarty failed to answer, dazzled by the glossy colors and the overwhelming scent of gardenia.

Peg, as always, supplied her own interpretation. She nodded grimly at the clothes. "It's that cook. I told her he'd be the death of us, but no, he's another lost lamb, in trouble through no fault of his own. Which we are all, if you think about it. So now he's got to live in our house, and we're all getting fatter. French cooks, I ask you! Where will it end?"

Moriarty scratched his cheek. He had no more voice in the matter of cooks than Peg. At least he got two or three hours of exercise every day to counter the effects. "I don't know," he said and went back the way he'd come, to be greeted by another round of shrieks.

A man's home should be his castle, but this one had been occupied by a superior force. Well, he had money. He could rent an office. He'd find something near those bastions of masculinity, the Inns of Court. He'd stop at Stamford's bookshop on the way and purchase a Chinese dictionary. He could at least live up — or down — to his housemaids' expectations.

He grabbed his hat and coat, patting his pockets to make sure he had his notecase, and jogged down the stairs. The knocker boomed three times as he reached the ground floor. More workmen, presumably. He'd let them in on his way out.

He pulled open the front door and tucked his chin in sheer astonishment. Instead of burly laborers in cloth caps, he found three gentlemen in top hats. One was a stranger, but the other two he knew, much better than he would like — Dr. John Watson and Mr. Sherlock Holmes.

# Chapter Two

"We've surprised you," the acclaimed detective observed.

"Indeed, you have." Moriarty regained his composure. "I never expected to see either of you again, least of all at my own front door."

Watson, ever the diplomat, offered a smile. "We parted on less than friendly terms, it's true, but we are both very pleased to see how well things have turned out for you. And your lovely wife, of course."

*Less than friendly terms?* That was rich. Holmes had accused Moriarty of cold-blooded murder and handed him over to the police, striding off to the train station without a backward glance. Circumstances had saved Moriarty's neck that day, but within the week, Holmes had threatened to pursue Angelina as well.

Nor had Moriarty forgotten the stunt Holmes had pulled at his wedding. Angelina hadn't noticed and he'd hoped to keep the secret hidden, at least until they found their balance together.

"I never followed through on that burglary matter," Holmes said. "In fact, it was I who recommended Scotland Yard drop the investigation once the burglaries ended. I knew there would be no further evidence."

"I have better things to think about than your affairs." Moriarty eyed his visitors with an unwelcoming gaze.

They hadn't changed a bit. Holmes, as tall as Moriarty, was still as restive as a racehorse, clean-shaven with that axe-like nose. Watson, shorter and stouter, wore the same old-fashioned moustache and genial expression. The third man wore a checkered jacket that barely covered his hips and a hat with a shorter than usual crown. A dandy, evidently.

Holmes met Moriarty's cool gaze with a twinkle. "Come now, Professor. Can't we let bygones be bygones? You went to Rugby — you can take a little rough-and-tumble in the course of a healthy competition. All's well that end's well, wouldn't you say?"

"What could you possibly want from me, Holmes?" Moriarty looked pointedly past him at the stranger.

Holmes stood aside to gesture at the fashionable young man. "This gentleman, Mr. Horace Wexcombe, has presented me with a most intriguing case, whose solution requires certain abilities beyond my capacity to supply. I believe you'll find the matter quite engaging."

"We won't take much of your time," Watson said.

Moriarty hesitated. His wrath had cooled over the summer. He hadn't given Holmes a single thought in months. And after all, the troubles of last May had won him Angelina — a prize worth any struggle.

In retrospect, being stalked and accused by Sherlock Holmes was rather like being buffeted by a summer storm. One didn't blame the wind for blowing. Holmes had followed a trail laid by someone else with deliberate intent to deceive. Moriarty might have reached the same conclusions in his place.

And the sorry truth was that he would rather listen to Holmes pomposticate than study Chinese in a rented office.

"Very well," he said. "I suppose I can spare a few minutes."

He stood back to allow them to enter. They shed their hats and coats, then stood in the empty hall, wondering what to do with them.

"We've only just moved in," Moriarty said. "Everything is still at sixes and sevens." He wished for a less observant guest, knowing his ignorance of his own home would show in every gesture. He waved them toward the room behind the dining room, in case the drapery people were still at work. "Shall we try the library?"

If he referred to the room by that name often enough, perhaps it would stick.

Moriarty assessed the sheet-draped shapes, seeking chairs to offer his guests. There was a bell pull near the mantel, but he dismissed the idea of ringing for tea out of hand. The mere sight of Sherlock Holmes would send the mousy housemaids gibbering into the attic. He ran a hand over his bald pate and cocked his head toward the dining room, but workmen's grunts sounded behind the door. No good.

Holmes chuckled at his discomfiture. He dropped his hat and coat on a crate and leaned his long frame against the mantel. "We're content to remain standing, Professor. And we don't require tea."

Watson adopted the waiting stance of a military man, holding his coat over one arm. Mr. Wexcombe retained his outerwear as well. He grimaced sympathetically at the mottled wall coverings, where yellowed rectangles revealed the absence of artwork. "It's kind of you to let us interrupt your work."

Moriarty planted himself in front of the dining room door. "I'll admit you've aroused my curiosity. What sort of case could require my services?"

"What sort indeed?" Holmes lifted an eyebrow. "Mr. Wexcombe came to me this morning with a curious tale. His aunt, Lady Georgia Estbury, died three days ago under circumstances he considers suspicious. The official verdict was death by misadventure, caused by an overdose of laudanum. Her ladyship was known to be a longtime user of that medicament and had recently returned from a private hospital specializing in the treatment of women with nervous complaints."

"I'm very sorry for your loss," Moriarty said. "But isn't that a common hazard with such drugs?"

"Not as common as the popular press would have you believe," Watson said.

Wexcombe nodded. "Aunt G would never make a mistake like that. She'd been using the stuff most of her life and knew her own tolerance to the grain. And don't think the other thing either," he added hastily. "Aunt G would never take her own life. They're trying to say that she suffered from melancholy. Well, who doesn't now and then? But she loved her life, even when she was down in the dumps."

"Then you don't believe the cause of death was an overdose of opium?" Moriarty asked. "Isn't that the main ingredient in laudanum?"

"Yes to the second question," Holmes said. "As for the first, the inquest will be held next week. That preliminary verdict was provided by the doctor who examined the body at the scene."

"It looks like an overdose, all right," Mr. Wexcombe said. "I believe that. But I don't believe Aunt G gave it to herself. I tried to ask questions, to get someone to listen to me, but Bertram had the constables throw me out."

"Who's Bertram?"

"Bertram Estbury, one of the heirs," Holmes said.

"Not her son," Wexcombe said. "Bertie and Nora are stepchildren. They came with Aunt G's second husband, Bertram Senior. A bit of a scoundrel, if you ask me, but he had a handsome face. The children were nearly grown when Aunt G married him. He died five years ago, but they stayed on in her house. More comfortable than making do for themselves, don't you know." He wrinkled his nose, bristling his short moustache.

12

"Do you suspect them of tampering with her ladyship's medicine?" Moriarty asked.

"Not directly," Holmes said with that infuriating smile that suggested he knew more than anyone else in the room. "Neither of the heirs were at home that week. Bertram was in Germany on business and Eleanor was in Norfolk visiting a friend. Their absence is significant, as you shall learn."

"Sometime today, I hope," Moriarty said.

Holmes chuckled. "I'll be concise. Mr. Wexcombe believes his aunt may be the victim of an extremely clever conspiracy of murderers."

"That sounds fantastic." Moriarty turned to Watson, expecting the stolid doctor to shrug or roll his eyes at Holmes's melodramatic tendencies.

He did neither, only nodding grimly. "I'm afraid it's possible. Implausible, but possible."

"Precisely so," Holmes said. "You'll recall that her ladyship had just returned from a month-long stay in a private hospital. Mr. Wexcombe believes that the doctor who owns that hospital, a well-known Harley Street nerve specialist named Robert Trumbull, has devised a scheme for disposing of unwanted relatives from a distance. There are many methods to choose from, including the manipulation of the tonics he sends home with his victims. The heirs, who have paid for this service, make sure they are far from home and thus free of suspicion."

"That's preposterous!" Moriarty said. "Forgive me, Mr. Wexcombe, but that sounds like a morbid fantasy."

"I would agree with you, Professor," Holmes said, "if Lady Georgia were the only case. But Mr. Wexcombe has heard of several other unexpected deaths of wealthy women with impatient heirs, occurring shortly after their return from Trumbull's hospital."

"I know how crazy it sounds," Wexcombe said. "I felt like a madman myself when I first told the story to Mr. Holmes and Dr. Watson."

"Who are these other women?" Moriarty made an effort to maintain a level tone. The poor young man seemed close to tears.

"Friends of Aunt G's," Wexcombe said. "Her cronies at the spas. You know — other old birds like herself with nervous complaints and time to spare."

Moriarty looked to Holmes for elaboration.

"Her ladyship was a habitué of convalescent retreats and health spas," Holmes said. "There's a circuit, here and on the Continent, frequented by the same persons year after year. Mr. Wexcombe is an aficionado as well."

Wexcombe said, "I know most of Aunt G's friends. The last time I saw them was a few weeks ago in Torquay. Aunt was in Trumbull's hospital by then. They warned me to look out for her when she came home, but I was too late."

Moriarty held up both hands in appeal. "With all due respect, Mr. Wexcombe, rumors from women with nervous complaints don't sound like solid evidence for a murder charge."

"Rumors sometimes contain a germ of truth," Holmes said, "however unlikely they may appear at first." He fished a cigarette and matches out of his pockets and indulged himself in his necessary vice.

Watson said, "I wouldn't dismiss the idea on account of the source. In my experience, these circles of invalids can be very well informed about each other's illnesses and treatments. It's their major topic of conversation and they often rely on each other more than on their relatives, who often treat them with the same skepticism you're showing now, Professor. Quite naturally, in your case."

"I am skeptical as well," Holmes said. "More precisely, I neither believe nor disbelieve. However, if Mr.

Wexcombe's suspicions are correct, that doctor must be stopped. Hence my decision to investigate Lady Georgia's death."

"I see," Moriarty said, finally understanding why they had come to him. "You'll want to start by examining objective forms of evidence. It should be possible to develop statistical data from the public archives. What is the expected rate of mortality in private hospitals among patients suffering from nervous disease? As a basis for comparison, I would also want to know the average mortality rates, by age and sex, at a public institution, like the Middlesex County Asylum."

"What did I tell you, Watson?" Holmes tossed a wink at his friend. "The professor might prove useful on this case as well."

"What do you mean, 'as well'? Didn't you ask for my help?"

"I never said that exactly." Holmes grinned. "As a matter of fact, it isn't your assistance we need. It's your wife's."

The words struck Moriarty like a slap. "You'd better explain yourself, Mr. Holmes, before I throw you right out into the street."

Holmes held out his palms. "My dear Professor! I meant no offense. On the contrary. My invitation should be construed as a compliment."

"A rare one," Watson said. "Holmes doesn't collaborate with women as a rule."

"I find them unpredictable," Holmes said, unruffled by his host's bristling hostility. "Once I realized the extent of your wife's operations last spring, I could only applaud her skill. Her gift for improvisation is extraordinary. She deceived the whole of London society."

"I'll accept the compliment on her behalf," Moriarty said. "What exactly did you want her to do? Not that I'll allow it, mind you. But she might find the idea amusing."

"I hope she'll find it intriguing. An artiste of her caliber won't be content for long with this sort of busywork." Holmes waved his hand at the unfinished room. "I also hope to stimulate her feminine compassion. If Mr. Wexcombe is correct, a trusted medical man is contriving the deaths of patients on behalf of their greedy heirs. Even the remote possibility of such perfidy would merit investigation, but I won't get anywhere by asking questions. No respectable doctor would discuss his patients with an outsider."

Watson said, "The mere fact of your asking would put him on his guard."

"The logical course," Holmes said, "would be to for me to become a patient and spy out the situation in person. Unfortunately, Dr. Trumbull's clientele is exclusively female, as is the circle of women who are our primary source of information at this stage. I pride myself on my talent for disguises, but even I could not pass the prolonged scrutiny of a group of sharp-eyed invalids. Only a woman will do."

Moriarty's jaw dropped at the sheer effrontery of the man. "Do you seriously expect my wife to become the patient of a man you suspect of cold-blooded murder?"

Holmes shrugged. "She'll be perfectly safe in the early stages."

"How many stages do you anticipate?"

"That will depend on what we discover."

"No." Moriarty shook his head. "Absolutely not. Under no circumstances will I permit her to have anything to do with this reckless scheme. My apologies, Mr. Wexcombe, but I'm sure you understand." He strode toward the door, scooping up Holmes's hat and coat as he went. "Allow me to see you out, gentlemen."

They followed him to the front door. Wexcombe murmured a polite apology for having interrupted his day as he and Watson tipped their hats and stepped outside.

Holmes accepted his belongings mutely but was incapable of walking away without getting in the last word.

He donned his hat and cocked a supercilious eyebrow. "Do let us know when your wife takes her decision, Professor. We shouldn't let the trail grow cold."

# Chapter Three

"I honestly cannot believe the man's nerve," James said as he brushed his fringe of hair. He leaned toward the dressing table mirror to tweak the curls at the ends of his moustache, then stood back to inspect the result. "To come here and ask us — us! — to participate in one of his daft schemes."

Angelina caught his sidelong glance as she smudged a touch of color across her lips. They were dressing for their first dinner party in their new home. She'd only invited two guests for this trial run — her sister, Viola, and Lord Brockaway, Viola's protector — but she intended to have many dinner parties, large, glittering, and sought after by all who mattered, once she wriggled her way back into theatrical circles.

James had just finished telling her about his visitors that morning. He'd resorted to this blatant fishing when she failed to display the expected degree of outrage. She didn't disagree about Holmes's cheek; the man had less shame than a fan dancer at the Gaiety. But she'd been *most* intrigued by the way James had told the story. She hadn't seen him so animated since their return from the Continent.

And wasn't *that* an interesting twist? This might be the new direction her brilliant husband so badly needed.

"Holmes is insufferably self-important," she said. "It shows a complete lack of feeling to ask you for any kind of favor after the way he treated you." Never mind that the favor would actually be supplied by her. That could be finessed later. "But how utterly vile if Mr. Wexcombe is right! A doctor, murdering his own patients? It's like something out of a gothic novel."

"You *are* interested." James moved to catch her gaze directly, no longer speaking over her shoulder to the face in the mirror. "Angelina, I forbid it."

She dropped her eyes to her jewelry box. He waited for one stiff moment, then blew out a sigh. They both knew that phrase had little meaning in this marriage. She tucked her tongue in her cheek and cast him a coquettish glance to ease the sting. He granted her a rueful smile.

She echoed the smile, waited a tick, and then said, "He didn't do us any lasting harm in the end though, did he? All's well that ends well, I always think."

"That's what he said." Suspicion narrowed James's brown eyes. "Please tell me you didn't arrange that visit. Surely you wouldn't conspire with that man solely to give me something to do."

"Of course not!" The idea hadn't occurred to her until this very moment. "Really, darling! You're fully capable of occupying yourself. Or you will be once you have time to settle in and look about you."

She drew out a string of garnets and held it against her throat, glancing up at him for approval. He shook his head and took them from her, replacing them with the pearls he'd bought her in Cannes. He fastened them behind her neck and then planted a kiss beside the clasp — for extra security, he always said.

She took his hand and kissed his palm, then held on to it. "We won't give the troubles of those poor, unhappy women another thought. I'm sure Holmes is perfectly capable of solving the mystery without our help. He must know his way around the records offices of London every bit as well as you do. He can look up his own mortality rates or whatever it was you suggested."

James grunted his assent, but his expression grew thoughtful. She bit back a grin. Competitive men were so

19

easy to manage. Trail a challenge under their noses and off they ran.

She rose from the dressing table and smoothed her skirts. James extended an elbow and she took it, allowing him to lead her down to the drawing room. James poured a small glass of sherry for each of them. He had taken charge of the wine purchases and done an admirable job. Unfortunately, that only needed doing every few months. She couldn't trust him to help with the furnishing. The man had absolutely no sense of style. If he had his way, their home would resemble a government institution — bland, sturdy, and functional.

They hadn't time to fall into one of their ongoing arguments about the house before the door cracked open. Rolly, the footman, peeked through the gap as if spying out enemy terrain.

James frowned, puzzled. "Who is that boy? I've seen him hanging about the hall lately."

"He's our new footman, darling." Angelina smiled at the lad. "Walk straight in, Rolly, and introduce the guests."

"Wery well, Missus." He flung the door wide and gestured like a barker at a seaside fair. "Miz Wiola Harcher and 'is lordship, Wyecount Brockaway."

His thick Cockney accent was nearly unintelligible. Angelina had grown up in the East End and even she could barely understand him. He'd done them several favors last spring when she'd been burgling gentlemen's libraries — all in a good cause, but still, technically, criminal. She'd needed expert advice and Rolly had supplied it.

The boy was as bright as a new penny, but had no family and no home. He lived by his wits, picking pockets and running the odd errand or two, but that life led nowhere. Angelina had brought him home and persuaded

Peg to outfit him as a footman. He'd get the hang of it soon enough.

Viola rolled her eyes as he backed out the door. "Is that really the best you could do, Lina?"

Now twenty-four, Viola had been a popular soubrette in London's grandest music halls. She'd parlayed her fame into a successful career as a courtesan, sought after by every fashionable young buck in the *ton*. Poems had been written about the sparkling azure of her eyes and the litheness of her figure as she rode through the park.

Tonight the seams of her dinner gown strained to cover the extra pounds she'd been packing on. Her hair was perfectly styled, thanks to her French maid, but the strands had lost their golden gleam and hollows shadowed her eyes. She looked like she hadn't slept for a week.

Her consort pursed his narrow lips at her rudeness. "Experienced footmen are hard to find these days."

Perry Wilton, third Viscount Brockaway, had won the contest for Viola's charms and supported her in luxury in a stylish flat in St. John's Wood. Angelina had only met Badger, as his friends called him, a few times. Tall, dark, and impassive, he reminded her of Mr. Darcy from *Pride and Prejudice*.

Angelina hoped a similar kindness lay hidden somewhere under that stoic facade. She and the twins, Viola and Sebastian, had been trained from infancy in the confidence game, where success depended on one's ability to read the mark's expressions. Yet both sisters had chosen men with marble faces. She chose not to dwell on what that might mean.

James shook hands with Badger. He looked so handsome in his evening dress; Angelina's heart swelled with pride. She'd stand her mathematics professor next to any peer in the realm — any realm, anytime.

"Good to see you again, my lord," James said. They had met for the first time two weeks ago in the private dining room at the Savoy, where they'd celebrated James's thirty-fifth birthday. They'd hit it off as well as two taciturn gentlemen could do in the midst of a family of actors loudly entertaining one another.

James poured sherry for the guests and they stood about taking tiny sips and smiling tightly for an unbearable length of time, measured out by the counterpoint of the ticking clocks.

Badger broke the awkward silence. "You have my sympathy, Moriarty. You must find it dashed difficult to get any work done with your home in a state of upheaval."

"Oh yes," James said, gamely pretending there was any such work. "But I have every confidence in the genius of the house." He smiled at Angelina. He and the viscount spouted empty phrases at one another about the news, filling the time until dinner was announced.

James led Viola downstairs while Angelina took Badger's elbow. He leveled a baleful glare at the back of Viola's head all the way down. Angelina chattered about her decorating plans, wondering if the two had had a fight in the coach. She'd bet a Renoir it had been Viola's fault. The girl grew more irritable by the day. If she wanted to drive Badger off, she was going about it the right way.

James paused inside the dining room, blinking at the brightness of the light. "Well, well! Isn't this a striking alteration!" His overly hearty voice rang against the walls.

The room had seemed so dull and dark Angelina had ordered a bigger gas chandelier to augment the sconces on either side of the fireplace. She'd thought the red flocked wallpaper good enough to keep, but under the flood of yellow light it glowed like fresh blood. Now the room looked a stage set for *Varney the Vampire*.

Viola snickered as James seated her at the table. "Striking isn't quite the right word."

Lord Brockaway's nostrils flared as he drew in a sharp breath, but he said nothing as he guided Angelina to her chair.

At least the table was lovely, covered with pristine linen that showed her new rose-patterned dinnerware to advantage. The cook had provided a centerpiece of polished fruit and Angelina herself had folded the napkins artfully at each place.

Once everyone was seated, Rolly poured the amontillado, then served the consommé. He had a natural grace and had been practicing under the cook's tutelage. As long as he kept his mouth closed, he really performed his duties rather well.

Angelina held her breath as the men took their first tastes.

"This is extraordinary," Badger said, frowning into his plate. "Truly exceptional."

"Delicious," James said. "Well done, my dear."

Angelina exhaled. Her first success. "I'm so relieved. They say consommé is the true test of a cook. I hired Antoine purely by reputation. Cook is such a tricky position to fill. He must be both a sensitive artist and a man who can work under pressure."

Viola sniffed at her full spoon but returned the portion to her plate. "I don't know why you bother. One can have anything catered these days."

Another topic deflated. They ate their soup in silence until Angelina caught James's gaze and said, "Why don't you tell his lordship about the hiking you did in Montecatini?"

"Oh yes," Badger said. "I would find that tremendously interesting."

James proceeded to tell him the same story he'd told at his birthday dinner, in nearly the same words. Badger

23

made the same comments he'd made before and then retold his own Alpine story. The men discussed hiking as if the subject were entirely fresh, branching on to Switzerland and Austria with only a hint of doggedness in their tones. Thank heaven for the automatic courtesies of the upper classes!

The Alps got them through the fish and on to the main course. Viola was no help whatsoever. She'd been Lord Brockaway's London hostess for two years, entertaining the most important men in European financial circles at her weekly salons. One of a courtesan's most important jobs was facilitating conversations, for pity's sake! But tonight she mutely poked at her plate, emanating a sullen sulkiness that dampened everyone's mood.

The men's conversation faltered as they focused their attention on the beef Wellington. Antoine had outdone himself. The pastry fairly floated off the fork and the roast melted on the tongue. Asparagus *al dente* and small roast potatoes made the perfect accompaniments along with a rich mushroom sauce that Rolly ladled out with a generous hand. The meal deserved silent devotion.

Viola pushed bits of food around her plate with a melancholy air. Badger's gaze dropped to her restless fork every few seconds, although he never looked directly at her, nor she at him, in spite of their sitting opposite one another. It took real effort to sit across from a person and never meet their eyes. *What* was the matter with those two?

Even James could feel the tension, judging by the forced jollity in his voice as he offered more wine.

At last, they reached the final course. Rolly served slices of Napoleon cake on small crystal plates and poured glasses of a fragrant Riesling. Angelina recognized its quality, but she'd drunk too many glasses of wine already in her effort to brighten the mood and she'd eaten too much beef to appreciate the cake. She wanted nothing more than a cup of strong coffee and a softer chair.

She tried to catch her sister's eyes, which had fixed upon a bunch of white grapes as if they were portents of her doom. Angelina mustered a cheerfulness she didn't feel and said, "Viola, darling, shall we leave the men to their port?" She had to call her name twice before catching her attention.

Viola struggled out of her chair with the grace of an exhausted charwoman. Badger watched her with furled eyebrows as she shuffled toward the door.

Angelina walked around the table to place a hand on her husband's shoulder and bent to plant a small kiss beneath his ear. "Take your time," she whispered. "Please!" She smiled at Badger as if nothing were amiss and followed her sister out of the dining room.

Viola clung to the mahogany banister as she hauled herself up each step. "What possessed you to choose such a big house, Lina? People like you and James usually live in a flat, like mine. It's easier to furnish, and you only need a couple of servants."

"There aren't any other people like me and James," Angelina said. "Professors don't marry actresses."

"Good thing you're not really married, then."

"Shh!" Angelina hissed. "This stairwell funnels voices like a monster ear trumpet."

Viola flinched dramatically and tiptoed the rest of the way up. She paused inside the drawing room to catch her breath. "This room is too empty; that's the first thing that's wrong with it. You don't even have any plants."

"Oh, I can't cope with plants yet!" Angelina stood next to her sister and tried to view the decor through Viola's sophisticated eyes. It positively shouted 1865, which was when it had last been decorated. "At least I've gotten rid of all the paintings of winsome tots and picturesque farms."

"But now you've got bald patches on your walls."

Angelina laughed, enjoying the shared moment. "This paper will come off eventually. I'll have to find some artwork to hang too. I hadn't realized how little James and I actually possess in the way of furnishings."

"Three trunks of dresses on your side," Viola said. "What did he bring?"

"Only that chair." Angelina pointed at an armchair upholstered in a dull brown fabric, worn shiny in patches with scorch marks up one side from being pulled too close to an open fire. "He's had it since Cambridge. He loves that hideous thing almost as much as he loves me."

"Oh dear," Viola said. "I begin to comprehend your problem."

"It'll all come together eventually." Angelina waved her sister toward the sofa and went to the well-stocked side table to pour small cups of coffee from her new silver service. The rooms might be ugly, but they were clean and the refreshments were tip-top.

She stirred sugar into each cup and handed one to Viola. She assembled a small plate of petits fours, then sat in one of the Louis Quinze chairs. "I'll confess I had no idea how much work this would be. And I'm no good at hiring servants. I have only the fuzziest idea of what sorts do which jobs and no notion at all about fair wages."

"So you hire the ones with the saddest stories and pay them twice the going rate." Viola grunted as she lowered herself onto the sofa.

"I can't seem to help it." Angelina had always been a soft touch. It hadn't mattered so much when she'd changed hotels every few months.

Viola took a tentative sip from her cup, blinked, and took another, rolling it on her tongue. "This coffee is perfect."

"Antoine is a genius. My methods work some of the time."

"Where did you find him?"

"Madame Vivier recommended him." A dressmaker by trade, Madame Vivier supplied fashionable ladies with the latest Paris styles. She also helped them turn the odd bauble into ready cash when they overspent their allowances.

"Oh, Lina! Is Antoine a pawnbroker too?"

"No, he's a forger. Quite the *artiste,* apparently. He took up cooking to relieve his nerves. He's wanted by the French Sûreté and is certain they'll track him to London any day now." She swallowed a sip of the coffee and hummed with pleasure. "I'm not sure what he did, to be honest. But there are advantages to having servants who are afraid to leave the house."

Viola laughed with a hint of her old gaiety.

Angelina seized the moment. "I could use help with the decorating, if you have the time."

Her ploy fell flat. Viola heaved a weary sigh. "I can't imagine taking on a place this size. Big houses are for people with herds of children."

Angelina didn't bother to answer that. There weren't going to be any children, as her sister knew perfectly well. "Fine. I'll get James a copy of Eastlake's *Hints on Household Taste.* Maybe I can present it as a challenge in domestic economy."

Viola leveled a warning look from under her arched eyebrows. "You can't put him off with busywork, Lina. That man doesn't need hobbies. He needs a profession. Trust me, I know the type. He wants challenging work to give him status and a sense of purpose."

"You're right. I know you're right." Angelina bit her lip. "But what can he do? After the scandal last May, all the usual avenues are closed to him. I've ruined him, Viola."

"Nonsense. Only a handful of people know the whole story. People were shocked when the famous American heiress married a humble patent officer, but beyond that . . ." Viola lifted one dismissive shoulder.

"Beyond that, we were both arrested, a company went bankrupt, and a noble family departed in the middle of the Season in unseemly haste."

"Scarcely half a dozen people know any part of that. If you live quietly for a year or two, the scandal will die down, you'll see."

"And there is the rub," Angelina said. "I can't live quietly. I've simply got to get back on the stage. It's like a *hunger*." She snatched up a petit four and popped the whole thing into her mouth as a feeble substitute.

"Oh my! What brought this on?"

"It's always been there, underneath. But we saw *The Lights o' London* at Princess's Theater last week. I played *La Périchole* there, remember? When I was seventeen? The smell of the place brought it all back to me — the lights, the crowd, the orchestra." She shivered with pleasure. "The applause gave me gooseflesh. It was as thrilling as if it were me up there taking the bows. James slept through the second act, but the whole thing left me with the most appalling case of footlight fever."

"You were marvelous in your day," Viola said. She sounded as if she thought those days were gone forever. Ancient history.

"I want another day. I want a new career. That's why I need this house. I mean to rebuild my acquaintance among the theater crowd and work myself back into the swing. That means *lots* of entertaining."

"Have you mentioned this fever to your husband?"

"Of course not. He can barely find his way to the bathroom and he startles every time he catches sight of a servant. One step at a time, darling. He won't object, I don't think. But once I land a starring role, he really will be ruined. No university would hire a man whose wife stands up on a stage and sings in public."

"Nor would any government office. There's nothing stuffier than the respectable middle class." Viola clucked her tongue. "I don't know *what* possessed you to choose a vicar's son, Lina. If you'd taken one of the lesser peers hanging about you last spring, you'd have no trouble at all. He'd set you up in a flat, visit you every second Tuesday, and send flowers to your dressing room on opening nights."

"Ugh! I couldn't abide those useless fops. *Too* boring, darling, especially with James lurking around the fringes looking all intense and interesting." Angelina sighed. "I do love that man. And I want him to be happy, if I can figure out how."

"Funny how we both go for the serious type." Viola's face grew so sad she seemed on the brink of tears. She gave her head a little shake and the expression vanished. "James won't tolerate idleness for long. Few men will; you have to be bred to it. Mark my words, his temper will turn sour, and he'll blame you."

"That's my deepest dread." Angelina ate another petit four, taking two tiny bites this time. "Between you and me, I have had the glimmer of an idea. I'm not quite ready to share it, but it could be just the thing."

The glimmer came from a spark lit by the unexpected visit of Sherlock Holmes. Angelina didn't trust the man and never would, but James had been his old confident self while telling her that story, his magnificent brain responding to the challenge in spite of his distaste for the source.

Her inspiration went beyond this particular case, however. She could see a whole new career for her brilliant husband. If Holmes could set himself up as a consulting detective, why shouldn't James? The work seemed chiefly to involve a bit of poking around followed by a spot of clever thinking. James could do that as well as anyone. Better.

He could start by helping Holmes with this nerve doctor business, learning the tricks of the trade, so to speak. Then they could let it be known that Professor Moriarty was available to solve ticklish problems of a confidential nature. Theater people were always getting into trouble one way or another. Clients would beat the door down.

Viola cocked her head and regarded her with a calculating look. "Don't blame me when James stamps out your bright idea with both feet. We tell ourselves that our cool intellectual men have warm hearts hidden deep inside, but they don't. They're cold all the way through. The minute their needs fail to be met, they walk away."

"Nonsense," Angelina said, although she often feared James would leave her if he ever learned all the sordid secrets of her past. She pushed away that thought with another sweet. "I can't stop eating these things. They're exquisite. Do try one. You hardly touched your dinner." She pushed the crystal plate an inch closer to her sister.

Viola flinched as if she'd offered her a dish of squashed bugs.

"What's wrong with you, Viola? You're all out of sorts tonight."

"Tonight and every night." Viola leaned back against the cushions, rubbing her midsection as if soothing a bellyache. "I'm an utter ruin. I can see it every time I look in the mirror. I'm past my prime. I have no sparkle and my looks are gone."

"Don't be absurd!" Angelina pretended disbelief, but Viola really had let herself go. Her dewy complexion had turned sallow and her lips were parched. Her figure, once trim from riding and dancing, had gone pudgy and slack. The only thing holding her up was her well-boned evening corset.

30

Viola watched her make this assessment with a challenge in her shadowed eyes. Then she looked away and said in a small voice, "I'm afraid Badger wants to set me aside. He's tired of me being so tired all the time. I'm no use to him anymore. I can't do my job and I'm hideous."

"Nonsense! I'm sure he loves you as much as he ever did." Angelina spoke briskly. A less honorable man would have broken the connection already. A courtesan's first job was beauty; her second was boundless amiability. "But for the sake of argument, let's pretend he's lost his mind. It wouldn't be the end of the world, would it? You could take a holiday at some lovely retreat and come back better than ever. You'd have a new champion before you could unpack your negligees."

"Impossible. He can't let me go. I know too much about his affairs. His government work, you know. I've served cocktails to foreign attachés who weren't even supposed to be in the country. He can never allow me to be taken up by another man."

"Nonsense," Angelina said, her conviction fading. "You just have to pull yourself together, darling. Start riding again. You used to love that. I'll go with you."

Viola shrank into the sofa. "Oh no. I can't even imagine it. I barely have the strength to struggle into a loose dress by midafternoon. I honestly don't know what's wrong with me."

She looked so forlorn Angelina sprang out of her chair and sat beside her, wrapping her arms around her sister's shoulders. She rocked her a little, or made a gesture in that direction. Their dinner clothes didn't permit much flexibility.

She planted a kiss on Viola's temple. "Come live with us, darling. I'll take care of you. My marvelous new cook will fatten you up and put the roses back in your cheeks."

31

Viola jerked her head away with a peevish whine. "I'm already fat. I need more than possets and bland soups. Badger thinks I should see a nerve specialist."

"Does he?"

"Some doctor named Trumbull. He's considered the top man in the field. He has consulting rooms on Harley Street and everyone of importance goes to him. He even has his own line of tonics and a private hospital."

A shiver of fear ran up Angelina's spine at the sound of that name. "What does Badger know about nerve specialists? He's as healthy as a horse and utterly nerveless."

"The recommendation comes from his wife."

"Lady Brockaway? I thought he loathed her."

"He does, but this is her area of expertise. She's something of a professional invalid, you know. A complete hypochondriac. She absolutely lives on the spa circuit. It used to be her liver, apparently, but now that nerves are the thing, she has nerves. She swears by this Dr. Trumbull."

The famous Harley Street specialist with his own private hospital. A month of expert care away from the prying eyes of friends and relations. And after that? Home again, this time with a specially crafted supply of laudanum?

\* \* \*

The party didn't last long after the men joined them. Badger drank one polite cup of coffee and admired the petits fours without touching them. Within twenty minutes, he had ushered Viola down the stairs, wrapped her in her fur-lined cloak, and taken her away.

Now Angelina sat again at her dressing table, brushing her long auburn hair by the light of a single lamp turned down low. She'd left her clothes in a heap and pulled a warm nightdress over her head, buttoning it right up to the chin. She scuffed her feet into a pair of woolly slippers.

After four months, the honeymoon was over. They now ventured into uncharted territory.

She was James's first intimate relationship. She'd had other lovers but had never settled into this vast, unbounded domesticity. How long could it last? How long would it be before she dropped one too many straws on his broad back and he shook them all off, retreating to his bachelor lodgings in Bayswater?

She'd loved him from the day they'd met. Well, almost. He'd saved her life that day, but it was more than that. She had seen the warm heart inside the stoic exterior. The lonely man with love to give, but no idea how. James Moriarty was the wisest, kindest, strongest, bravest man she'd ever known. It was simply inconceivable that such a man would stay with her once familiarity stripped away her facades.

They weren't legally tied, after all. She'd signed a false name to the marriage license, not ready to tell him her whole complicated history. He'd thought her name was Gould, so that's what she'd written. She kept meaning to confess, but the timing was never quite right. Now it was too late to bring it up.

It might never matter. He might never need to know. But the secret lurked at the heart of their marriage like the villain in a melodrama, waiting to leap out at the worst possible moment.

James had hung his own suit neatly in his wardrobe. He wore a calf-length flannel nightshirt and fleece-lined slippers. She adored him in this homey costume; he looked so everyday and contented. He sat on a padded stool at the edge of her dressing table to tend to his fingernails. He visited the barber twice a week and did for

33

himself in between — thrifty bachelor habits ingrained since his frugal years at university.

They performed their little rituals in companionable silence for a while. This was one of their favorite times of day. She loved the peacefulness that smoothed his face while he watched her in the mirror. She felt the same way watching him, so attached to him it alarmed her. It was like falling into a deep well filled with something very, very soft. Lovely while falling, but would she ever be able to climb out?

Not without destroying the well.

She shook her hair behind her shoulders and drew forward another strand to work on. Then she broached the subject that had been brewing in the back of her mind all evening.

"James?" She gave the word a little uplift of intonation to warn him of a tricky topic. "Perhaps we should consider Holmes's proposal. We could at least have them for tea. I would rather like to hear Mr. Wexcombe's story for myself."

"I thought we'd settled this." He clutched his bit of chamois in his long fingers and frowned at her. "What are you thinking, my dear? You've got that crafty gleam in your eye."

"Oh, you know me too well." She set down her brush and faced him squarely. "I'm worried about Viola, James. She's terribly unwell."

"She did seem awfully feeble this evening. I wasn't sure she'd make it through the meal. That young woman needs a week at the seaside. You should take her."

"She's not just tired. I'm afraid something may really be wrong with her. But that's not all. Badger wants her to see a nerve specialist — that very same Dr. Trumbull that Holmes's client suspects of murder!"

"Ah, I see. But, my dear, you know that story is purest lunacy. Only Holmes could credit something so far-fetched."

Angelina pursed her lips. "I'm sure you're right, but I must know. If this doctor is murdering his patients, he isn't doing it to amuse himself; at least I hope not. He's doing it for money, to benefit someone else. The heirs in Lady Georgia's case, but mightn't it be anyone wishing to dispose of an inconvenient woman?"

"Ah. I do see. You mean someone like a viscount who does ticklish work for the foreign office, whose mistress no longer serves his needs."

"She's the only sister I've got, James. I can't risk her."

James nodded with pursed lips, then gave a little shrug. He took her hand and turned it over to plant a kiss in her palm. "Very well, my dear. If it will set your mind at ease, let's invite them back and see what the old sleuth hound has in mind."

# Chapter Four

Moriarty spent a good portion of the weekend in the libraries at Burlington House, reviewing the literature on nervous disorders. He'd sent a note to Holmes and Watson inviting them to bring their client to tea on Tuesday afternoon to tell his story, but he had no intention of twiddling his thumbs in the meantime. Nor would he accept Holmes's interpretation of Mr. Wexcombe's story without independent substantiation.

The English were fortunate to live in an age of rapid advancement on the scientific and medical fronts. The diagnosis and treatment of the so-called psychological illnesses improved constantly, as did the understanding of drugs and their effects. Better to brush up while he had the time than be caught wanting by Sherlock Holmes.

Moriarty's research turned up the name of an alienist with a scientific bent named Alan Fairchild. The doctor had published many articles in the *Journal of Mental Science*, among others. The articles supplied an address: the Second Middlesex County Pauper Lunatic Asylum at Colney Hatch. The village lay on the northwest fringe of the London metropolis. Bradshaw's Guide showed trains running direct from Paddington Station every hour.

Guessing that a large public hospital would operate on a similar schedule to a university, Moriarty calculated that he might find the doctor in his office around ten o'clock on a Monday morning. By then, he would have met with his staff and returned to his own desk to contemplate his weekly agenda over a cup of tea.

Moriarty rose on Monday morning with a revitalizing sense of purpose. He performed the usual ablutions at the washstand and dressed as he would have done for his old job at the Patent Office, in a well-brushed coat and striped trousers. He tucked a notebook into his pocket, thinking he might jot down his impressions on the return journey.

He ate a good breakfast, rising from the table without asking for that slothful third cup of tea he'd fallen into the habit of taking. He kissed his wife on the cheek and said, "Busy morning, my dear. Don't worry if I'm late for lunch."

She blinked at him as if surprised, but Moriarty had long since seen through her womanly wiles. She'd been worried about him since they'd come home, sensing his restlessness. Now she'd found a way to cure two birds with one tonic by involving him in this nerve doctor affair. She'd protect her sister and provide him with an intriguing challenge in one stroke.

Besides, nothing would give him greater pleasure than learning something to put Holmes's oversized nose out of joint.

Moriarty walked to Brompton Road and hailed a hackney cab to take him to Paddington Station. The westbound train pulled in only two minutes late. When he arrived at the Friern Barnet Station, he found another cab to drive him to the hospital. The whole journey, door to door, took less than an hour. While he had thoroughly enjoyed exploring the capitals of Europe in the company of his cosmopolitan wife, nothing on the Continent could compete with the sheer efficiency of the British transportation system.

The drive from the northeast corner of the hospital to the main entrance in the middle took nearly as long as the drive from the station to the hospital grounds. The place was huge; quite simply enormous. Moriarty had read about it, but the article had not prepared him for the full impact. This asylum had been the most up-to-date facility in Europe when it was built in 1851, meant to embody the best principles about the care and treatment of lunatics. Demand had rapidly outstripped the founders' intentions. Designed to house a thousand patients, it now held more than twice that number, most of them drawn from the neighborhoods in east London.

From the outside, the hospital looked like an elongated Italian palace with two wings extending from a central tower topped with a graceful cupola. Smaller towers, most likely administrative blocks, punctuated the long runs of wards. Rolling parkland filled the scene behind it; the very picture of a wholesome situation.

A nurse at the desk in the lobby offered to guide Moriarty to Dr. Fairchild's office. He followed her into a corridor that seemed to stretch to the horizon — an infinite tunnel smelling heavily of carbolic, arched windows on one side and an occasional door on the other. White paint peeled on the walls. Gas lines ran the full length, making it feel like a basement in spite of the windows. Moriarty could hear women's voices behind the wall on his right, crying, wailing, shouting. The windows looked on to an airing yard where a nurse in a white cap led some fifty women in a series of exercises.

A male orderly picked up trash in a corner of yard. He turned to watch Moriarty through the windows and flashed a brief smile. *Holmes!* It was impossible to get ahead of that man.

After a walk of many minutes' duration, Moriarty and the nurse reached the administrative hub of the east wing — the women's wing. She led him up a scuffed staircase to the first floor and opened a door labeled "17." She poked her head in and said, "You have a visitor, Doctor." Then she granted Moriarty a short nod and clacked away.

The office was a large one, evidently shared by several doctors, although two of the three desks were unoccupied. Dr. Fairchild, a slender man with blond hair and a Van Dyke beard, sat behind the messiest of the three desks, surrounded by stacks of papers. He probably spent more time filing reports than seeing patients and might resent this interruption. But no, he leapt to his feet and extended a welcoming hand. "Good morning! What can I do for you, Mr.—?"

"Moriarty. James Moriarty. I apologize for the intrusion."

"Not at all! Not at all!"

Another stroke of luck. The good doctor would clearly rather chat than do paperwork.

"I promise not to take much of your time," Moriarty said. "I read an article of yours in the *Journal of Mental Science* the other day and found it intriguing. I thought I might trouble you with a few questions."

"By all means! Sit down, sit down." The doctor indicated a chair facing the desk, then returned to his own seat. He leaned forward, setting his elbows on his desk and giving Moriarty his full attention. "Are you a medical man, Mr. Moriarty?"

"No, I'm a mathematician with an interest in statistics. A personal matter turned my attention toward nervous disorders."

"I see. Well, I do take a few private patients, but not on these premises. Of course, the place to start is always with your family physician."

"Oh no. I'm not seeking a consultation." Moriarty chuckled to cover his embarrassment at the misinterpretation. "No, I'm interested in the larger picture. One hears so much about nerves these days, yet the term seems to mean different things to different people. How is a nervous disorder diagnosed?"

Dr. Fairchild had started shaking his head and his hand before the end of the question. "That is *the* fundamental problem. There are no typical symptoms. Every case is unique. Where, for example, should we draw the line between temporary conditions, such as a response to difficult circumstances, and the beginnings of serious illness? How do we distinguish the trivial from the acute? Insomnia might be the first sign or, contrarily, excessive drowsiness. Other diagnostic symptoms include bad dreams, noises in the ears, numbness in the extremities, irritability, unwarranted fears, indecisiveness, feelings of hopelessness, feelings of grandiosity, and impotence."

"Great Scott," Moriarty said. "I begin to see the scope of the problem. Do you postulate an equal variety of causes?"

"One might, at first glance. This patient drinks too much, that one works too much, this one has a family history of mental disturbance. But dig beneath the surface and you'll find a common underlying cause." Fairchild flashed a smile. "You're a man of science, Mr. Moriarty. You'll appreciate this analogy. Compare the human brain to a voltaic battery which generates nerve force rather than electricity. Like a battery, the brain can be drained by overexertion, whether mental or physical. When this happens, the patient feels listless and out of sorts. He has trouble making decisions and is unable to enjoy his former activities. He no longer has the vigor he needs to perform his usual professional and domestic roles."

"You say 'he,' Doctor, but aren't women more susceptible to nervous disorders?"

Fairchild puffed that away with a dismissive snort. "That's the old cliché about the useless middle-aged spinster or the widow with grown children, blessed with independent means but with no fruitful occupation. The so-called 'superfluous woman.' That's far less common than you might think. A healthy woman can always find something useful to do." He leaned back in his chair, hooking his left thumb in his vest pocket and gesturing with his right hand. "But it is true that a woman's nervous system is more fragile than a man's and more volatile. Imagine the greater play of finer wires strung more loosely, to continue our electrical analogy. They would be more sensitive to pressure and more quickly burned up by strong currents."

Moriarty reflected on the two women he knew best — his wife and his mother — both of whom had nerves of steel.

Dr. Fairchild sat forward with startling energy, stabbing a finger straight at Moriarty. "But don't imagine men have any natural immunity. Not so! Given the rapid pace of modern life, with society and technology changing before our very eyes, the male of the species is more vulnerable than at any other time in history. Educated, intellectual men like you and and me, Mr. Moriarty, are especially at risk. The pressure to succeed, to excel, is relentless. Many men overdo it and find themselves drained of their essential vigor, suffering a profound exhaustion exacerbated by anxiety about the failure to provide for the moral needs of their spouse. No, no. Mental illness is no respecter of persons. Even strong men can succumb if the pressure is great enough."

"I am duly warned." Moriarty tried to look chastened, although the last thing he had to worry about was an excess of work.

Dr. Fairchild gave Moriarty a penetrating look. "It's best to seek treatment at the first sign of trouble, you know. Neglect only leads to a vicious downward spiral, which can result in a breakdown of the system and a complete collapse of normal function."

"That's a dire prognosis. What happens then?"

"You end up in a hospital, my dear man — if you're lucky. That's why early intervention is so important."

"What treatment can the hospital provide? How can the battery be recharged?"

The doctor nodded, smiling at the use of his favorite analogy. "We have a variety of methods, constantly being refined. Diet, of course, is the backbone of any sound therapeutic regimen. Some doctors advocate complete rest, but I believe nothing is as beneficial as fresh air and exercise, which cost relatively little to provide. Then, when possible, we add additional treatments according to the specific complaint. Hydrotherapy is effective for anxious or depressed persons. Electrotherapy is recommended for nervous exhaustion."

Moriarty nodded, absorbing the information. "You don't mention drugs. Is medicine no longer recommended for the treatment of mental disease?"

"Naturally drugs remain an essential tool. There are some promising improvements in that area, as matter of fact. Heroin, for example, is a new derivative of opium that is highly effective in treating pain. Its application to nervous diseases remains to be explored."

"It sounds promising, especially if it's less addictive than laudanum. I understand that can be a serious side effect."

Fairchild scoffed at that. "The fear of addiction is wildly overblown. It should never prevent anyone from obtaining relief from a serious complaint. All methods have their hazards. But when properly prescribed and administered, nothing works as quickly as the right regimen of drugs to bring the patient into a state where less intrusive methods can become effective. It's the combination of methods that does the trick; not any one alone."

"That makes sense." It also supported Moriarty's skepticism about Holmes's case. Lady Georgia had undoubtedly failed to follow instructions after leaving the hospital. "Do you craft an individual suite of therapies for each patient while they're in hospital?"

"Not here, I'm afraid. Our county hospitals are not that well funded. But my practice isn't limited to this institution. I also consult at an exclusive private hospital in Hampstead called Halcyon House, equipped with the latest in therapeutic resources."

Moriarty blinked to cover his surprise at that name. He hadn't seen any references to it or Dr. Trumbull in Fairchild's publications. "That must give you an exceptional view of the field as well as unique opportunities for observing the effectiveness of your treatments."

"Oh yes. In fact, I'm currently conducting a survey of drug-based therapies for nervous diseases that takes me into every asylum in the London area, public and private. It's a fascinating topic and should make a useful contribution to the literature."

"I look forward to reading it," Moriarty said. Such an investigation would allow this doctor to get his fingers into the tonic bottles of nearly any patient he pleased. Perhaps Dr. Trumbull wasn't the right target for their investigation. "One thing I'm curious about, Doctor. What happens after they're discharged?"

"What do you mean?"

"Don't people tend to fall back into their old ways once they leave the nurturing environment of the hospital? I'm curious about the mortality rates among patients who have been released from care."

"Mortality rates!" Fairchild frowned. "My goodness, you have a morbid turn of mind."

Moriarty feared he had gone too far. He backed up a step. "I didn't mean mortality exactly. I only meant, are patients able to continue the good habits they learn in the hospital once they come home again?"

"Ah! I think I understand you. You're wondering how you — the hypothetical you, of course," the doctor said with a wink, "can learn to maintain that old battery on your own. Well, that can be a problem for some people. Patients are never alone in a private hospital, you see. A personal attendant watches them constantly, and the round of treatments makes for a full day. Once home, of course, the patient receives far less attention and might, as you suggest, fall back into the old destructive habits. In many cases, the family itself is a major cause of stress. But I shouldn't worry too much, Mr. Moriarty. We're pretty good at judging when our patients are ready to get back into the fray."

"Do you send them home with a set of exercises or medicines?"

"If they need them, certainly. Most people leave Halcyon House refreshed and ready to get back into the rhythm of family life." He winked again.

Moriarty decided to push a little harder while he had the chance. He licked his lips, then leaned forward in a confiding posture. "Frankly, Doctor, half of the things you've said might apply to my wife. She's irritable all the time. Every little thing I say! She seems to think I'm not doing my job, not holding up my end of the domestic compact. Not performing my husbandly duties." His voice held a note of real disgruntlement. Angelina never appreciated his attempts to provide guidance concerning their staff, for example.

Fairchild nodded, his genial expression transformed to a professional mask. "I see. How long have you been married?"

"A little over four months."

"Well, some couples take more time to find their way with one another. Many have no experience with such intimate relationships."

44

"It's certainly not what I expected." That much was true, to say the least. "She spends money like water." He added in support of his fictional role, "Of course, it was hers originally."

The doctor frowned, quirking his eyebrows as he studied Moriarty. "I understand. Your complaint is not uncommon."

Someone knocked on the door and opened it a crack. "We're ready to make the rounds, Doctor."

"I'll be right there." Fairchild rose from his chair. Moriarty did the same.

The doctor paused and said, "I wouldn't take these early difficulties too seriously, Mr. Moriarty." The doctor regarded him with a knowing twinkle in his eyes. "Don't brood. Give yourselves time to sort things out. But I'll tell you what." He went to a glass-fronted cabinet and extracted a small bottle. "Why don't you give this a try? Don't worry, there's no risk of addiction. I think you and your wife will be pleased with the results." He handed it to Moriarty with one last wink.

Moriarty thanked him and tucked it into his pocket as the doctor ushered him out. He exited directly from this wing, not wishing to encounter Holmes again, and walked across the gravel drive to meet his driver. So it wasn't until he had settled into the cab that he pulled out the bottle to see what he'd been given.

He barked a surprised laugh. No wonder the doctor had been winking like a man with a nervous twitch. The label read, "Dr. Trumbull's Stimulating Nerve Tonic for Male Enhancement. Guaranteed to restore the debilitated to their former masculine zest and vigor."

# Chapter Five

Angelina placed a vase of chrysanthemums on the tea table in the drawing room, then picked it up again and moved it to the console table by the door. Her guests this afternoon were gentlemen. They wouldn't appreciate anything getting between them and the sandwiches, however cheerful the color or fresh the fragrance.

She checked her hair in the mirror over the mantel and smoothed an invisible wisp back into the curls piled on top of her head. She flicked an invisible speck of dirt from the lace around her neck and pinched her cheeks to bring out the color. Then she laughed to see her husband watching her from the doorway. "I think we're ready, darling."

"Is it time, then? Thank goodness. I'm famished." James had affected a lack of interest in this meeting, but he'd polished his shoes and brushed his coat again after lunch. He sauntered to the tea table and inspected the offerings. He selected a sandwich, took a bite, and grunted with pleasure. He polished it off and reached for another one.

"Do leave a few for the guests, James."

"These are too good for Holmes."

"Then think of Mr. Wexcombe and Dr. Watson."

The door knocker echoed up the stairs. Angelina arranged herself on the sofa. In a few minutes, Rolly led their guests inside and left without attempting to introduce them.

Angelina observed the three men with interest. She had seen Holmes and Watson before, though they had not seen her. She painted an expression of anticipation on her face, shaded with a touch of reserve. Her husband might consent to collaborate with these men for a short time, but he would never consider them friends. Therefore, like a good wife, neither would she.

James walked forward to do the honors. "Welcome to my home, gentlemen. Allow me to present my wife."

Mr. Wexcombe had a diffident air, but he wore the latest fashions like a man who made a point of always being *au courant*. He had a short, stiff moustache and thick mouse-brown hair that looked as if he'd given it a generous application of pomade and then run both hands through it like a madman in dismay. Angelina had noticed that anti-style among fashionable youths in the south of France.

She held out a hand, over which he made a short bow. "Thank you for inviting me into your lovely home." Wexcombe spoke without a trace of irony.

Angelina returned the favor. "It's so kind of you to take time from your busy schedule."

They smiled at one another in perfect, companionable understanding.

James said, "My dear, I don't believe you've ever met Mr. Sherlock Holmes and Dr. John Watson."

"At last, we meet!" Holmes said, performing a dramatic half bow. "The famous — or should I say infamous — Angelina Gould."

"That's Mrs. Moriarty now," James snapped. The poor man really *must* learn to stop leaping at the bait.

Holmes grinned. "But the fame belongs to the former name."

Had he not learned any of her earlier names? They'd been much better known in their day. Lovely Little Lina, Lina Lovington, Lionel Lockwood, Angelina Della Rosa . . . Photograph cards had been made of her as *La Périchole*, not to mention Angelina and her Little Angels. They'd

47

sold well. There must be lots of them still about. Either Holmes hadn't bothered to explore her past or he was saving the knowledge to spring it on them when it would be most impressive.

Holmes's coat and loose trousers were two steps closer to current fashion than anything James could be persuaded to wear. And Holmes was clean-shaven in the style of the aesthetes. That puzzled Angelina for a moment, but then she remembered how much Holmes loved disguises. It was so much easier to glue false whiskers to a bare chin.

"You flatter me, Mr. Holmes. Your fame, of course, outshines us all." She turned to the man beside him. "Then you must be Dr. Watson. James has told me *all* about you."

"Not all, I hope." The doctor frowned as if he had a great store of secrets to conceal. Nothing could be less likely. Every detail, from his brushy sideburns to his sensible boots, declared him to be a simple family doctor.

"Please sit next to me, Mr. Wexcombe." Angelina patted the sofa. "And do sit down, gentlemen. Anywhere you like."

Holmes made a beeline for James's chair. The clues were too obvious to merit comment, but how typical of the man to take his rival's favorite spot! Watson seated himself in the walnut rocking chair and grunted in surprise when it tilted backward. The doctor was either nearsighted or blissfully unobservant; either way, an ideal companion for Sherlock Holmes.

James took the spindly Louis Quinze armchair. He hated the thing, but it stood the closest to her. Heaven forbid that she be left undefended with barbarians in the room!

Holmes regarded his client with a twinkle in his dark eyes. "Mr. Wexcombe had just returned from his club when we collected him. Did you win your game of billiards?"

"Oh!" Wexcombe startled, then wagged his finger at the detective. "There you go again, Mr. Holmes. I suppose I picked up a speck of chalk that only your sharp eyes could spot." He bent toward Angelina and said, "He gave me my whole history when we first met, just by looking at me. Everything but the name of my fourth-form Latin master! That's quite a trick he's got."

Holmes's eyes narrowed at the word "trick." He regarded his observational prowess as a science, James had said, considering himself its sole practitioner. He wasn't, of course. Angelina, both twins, and the father who'd trained them were every bit as good. But the best confidence tricksters didn't advertise their skills. Letting the marks know how easy they were to read only put them on their guard.

Rolly returned with the tea tray and departed without a word. Holmes's eyes followed him, then he shifted his gaze to James, twitching an eyebrow to signal his awareness of the boy's origins — to no avail. James hadn't a clue. He responded to Holmes's inexplicable signals with a frosty glare, his usual response to anything he didn't understand.

Angelina poured tea. James passed the cups. Watson and Wexcombe kept up a bit of light chatter while she offered around the sandwiches and cake. She loaded an extra plate and prompted James to place it on the table between Holmes and Watson so they could help themselves at their pleasure.

Once everyone had taken some refreshment, she nodded at Holmes. "Would you like to begin?"

"Yes, it is time." He set down his teacup and placed his hands on his thighs — a masculine pose, indicating his taking control of the meeting. "This case, if indeed there is a case, is potentially the most complex and baffling that I have yet encountered. Our first task is to determine whether any crime has actually been committed."

"We must be careful," Moriarty said, "whatever we do. This Trumbull appears to be a highly respected medical man. We must not risk anything that could be construed as slander."

Watson let out a low whistle. "He could sue us all into the poorhouse if we're wrong."

"But we can't allow this terrible man to keep murdering his patients," Angelina said.

"If that's what he's doing," James said.

She fluttered her lashes at him, smiling through her teeth. "*If* that's what he's doing, of course. But we must *know*, James. Surely you can agree to that."

"I said I did." Their eyes met in a silent contest of wills.

Holmes pressed his lips together as if resisting a grin. "It's a wise cautionary note, Professor. I recommend that, apart from Mrs. Moriarty, we keep our distance from Dr. Trumbull and his staff until we have more to go on."

"What's your plan?" James asked.

"I propose that Mr. Wexcombe, Watson, and I attend the inquest in Richmond this week and pursue whatever we can there. Then I suggest that you and Mrs. Moriarty visit one of the spa retreats Lady Georgia frequented to see if you can pick up a trail. My hope is that you'll be solicited by one of the touts Mr. Wexcombe mentioned."

"If I may be so bold," Wexcombe said, "I would recommend Torquay. It's lovely at this time of year and the Beaumont Hotel is a favorite of Lady Georgia's set. Look for the old tabbies — that's what they call themselves — on the terrace on the east side of the hotel. It's in the sun but out of the wind."

"Capital!" Holmes said.

"I remember groups of women like that," Angelina said, "clustered together in deck chairs, anywhere with a pleasant view. I never spoke to them beyond the usual 'Good morning.'"

"I remember them too," James said. "I suppose I met many of their husbands at the card table."

"That's where you'll find them," Mr. Wexcombe said. "Or in the billiard room after dinner. That's where the fellow told me about the Clennam treatment."

James frowned at him with that cold glare that made people feel like idiots. Angelina patted Mr. Wexcombe's hand. "I don't think you've told us about that part yet. What fellow was this?"

"I'm sorry." Wexcombe gave her a twisted smile. "I'm not much good at making sense. My cousins think I'm the most frightful pumpkin-head."

"Not at all!" Angelina protested. "You're very brave and perceptive. We just need to take things step by step. You met this fellow in the billiard room?"

"Yes. Us younger fellows, nephews and sons mostly, tend to gather around the table, although not many of us play. The older blokes sit in front of the windows. They don't stay up very late." Wexcombe screwed up his face as if trying to remember. "There we were, smoking and chatting, when Bertram came in and flopped down in the chair next to me in the foulest temper! He'd come down to Torquay to beg Aunt G for another loan. She'd said no, of course. Bertie has no head for money. Besides, it's hers to do with as she pleases."

Angelina smiled patiently. "That's very clear. Now who is Mrs. Clennam?"

"Oh yes. Let's see. Well, here's Bertie ranting on about useless old women and their tight purse strings. Same old rot. Then this other chappie pipes up and says, 'If you really want to change things — I mean once and for all — get the old bird into Dr. Trumbull's private

51

hospital. Write the letter yourself, mind you, and ask for the same treatment they provided Mrs. Clennam. Use those words exactly. They'll let you know what to do next.'"

"Mrs. Clennam," Holmes said. "Did you recognize that name?"

Wexcombe shook his head. Angelina frowned, searching her memory. The name did sound vaguely familiar, but she couldn't put her finger on it.

Watson burst out, "By gad, it's ingenious!" He grinned at them. "Do none of you read novels? Mrs. Clennam is the dictatorial invalid in *Little Dorrit*. By Charles Dickens? Surely even you have heard of *him*, Holmes."

Angelina gasped. "Oh my stars!" Dickens was too sentimental for her taste. She preferred Mrs. Braddon and Wilkie Collins. "What happened to Mrs. Clennam?"

Watson said, "I believe she dies of overstimulation. She wasn't murdered, in any event. But she's a well-known example of an old woman standing in the way of a young person's happiness."

"My word, you are the cleverest people!" Wexcombe gazed at Watson with admiration.

Watson preened his moustache, deservedly pleased with himself. Holmes gave him an approving nod. James, on the other hand, lowered his eyelids in that slight flutter of lashes that meant he was less than impressed. A more expressive man would scoff openly, saying, "Great Scott, man! What a load of balderdash."

His natural skepticism kept him from making the intuitive leap Angelina and Holmes had managed with ease. James liked to see everything lined up like a neat mathematical equation. Well, things in the world of human beings didn't often work that way.

"How did Bertram react to that advice?" Angelina asked.

Wexcombe said, "I don't remember him saying much of anything. The other chappie just dropped the butt of his cigar in the ashtray and stood up. As he walked by, he put a hand on Bertie's shoulder and said, 'Look me up before you go. I'll be around for a few more days.' He winked at the rest of us and left. The conversation moved on. I didn't think much of it at the time, but then Aunt G went into Trumbull's hospital and came home and died a few days later. Then I remembered and started wondering if it hadn't meant something after all."

"And that's where we come in," Holmes said. He took a cigarette from his pocket and lit it. Forewarned of his habit, Angelina had placed ashtrays everywhere. "I hope you and your wife won't mind a short holiday, Professor."

James traded glances with Angelina before answering. "Not at all. But my role sounds rather vague. Am I expected to loiter about the billiard room in the evening complaining about my wife? That sounds like a very uncertain method to me."

"That is often the nature of investigative work," Holmes said. "If it were certain, subtlety and ingenuity would not be required. We could simply summon the police. Do you fear the task will be too challenging for you?"

Angelina nearly spat out her tea. But James merely smiled and said, "Not at all. It's well within my scope. After all, I bought this house with the proceeds of gambling in spa retreats."

Holmes's dark eyes twinkled. "This time, however, you must lose, or your complaints about your wife's money will be unconvincing."

James's eyes narrowed, but he said nothing.

Angelina rescued him. "That leaves my role to prepare. How does a woman suffering from nervous disorders act?"

"Oh my," Wexcombe said. "Well, there's all sorts, aren't there?"

"The symptoms of neurasthenia," James said, jumping in before Watson could open his mouth, "include insomnia, excessive drowsiness, anxiety, fearfulness, headaches, irritability, feelings of hopelessness, fear of contamination, bad dreams, indecisiveness, and grandiosity, among others."

"I see you've been boning up on the subject," Holmes said with a twist of his upper lip.

James smirked at him.

"Yes, dear," Angelina said, "but that doesn't help me. No one person can exhibit all of those symptoms. Some of them contradict each other!"

Watson said, "Neurasthenia is a vague diagnosis. You can choose almost anything you like, Mrs. Moriarty. I'm sure you'll do an excellent job, whatever you decide."

"Be fussy," Wexcombe said. "Ask for special everything. Send things back. You know the sort of person I mean. Create a bit of a stir in the dining room. Then the professor will have something obvious to complain about."

"If I may make a suggestion," Holmes said. "Your goal is to portray a woman whose husband wants to eliminate her. In that case, you might try to play a woman who is at odds with her spouse."

Angelina leveled a dry look at James. "I should be able to manage that, Mr. Holmes."

# Chapter Six

James Moriarty chose a cigar from the selection offered by the waiter at the Beaumont Hotel. He clipped the end, accepted a light, and drew in a mouthful of pungent smoke. He had better at home, but for a hotel, this one was not bad.

He strolled over to watch a billiard game in progress, making it clear by his manner that he wouldn't mind a game himself. The truth was that without the focused gambling he'd engaged in on the Continent, he found the evening ritual of lounging about after dinner with a group of men in formal dress to be completely pointless. He would rather be up in his room with a glass of port and a good book.

But he and Angelina had come to Torquay to verify as much as they could of Mr. Wexcombe's implausible tale, so he must hang on as best he could for at least a couple of hours. At least he needn't struggle to suppress his boredom. Angelina had told him that an air of infinite ennui would help support his role.

The game ended. One of the players said, "That's it for me tonight," and took his leave. The other caught Moriarty's eye and gestured at the table, inviting him to take a turn. They played in comfortable silence, only speaking to express the necessary, with a wager of one guinea. Moriarty managed to lose in spite of his opponent's lack of skill. Angelina had tied a thin bandage around his left thumb to remind him to play badly. A neat trick, though it made him feel like one of those professional hustlers.

As he handed over his guinea, he shrugged and said, "Well, the wife can spare it, although she keeps me on a damned short leash."

The other player merely grunted and offered a game to a fresh opponent. Moriarty wandered over to join a group of men in club chairs, smoking and drinking brandy from oversized snifters. He continued his grumbling after accepting a glass from the hovering waiter. "Seems like I've spent half my life hanging about these damned health retreats. They might be good for her health, but they don't do mine any good."

That earned him a dark chuckle or two.

"No, sir," he went on. "A man can't do a thing for himself in a place like this. But if she would loosen those damned purse strings a little, I could make my mark, I don't mind telling you. All a man needs is a little starting-off money in today's market."

A couple of the men nodded at that. One of them launched into a short lecture about Brazilian railways and the wave of the future. Moriarty listened with grave attention. At a pause in the spate of nonsense, he said, "That's good advice, friend. Thanks for the tip. I was thinking about South Africa myself, but you make a good case for South America."

"Glad to help." The man downed the last of his brandy, stubbed out his cigar, and bid the rest good night. Another man went out with him, leaving Moriarty and a red-faced fellow with a pair of diamond-studded cuff links that winked in the soft light of the chandelier every time he raised his cigar.

"It's one of the greatest crimes in our society," he said, leaning toward Moriarty, "that so much of our investment capital is in the hands of women who can't seem to think of anything beyond their own whims."

"That is a profound truth," Moriarty said. "Take my wife, for instance. Thanks to a Parliament with more sentiment than sense, she's allowed to retain full control of her inheritance. Full control! Does she then invest those funds in coal production or shipping ventures or colonial railways to make Britain greater than it is? No, she does not. She fritters it away on hydro-baths and saltwater treatments — whatever the latest fashion is. Money thrown down the drain, if you ask me."

"You could change that, you know," the red-faced fellow said. He leaned even closer and spoke in a low voice. "Once and for all, if you catch my meaning. Get your wife into the care of a Dr. Trumbull. Nerve specialist, Harley Street man, very popular. You'll find him easily enough. Write him a letter asking for an appointment for your wife at his earliest convenience. Tell him you want the Clennam treatment. Got that?"

"Clinic?" Moriarty said, trying to restrain his excitement.

"No, Clennam." The man spelled it for him. "Some Dickens character. Never heard of it myself. But use that name in your letter. They'll send you instructions as you go along. In a few short months, you'll have those funds in your own hands to invest as you see fit, and no more nagging and nattering in your ear while you go about your business."

He let that sink in for a minute, then drained his snifter and stood up.

"That's an interesting suggestion," Moriarty said. He took a draw on his cigar and blew it upward, using the smoke to cover any inadequacies in his expression. "Intriguing, one might say." He showed the man a hard smile. "Shall I send you a postcard to let you know how things turn out?"

The red-faced fellow shot him a wink. "Don't bother. We'll meet again, here or there. If you like the results, pass the word on to another fellow in the same boat." Then he left Moriarty alone to ponder his advice.

And strange advice it would seem, if he didn't already known what it was about. Would every man who received it recognize it as means to commit murder by another's hand?

\* \* \*

"Thank you, my dear." Angelina accepted the cashmere shawl from the maid. Her name was Semple, but it seemed a bit proprietary to refer to another woman's personal servant by name. "What a treasure you are!"

Semple's mistress, Mrs. Elizabeth Parsons, was seated on Angelina's right, fourth in the row of women stretched out in deck chairs, bundled to the chins, enjoying the sea breeze on the terrace. Angelina had joined the group after lunch yesterday, introducing herself by complaining about the cold. She'd been roundly assured that it would be *much* colder in a month. Positively unbearable! She'd allowed that the sun was truly lovely and snuggled into position.

They'd interrogated her gently but thoroughly. She'd ended up giving them most of the symptoms from James's list, which they seemed to accept as a perfectly natural assemblage. In fact, most of them suffered from the same exhausting suite of vague complaints. They were so cheerful about it though, that she warmed to them at once, gradually relaxing into a sort of exaggerated performance of herself. An Angelina who reserved nothing, delivering a constant report of her interior and exterior condition. Hot, cold, hungry, sleepy, caught in the shreds of last night's dreams . . .

Mrs. Parsons, her new best friend, was about fifty years old, though very well tended. Her graying blond hair had been charmingly styled, probably by the ever-attentive Semple, but her gray eyes held a saddish cast, even when she smiled. She fussed about every little thing, but perhaps that covered some deeper pain.

The hotel attendant brought Angelina the chocolate she had ordered, though she would secretly prefer a gin and bitters. But none of the other women had alcoholic drinks on the terrace — just herbal teas, fruit juices, and hot cocoa. Each one also had her own little brown bottle or enameled pill box. Angelina hadn't had one the first day. Luckily the hotel carried an assortment, and she and James had chosen one that didn't look too dire — Ollie's Jolly Female Strengthener, which tasted like cherry syrup with a touch of something fizzy. As far as Angelina could tell, it did nothing at all, which was just what she had hoped.

Now she took a sip of the chocolate and made a great face. "Oh my stars! Now it's too sweet! It makes my teeth ache, just that tiny little sip!" She thrust the cup at the stoic attendant. "Perhaps we should forget the chocolate today."

"No, no," Mrs. Parsons said. "Let Semple make it for you. She'll get it just right, I promise."

"Well, if it isn't too much trouble . . ."

"Not at all, Miss," the maid said. "I'll fix it the way my missus likes it. Not too sweet nor too bitter. It'll only take half a jiffy."

Angelina watched the young woman bustle off with the hotel attendant. Then she lolled her head toward Mrs. Parsons. "Wherever did you find that absolute treasure of a girl?"

Mrs. Parsons smiled at the compliment to her hiring skills. "I stole her." They traded shocked expressions before she explained. "I found her in a private hospital called Halcyon House. Have you been there?"

"No," Angelina said, ears perking. "Is it lovely?"

"Very." Mrs. Parsons lowered her voice to a confidential level. "Better than here, apart from the sea.

59

Which I do adore. That's why I came here instead of going straight home. Halcyon has the best treatment, but it's a private estate, you know, in Hampstead, behind a great wall. It feels very snug and private, and, of course, that's what it is, that's the whole point, but I do love a view of the sea."

"So do I," Angelina said, although she couldn't think of anything more barren or unwelcoming. Give her a London street — the busier, the better. Or better still, a theater seen from center stage. "But do you recommend Halcyon House for a rest?"

"Oh yes. Well, not so much a rest. They're better at that here, frankly. At Halcyon, they're very intent on making you better, so they're always dragging you from one treatment to another, coaxing you to try some needlework or play badminton, of all things."

"Badminton!"

"Exercise, my dear. It's the latest thing."

Angelina made a face. "I prefer doing nothing when I need a rest."

Mrs. Parsons laughed. "Then Torquay is the place for you. If you manage to take a turn around the garden in the morning here, they're satisfied."

Semple returned with Angelina's chocolate on a tray. "Try this, Madame."

Angelina took a judicious sip. It tasted the same as the last cup, but then she was not a great lover of chocolate. She closed her eyes and licked her lips. "Perfect. Absolutely perfect." She smiled up at the maid. "Best be careful, Semple. I may try to steal you again."

"Never, Madame, with respect. I'm that fond of my missus; I would never leave her."

"Not until your young man is ready to give you a home of your own," Mrs. Parsons said.

Semple grinned and stepped back to the edge of the terrace, where the maids and hotel attendants awaited a

60

signal from the ladies in the chairs. Angelina sipped her
sticky drink in silence for a little while, wondering if Mrs.
Parsons were one of the Clennam patients or not. Would
they allow her to wander off like this instead of going
straight back to her house? Or would they have the
audacity to try their tricks here?

She set the half-finished cocoa on the small table and
allowed herself to close her eyes for a minute or two. She
was abruptly awakened by terrified shrieks from her new
friend, who was flailing in her chair, flapping her hands
over her face.

"Bees! Bees! Semple! Help me!"

Semple dashed over and began swatting at the air with
a napkin, crying, "Shoo! Shoo!"

Other women began to whimper and cry, "Oh! Oh!"
Angelina nearly jumped out of her chair to help but
remembered her role and cowered down instead,
covering her head with the shawl, peeking out to
whimper, "Is it gone? Is it gone? What was it?"

Hotel staff leapt into the fray, some comforting the
old tabbies, another helping Semple disperse the invading
insect. Someone said, "It's all right, ladies. It was only a
fly. Beastly thing, but it can't you hurt you, and it's gone
now. It must have been attracted to the chocolate. We'll
take that away and then we'll be right as rain again."

Gradually the coterie of nervous women recovered
from the crisis. Mrs. Parsons patted her cheeks and
smoothed her hair, still a bit pale and breathless, but
calmer. She seemed a bit embarrassed as she confided in
Angelina, "My husband gets so annoyed with me when I
panic like that. But I am simply terrified of flying insects!
I've been stung by a hornet once and bees another time.
My face swelled up like a balloon! Horribly unattractive,
as you can imagine, and *so* painful. It made me short of
breath and light-headed."

"How frightening for you," Angelina said. She reached over to pat the blankets in the general area of her neighbor's hand.

"You're so kind," Mrs. Parsons said. With a sidelong glance at the other women, she added, "They call it an irrational fear. But it isn't irrational if it really hurts you, is it?"

"Of course not." Angelina felt a shiver that had nothing to do with the ocean breeze.

"Good afternoon, tabby darlings!" a plummy voice sang out as an older woman in an elegant tea dress approached the group. "Is there a free chair anywhere?"

An attendant brought one, positioning it to bring one end of their half circle around to facilitate conversation. The newcomer got herself settled while exchanging a few individual greetings. Her name was Mrs. Northwood. The tabbies tended to call one another by full title.

"I've just come from Vichy," she informed the group. "Really not what it used to be, is it? I don't mean the scenery or the food, of course. It's still France, isn't it?" She tittered. "But the services have gone sadly downhill. It's almost not worth it."

That started a general conversation about masseuses and bathing attendants at the most expensive spas in Europe. The consensus seemed to be that such persons expected far too much in the way of tips, considering the simplicity of their work. Anyone with strong hands could give a massage, for example.

"Well, I wouldn't go *that* far," Mrs. Northwood said. "But if you really want to be pampered from head to toe without having to tip everyone you see, you really should try Dr. Trumbull's establishment, Halcyon House. It's *so* convenient to London. Your menfolk can stay in town and not hang about grumbling in the smoking room. If you haven't tried it, my dears, you positively *owe* yourselves the treat."

An attendant came over and whispered something in Mrs. Northwood's ear. "What?" She looked at the jeweled watch pinned to her jacket. "Is that now?"

The attendant nodded and helped her out of her nest of blankets, then guided her back to the main hotel.

A short silence followed her departure. Then one of the older woman sniffed and said in a stage whisper, "Trumbull again! Why doesn't she move into Halcyon House if she's so fond of the place?"

"She's probably in love with that doctor," another one said. "Happens all too often, don't you know."

One of the other women snickered while another one sighed. A mixed bag on that score, then.

"Isn't it a nice place?" Angelina asked, all innocence.

Another short silence met her question. Then Mrs. Tattersall lowered her head in that confidential pose they adopted for delivering especially juicy bits of gossip. "You're new, Mrs. Moriarty, so you won't know. But most of us would rather spend a month in prison than in Dr. Trumbull's hospital. Odd things happen to his patients, more often than they ought."

"Odd?" Angelina asked. "In what way?"

Lady Pembrey shifted into the confidential pose. "No one ever listens to us. We're just a bunch of silly old women. But we hear things, my dear. Oh yes. Mrs. Atlee, for example. Does anyone remember her?" She looked around the group, collecting nods of agreement. "Well, she died four days after leaving Halcyon House, from mixing up her blue pill, they said. How could anyone mix up their blue pill, for pity's sake? One a day, that's simple enough."

Mrs. Tattersall said, "She's not the only one. Remember that lovely Mrs. Delaney? The one that was so fond of riding? She died two days after leaving that hospital, on Boxing Day. From heart failure, the papers said, but she didn't have any trouble with her heart when she was here. She'd have told us."

Everyone murmured their agreement. Angelina trusted their knowledge. She had learned the essential facts of each one's physical and mental health on first meeting. These old birds could drive a person to distraction with their petty complaints and requirements, but they weren't stupid — not a bit of it. They were sharp-witted and observant, and they genuinely cared for one another. They seemed to rely on each other, in a tribal sort of way.

"That sounds ominous," she said, earning several dark looks.

Lady Pembrey said, "There's been another one, ladies. I'm sure we all knew Lady Georgia. Well, she's gone too now, just like the others, after a month at Halcyon House. The newspapers say she took an overdose of laudanum."

"Impossible!" Several voices spoke in unison.

Angelina shivered again. Mr. Wexcombe had been right. It was like a hidden epidemic, a secret disease that took women one by one. But since they were all "superfluous women," no one raised the alarm.

* * *

That night, alone in their room, Moriarty and Angelina donned their honeymoon nightclothes by unspoken mutual consent. They'd returned to the neutral ground of impersonal hotels, where their only decisions were what to wear and what to order from an extensive menu. The well-trained staff required no instructions from them to perform their duties. They barely noticed the luxurious decor, other than to recognize in a general way that it was luxurious.

Moriarty buttoned up his long linen nightshirt — the one with the ruffles along the front facing — and scuffed his feet into his fleece-lined slippers. He wrapped up in the quilted silk dressing gown Angelina had given him and tied the sash around his waist. He always felt vaguely theatrical in this costume. He appreciated the return of her lacy nightgown, however, whose sheerness remained imprinted on his mind even after she snuggled into her chenille dressing gown.

She had curled into one of the deep armchairs flanking the fireplace. The ruby flames found a mirror in her chestnut hair, which tumbled below her shoulders in its natural state. He loved to see her like this, without the artifice of bustles and pompadours. They rarely had a fire in their bedroom at home, so they didn't lounge about like this in their nightclothes.

He poured two snifters of brandy and handed her one, then settled comfortably into his own chair, stretching his feet toward the warmth of the fire. The setting promoted companionable conversation — another pleasure in short supply at home. Better, this nerve doctor business supplied them with a neutral topic, one that intrigued them both. Angelina had been right to push them into collaborating with Holmes. The whole project provided them with a respite from the nerve-wrenching enterprise of learning to live together.

"Well, my dear. Are you ready for a report from the billiard room?"

"Did you learn anything?"

"I did." Moriarty proceeded to tell her about the red-faced chap and his oblique suggestion. She listened with rapt attention, a light of intense interest dancing in her amber eyes. He made as much of the tale as he could.

"Oh, James," she said when he finished. "That is truly astounding. On your very first effort! You must have played your part to perfection. I wish I could have been there, but of course that would have spoiled everything."

"Your trick with the bandage on the thumb was very helpful, I must say. Every time I settled the cue into my hand for a shot, I was reminded that my objective was to miss the mark."

"I don't know what we could have come up with if the game had been cards." She gave him a smile filled with wifely admiration, warmer than the crackling fire. "But didn't you manage to get the chap's name?"

"Of course I got it." Moriarty's puffed-up pride lost a bit of air. "I asked the waiter. His name is Randolph Atlee."

Angelina drew in a sharp breath. "Atlee! Oh, James! Mrs. Atlee was one of the women the tabbies mentioned. One of their friends who died in a way they didn't believe could be natural."

She had told him about the gossip on the terrace while they were dressing for dinner. Moriarty asked, "Isn't she the one who died of an overdose of mercury, caused by taking too many of her blue pills?" Blue pill was a popular remedy for constipation. His mother had kept a box of them in a drawer of her dressing table.

"Yes," Angelina said. "A thing which they all agreed was impossible. And really, how could anyone take too many of a pill that they've been taking for years? Habit would guide your hand. You'd take one after dinner or in the morning or whenever you had established as your personal ritual and then put the box away."

"I don't know about that." Moriarty had decided to adopt the role of devil's advocate in this affair since no one else seemed ready to take it up. Holmes wanted a dramatic case and Angelina naturally empathized with Mr. Wexcombe. She had now extended that bounteous emotion to the tabbies on the terrace as well. His job, as he saw it, was to provide the needed check of a cool-headed, rational perspective. "I can easily imagine an elderly woman mixing up the time of day and taking a second dose. Or an apprentice at the apothecary making a mistake. How many pills would a woman of average size have to take to attain a fatal dose?"

"*Attain!*" Angelina uncurled her legs, planting her feet on the floor in a far less beguiling posture. "You make it sound like an achievement."

"I retract the word if it offends you. But we must be careful, my dear, as I pointed out at tea with the others, not to theorize ahead of our facts."

"We've confirmed three facts today," she said, tilting her chin in that combative pose that meant she was prepared to disagree with everything he said. "First, that men who are tired of their wives are passing the word about Trumbull's private hospital and the special Clennam treatment. Second, that a disagreeable woman is touting that same hospital. And third, that a group of keen-eyed, attentive friends are convinced something is wrong with the unexpected deaths of several of their number."

"Three, I believe you said. This Mrs. Atlee, the horse-riding woman, and our Lady Georgia." He decided not to be led into a debate about the significance of the first two "facts." It was easy enough to see how credulous persons like Wexcombe and, sadly, Angelina could interpret those separate events as a fiendish conspiracy, but he found it easier to see them for what they were — two ill-humored persons promoting themselves by professing inside knowledge. They did not as yet have any reason to connect the red-faced fellow in the billiard room with the haughty woman on the terrace. But he kept that to himself for now.

"Doesn't all this strike you as significant?" Angelina demanded.

Moriarty shrugged his shoulders. He didn't want to appear unsympathetic — the greatest crime in Angelina's book. "I agree that it seems to be significant, considering the size of the group, but I must remind you that these are women who suffer from a range of complaints, both mental and physical. One would expect a greater rate of mortality than one would find in the general population."

Angelina glared at him over the rim of her brandy snifter. For an intelligent woman, she showed a surprising resistance to the rational view. She took a sip and rolled it on her tongue before swallowing it. Moriarty watched the working of her alabaster throat with unabated desire. That never changed, however much she might exasperate him during these stimulating debates.

"All right, then," she said. "We don't know the *normal* rate of mortality for a group of old darlings like the ones I've met here. But we do have suspicions. We have many small things, perhaps easy enough to dismiss each on its own, as you persist in demonstrating, but add them all together and we have something worth investigating, as you yourself agreed."

"Indeed, I did. And I continue to agree. That's why we're here." This need to repeat the obvious always baffled Moriarty. "We'll follow it through to the end, now that we're committed. I'm only warning you that we may end up learning that all these deaths were in fact no more than they appeared to be. That the official verdicts were correct and we have no mystery at all."

She said nothing for a while, staring at the fire. But then she leaned forward, an intense posture. "You spoke of warning. I appreciate your caution, darling; honestly I do. But shouldn't we warn Mrs. Parsons of our suspicions?"

"The woman who dined with us tonight?"

"Yes. She's such a sweet thing, so thoughtful and kind. But you know, James, she's the ideal candidate for the Clennam treatment. Her husband doesn't seem to like her very much, from what she told me. She has a variety of complaints, easily exploited. And she just left Halcyon

House after a month's stay. She said she was expected to go straight home but came down here on a whim for the air. What will happen to her when she goes home?"

Moriarty was nonplussed by this anxious spate of words. "This is the woman you mentioned before dinner, isn't it? The one who was afraid of bees and flies and other things?"

"Yes."

"My dear Angelina, what do you propose we say to her? Should we tell a woman beset with fears to be even more fearful? That would be irresponsible, even a little cruel, especially when we know nothing for certain."

Angelina wrinkled her nose the way she did to acknowledge an undesirable truth. "Well, we've got to do something."

"We will. We'll keep doing what we're doing. Only now, thanks to your subtle interrogation skills, we have two more names to pursue. One unexpected death, possibly caused by mercury poisoning, and one death from heart failure, induced by an as yet unknown cause. There may be more information in the inquest reports, which I should be able to find in the British Museum archives. You'll visit Trumbull in his lair on Harley Street and see what you can turn up. We have a trail to follow." He smiled at her, trying to show his willingness to play the game to the end.

Angelina wrinkled her nose, this time indicating that she didn't appreciate his attempt to lighten the mood. "We'd best tell Holmes at once when we get home, so that he can get started right away."

She couldn't have chosen anything more deflating. "Oh, there's no rush on that front, surely? Let's you and I scout around a bit first and see what we can turn up. No need to show all our cards in the first round, is there?"

# Chapter Seven

"Here, ducky. Hop into these."

Angelina accepted the muslin combinations from her old friend and dresser. She shook them out, started to step into them, then stopped with one foot in the air. "Oh, not these, Peg! They have too much lace. It tickles me under the arms and itches like fury behind the knees when I sit down."

"That's the idea. It'll make you peevish. You're supposed to be the fussy sort."

Angelina flashed a grin. "Aren't you the clever old fox?"

"My job, ducky. Make it easy for you to play your part."

Angelina surrendered to necessity. She climbed into the combinations and buttoned them up. Peg was dressing her for her first performance as Mrs. Nervy. She would meet the infamous Dr. Trumbull in less than an hour. She didn't plan to do any snooping on this first encounter — unless she got a chance too good to pass by. Her main concern was convincing the famous specialist that she needed his help. She'd pretended many things to many people over the years, but usually they were more interested in themselves than in her. That made it a sight easier.

Peg wrapped a corset around Angelina's torso. "I'll lace it tighter than usual to make you a touch breathless."

"Oh, you *are* heartless!" Angelina gasped as Peg gave the laces a powerful tug. She adjusted her breath before stepping into her petticoat and turning so Peg could tie on the bustle. "I won't need to pretend at all. I'm feeling a bit of a shiver already. I'm sure he won't murder me on the spot, but what sort of man must this Dr. Trumbull be?"

"A cheeky one," Peg said. "He charges two pounds an hour for listening to women talk about themselves. That's robbery right there."

"It does rather add insult to injury, doesn't it? Especially since he's asking two thousand quid for Mrs. Clennam's special treatment."

James had written the letter as soon as they'd come home from Torquay. They'd gotten a response the very next day. The doctor must be eager for new patients, having dispatched of Lady Georgia. The note told James to bring his wife to Harley Street on Tuesday morning for a ten o'clock appointment, returning to collect her in one hour. In a few weeks, it said, the patient would be advised to enter the hospital for a month-long stay. At that time, James would receive another letter with instructions for delivering payment for the special services. This would be one thousand pounds before the event and another thousand after the will was proved.

Two thousand pounds was a breathtaking sum. James had only earned three hundred pounds a year as an assistant examiner at the Patent Office. He'd expected her to live on that when they first married, bless his innocent heart!

Peg gathered up the skirt of a violet silk walking dress, then paused to catch Angelina's eyes. "Promise me you won't set one foot in that hospital, Lina."

"It won't come to that." Angelina's gaze flicked toward the mirror. She hated making promises she couldn't keep, but she intended to see this through. Not just for Viola. She felt so sad for Lady Georgia and all the other "superfluous women" being so callously disposed of.

71

"Forewarned is forearmed, Peg. I'll keep my wits about me and my eyes open."

"Hmph." Peg pulled the skirt over Angelina's head and adjusted the folds over the bustle. As she helped her into the snug jacket, she said, "That doctor will ask about your childhood, I'll wager. What're you going to tell him?"

"I haven't decided." Angelina buttoned the jacket and checked her costume in the mirror. "I'll be vague about details until I know how confidential our conversations will be. What if he's one of those doctors who turns around and tells your husband everything you've said?"

Peg clicked her tongue. "Better to hear it from you, Lina."

"I know. But we can't go into all that now, not with this nerve doctor to deal with."

"Oh no, of course not." Peg gave her that look that meant she could say plenty more if she thought it would do any good. "Later is always better."

Angelina sat down to have her hair done, avoiding Peg's eyes in the mirror. They'd played some risky games over their twenty-five years together, but usually in theater circles where no one cared about your past. And she'd never deliberately put herself in the path of a murderer.

"I'll make it up as I go along," she said. "You know how this game is played. If I'm going to keep the story straight, it'll have to be fairly close to the truth."

Peg grunted again. "More than you've told your husband, then, eh, ducky?"

* * *

Angelina descended from the cab as awkwardly as she could without falling on her face in the street, fumbling her handbag and her umbrella. A nurse in a gray uniform trotted down the front steps to take her arm, gripping it tightly with one hand and relieving her of the umbrella with the other.

She ushered Angelina up the steps, which were tiled in blue to match the indigo front doors. This grand portal sported large brass knobs, a pair of lion's head knockers, and a fanlight. The spiked iron railing around the area also looked freshly polished, gleaming and dust free, like the white painted trim around the front windows on each floor.

It must take an army of servants to keep it looking so spruce. No wonder the doctor charged two pounds an hour!

The interior was even more elegant. Trumbull made sure his patients were duly impressed from the moment they entered the house. The marble tiles of the stoop changed to black and white chequers inside, with burnished oak trim everywhere and portraits of solemn gentlemen on either side of an ornate mirror. Was she expected to compare herself to these august individuals? She'd come up wanting, especially in the silly hat Peg had chosen.

The nurse whipped off her cloak and hustled her into a small drawing room, where she waved at a stiff-backed chair. "Sit down, please, Mrs. Moriarty. Would you like a cup of tea?"

"No, thank you," Angelina said in a small voice. "Will the doctor see me in here?" She looked fearfully about the dimly lit and lushly furnished room. It felt very impersonal, and she had a sense of other small drawing rooms on either side. They must be used to prevent patients from seeing one another as they came and went.

"No, you'll go upstairs. But first Dr. Fairchild, one of our consultants, would like to ask you a few questions."

"Oh!" Angelina had no need to feign surprise. Hadn't James visited a Dr. Fairchild last week? He had given

James that little bottle of male tonic. They'd thrown it out. They never had problems in that arena.

She didn't have time to remember what he'd told her about that visit. A thin man with longish blond hair in a dark coat opened the door without knocking. He wore a Van Dyke beard and was handsome enough, in a pinched sort of way. Angelina judged him to be about James's age — thirty-five-ish. He carried a notebook and a fountain pen.

James had described Fairchild as "geniality incarnate." This man looked as though he'd never had a happy moment in his life and resented it deeply.

"Good morning." He granted her a stiff smile and seated himself in the chair closest to her. "I'd like to ask you a few questions, if I may."

"What sort of questions?" Angelina put a little thrum of fear into her voice.

"Nothing difficult. We like to get a well-rounded picture of our patients here. I'm a colleague of Dr. Trumbull's, a nerve specialist as well. I collect the admitting data myself to ensure consistency with a larger study I'm conducting as part of my private research."

"I see," she said, sounding confused. James had mentioned that part. It sounded like the perfect ruse for identifying victims.

He opened his notebook and wrote something at the top of a fresh page. "Let's see, you're Mrs. Angelina Moriarty, is that correct?" He gave a short laugh, then choked it back. But his eyes twinkled a little as he jotted down the name. "I'm glad to see you here."

What *had* James told him about her? He said he'd gone to ask about methodologies and treatments. He hadn't said anything about discussing personal matters. Angelina stretched a smile on her lips. Two could play at that little game. She wouldn't tell him about her consultations either.

Without looking at her again, Fairchild asked, "What is your husband's occupation?"

"He hasn't one; he's a gentleman. Or do you mean how does he spend his time?"

"Mm-hmm."

"Well, he has his books and his clubs. He likes to play cards." She smiled brightly, as if that were an accomplishment.

"And his family?"

"I don't think they play cards. Croquet, perhaps. I scarcely know them. They're in Gloucestershire and they loathe the city."

"I meant where are they and you've just told me." He jotted down her answers. "Maiden name?"

"My husband's?"

"Yours, Mrs. Moriarty." He sounded as though he could barely tolerate her stupidity. He seemed to be one of those men who took it for granted that women were simple-minded.

"Oh! Of course!" Angelina tittered. She always enjoyed playing it dumb. "My father's name was Archibald . . . Battle." That was close to Buddle, his real name and hers, and not a bad description of their relationship during her last years under his thumb.

"Parents still living?"

"No, both gone." She cast her eyes sadly to her hands. "Father died when I was only a child and Mother passed away a year before I married. If it weren't for my darling James, I'd be all alone in the world."

"Cause of death?"

"James?" She let her voice spiral up in alarm.

Fairchild drew in a long, irritable breath. "Your parents."

"Oh my! Well, I don't know how Father died. He was terribly sick for simply ages. Then I suppose Mother died

of loneliness. That can happen, you know." She batted
her lashes with a pious smile.

His upper lip curled with contempt. "Father's
occupation?"

"My father?"

"Yes, Mrs. Moriarty. Your father." He bit off each
word. She should probably cool it down a touch.

"Daddy was a gentleman too. Although sometimes he
went to the mill with the manager to look at something or
other. The money was Mummy's. It's mine now."

"And where did that come from?" He sounded like
he was asking about a boil on her thigh. She would have
expected the word "money" to light at least a tiny spark
in those cold eyes.

"Well, the mill, I suppose. Cotton, you know." Then
inspiration struck. "And, of course, the plantation in
Jamaica." Difficult to verify if anyone tried.

"I see." Fairchild wrote it all down with the same air
of disapproval. How could James ever have considered
this man to be amiable?

"Any history of nervous disease in the family?"

"Oh! Well, no. Unless you count fainting spells."

"Who and under what circumstances?"

"Mummy. And only when I was naughty and refused
to behave." That seemed another clever touch, but he let
it pass without comment.

"What medicines do you take regularly?"

"Well, none. I don't like tonics. They have a nasty
taste and make me feel sillier than I already am. James
hates it when I'm silly." She frowned sadly at her hands
again.

"I see. Well, you'll like Dr. Trumbull's tonics.
Everyone does. And they won't make you silly; quite the
contrary." Fairchild replaced the cap on his pen, closed
his notebook, and stood up. He twitched his lips in that
grim smile and tilted his head in the briefest of bows.

"Never fear, Mrs. Moriarty. We'll get to the bottom of your troubles and devise the best possible treatment for you. I'm sure your husband will be completely satisfied with the result."

He left without giving her a chance to respond. She heard footsteps and voices in the corridor, muffled by the thick oak door and plush furnishings. The last patient must be going out. She listened to the clock on the mantel ticking while she rehearsed the answers she'd given, drilling them into her memory. In a few minutes, the slim nurse reappeared and said, "Dr. Trumbull will see you now. If you'll follow me?"

She led the way up the carpeted stairs to the front room on the first floor. She rapped a knuckle on the door and opened it without waiting for an answer. "Mrs. Moriarty," she said, standing back to let Angelina pass her. She closed the door behind her as she left.

"Come in, come in. I'm Robert Trumbull." A short, plump man in a morning coat with narrow trousers came toward her with both hands extended. She let him draw her into the room and guide her to a silk-covered chair, wide and soft, the essence of luxury.

He stood over her for a moment, nodding, his blue eyes twinkling at her with such warmth she knew at once that she could tell this man anything — anything at all — and be fully understood. He was sympathy personified. He looked like Father Christmas, but with luxurious side whiskers instead of a curling beard.

He offered her sherry or a cup of tea. She declined them both, determined not to eat or drink anything in this house. Then he sat next to her and leaned forward, clasping his hands between his knees. "Now, my dear. Why don't you tell me what's been troubling you."

She blinked at him. She'd expected more questions, which she could answer one at a time. After the interview downstairs, she'd expected another crisp professional man with a superior attitude. She licked her lips, hesitating. He waited in silence with a patient smile on his pink lips.

She let her eyes wander while she collected her thoughts. The large room was filled with intriguing textiles and *objets d'art* that had been chosen with care, over time, by a man with eclectic tastes. Silk draperies muted the light from the front windows while two gas lamps banished the shadows from the back of the room, where a mahogany desk stood in front of a tall cabinet. This was the most comfortable, functional, tasteful gentleman's library she'd ever been in. She wished she could hire the nerve specialist to decorate her house. And that gave her a theme.

"This may sound terribly silly, Doctor, but it's my house. Well, my husband and my house. The house and James. I can't seem to make anything go right with either of them."

"Tell me all about it," he prompted in a rich tenor voice.

So she did. She cast James in the role of a man whose ambitions demanded a showplace with a wife to match. She used her real guilt about her own ambition to return to the stage to color her performance. She didn't have to pretend that decorating, furnishing, and staffing a large house for the first time in her life was driving her mad. And it wasn't at all difficult to focus her frustration on the husband who had no appreciation for the effort.

She concocted a mixture of truth and fiction, seasoned with genuine feelings of frustration and self-doubt, even throwing in the skittish housemaids and the French cook. Dr. Trumbull listened with unobtrusive attention, his face turned slightly away, wearing an expression of neutral understanding. When she paused or floundered, he nudged her gently forward. She found herself telling him things she hadn't even realized were bothering her until the words flowed from her lips.

She wound down after a while with a few sniffs. He handed her a handkerchief and nodded as she dabbed her eyes. She looked up at him, smiled weakly, and sighed.

"Feel better?"

"Much," she said with utter truthfulness.

"Good. You have a lot to cope with, my dear. We men grossly underestimate the pressures we expect our women to bear. It isn't easy to meet everyone's expectations, is it, especially when they're not very clear about what they want."

She shook her head, agreeing with him. She understood why this man was so popular. She'd never felt so deeply understood. She had to bite her lip to remind herself why she had come here.

She sniffed and plied the handkerchief again, then tilted her face down to peer at the doctor from under moist eyelashes. "The truth is, I'm afraid my husband wouldn't love me at all if he knew who I really am. I don't think he loves me now. In fact, I think he thinks that he'd be better off without me." She dropped to a whisper at the end.

"Nonsense!" Dr. Trumbull grasped both her hands. His blue eyes caught and held her gaze with nearly hypnotic intensity. "Your husband loves you very much. I know because if he didn't, he wouldn't be willing to pay my exorbitant fees." He smiled at his little joke. "I'm going to help you, Mrs. Moriarty. I'll put the roses back in those cheeks. It might take some hard work for both of us, but never you fear. You and your husband will be happy again."

She clung to his strong hands and gazed into his kindly blue eyes. This Dr. Trumbull was either the genuine article — a skilled and sympathetic alienist — or the most fiendishly gifted old confidence trickster she had ever met.

A chill ran up her spine. *Be careful, Lina!*

# Chapter Eight

James Moriarty trotted up the stairs inside St. Bartholomew's Hospital in Smithfield, as keen as a student ready for a school treat. Holmes and Watson had invited him to join them in analyzing an assortment of medicinal tonics to explore the possibilities for effecting murder by such means.

He wasn't eager to spend a day in Holmes's pretentious company specifically, but he had been buried in records offices and newspaper archives for the past week, poring through stacks of dusty paper and learning very little. He had noticed advertisements for tonics everywhere, now that his attention had been drawn to them. He'd had no idea. Colorful cartoons of plump toddlers and muscular men appeared on nearly every page. On billboards too, on the sides of buildings. They'd received two telegrams in the last week urging them to buy a box of Ollie's Jolly Liver Pills. Funny how a man could fail to notice such things day in and day out.

Moriarty found the chemistry laboratory as much by following his nose as by noting the room numbers marked over each door. He walked into a well-lit room divided into workspaces by stands of open shelves filled with glass bottles and canisters, set down the middle of scarred oak tables. Each station included a pair of stools and an assortment of implements like mortars and pestles, racks of tubes and pipettes, tongs and small knives — the superficial disarray and underlying order of places in which men conducted serious research.

He inhaled the acrid aroma lingering in the room with pleasure. He loved laboratories the way Angelina loved draper's shops. All the possibilities contained therein!

Holmes and Watson had commandeered a table about midway into the cluttered room. Watson sat on a stool by the window studying a large leather-bound book. Holmes puttered at the worktable, stirring a dark liquid in a large flask over a Bunsen burner. They looked as cozy as if they were sitting in their bachelor digs on Baker Street.

For a moment, he envied them. Up until recently, he too had spent his days in the company of educated men engaged in intellectual pursuits. He missed it.

"Ah, Professor!" Holmes cried. "You found us."

Moriarty and Watson exchanged conventional greetings. Then Moriarty pointed his chin at the bubbling liquid. "Have you started without me?"

"By necessity," Holmes answered. "This process takes an hour at least."

Moriarty peered at the concoction. It smelled like mulled wine with metal shavings. "What are you cooking?"

"I'm testing a sample of Trumbull's Stomach Bitters for mercury and other metals."

"Interesting." Moriarty took another tentative sniff. "Why mercury?"

"Because it's a relatively easy test." Holmes chuckled. "We can't perform full analyses of the doctor's complete range of products. We have neither the time nor the resources."

"They don't want it to be easy," Watson said. "If it were, imitations would spring up right and left. These tonics tend to have a lot of ingredients and the manufacturers guard their recipes closely."

"Just so," Holmes said. "But we can make a more direct assessment of their qualities." His dark eyes twinkled with mischief.

He obviously wanted Moriarty to ask, so he obliged. "How is that?"

"By tasting them!" Holmes gestured at an assortment of bottles arrayed on the table. "A sophisticated palate may reveal as much as a chemical reagent." He selected a bottle and poured a tot into three small glasses. He handed one to Moriarty and took one for himself. Watson declined.

Holmes raised his glass. "To your good health, gentlemen!" He took a sip and turned his gaze toward the smoke-mottled ceiling, working his tongue to evaluate the flavor. "Hmm. What do you think, Professor?"

Moriarty shrugged at Watson and took a swallow. He refused to seem a coward over so trivial a test.

Watson gave them both a wry look. "You've just taken about ten times the prescribed amount, you know."

"Tush, Watson!" Holmes said. "That prescription is for children. We want to evaluate the effects in one dose."

Moriarty noted a pleasant warmth spreading from his stomach to his head. "An interesting sensation, I must say. It tastes like sarsaparilla-flavored gin." He chuckled. "Add a slice of lemon and some shaved ice and they could serve it as a cocktail at the Savoy." His chuckle grew to a laugh, although it really wasn't that funny.

Watson said, "More likely plain grain alcohol. It's cheaper. Some tonics have as much as eighteen percent alcohol by volume — as much as a strong wine."

Moriarty took the rest of his ration into his mouth, curling his tongue and clucking a little as he tried to discriminate another element. He swallowed it, thought for a minute, and asked, "Do I taste hops?"

"Possibly," Watson said. "It causes a tingle that patients often interpret as the medicine working its magic."

"Well, I do feel more relaxed," Moriarty said. "Is that the purpose of this elixir?" He reached for the bottle and read the label: *Trumbull's Nerve Strengthener and Brain Food.* "Brain food? I say!" He cocked his head, assessing his interior state. "No, I feel a little lazier than usual. I wouldn't choose this potion to fortify me for an examination, for example."

"Nor would I," Holmes said. "I believe this tonic contains one of the opioids. Opium, most likely. Nerve tonics typically contain about five grains of the pure drug per dose, assuming a dose of one teaspoon."

"Is that a lot?" Moriarty asked, suppressing his alarm.

"No," Holmes said. "An accustomed user like Lady Georgia would take ten times that amount, and a confirmed addict of strong constitution could tolerate an even larger dose."

Watson studied the label. "This says it's meant to calm a nervous patient and reduce mental agitations that prohibit normal concentration."

"Ah, well, then," Moriarty said. "It accomplishes that goal handily."

"Let's try another one," Holmes said. "We'll rinse our glasses with plain water first."

Moriarty swirled the splash provided in his glass, then swished it around in his mouth to clear his palate, as if conducting a wine-tasting.

Holmes grasped a tallish bottle in such a way as to obscure the label and poured a good two ounces for each of them. He raised his glass. Moriarty followed suit. "To the queen!"

Holmes drank his ration in two swift swallows. "Ah." He closed his eyes to savor the effects.

84

Moriarty took a smaller sample. "Why, this is wine! An undistinguished Bordeaux, I should say. With a rather unpleasant aftertaste, although that could be from the smell of chemicals in this room." He drank down the rest of his portion. "No, it's definitely the tonic."

Holmes watched him with glittering eyes. "Does it affect your mental state at all, Professor?"

"It believe it does. More than the other. In fact, my head now seems quite clear. I feel more awake and ready to learn than when I first arrived."

"Yes," Holmes said. "That's the cocaine working."

"Cocaine? Give me that bottle!" Moriarty read the label with a frown: *Vin Mariani — Peruvian Coca Wine. Stimulates the internal organs and enhances masculine vigor.* He'd discovered in May that cocaine was Holmes's favorite shield against boredom. Though he had little tolerance for that condition himself, resorting to a drug suggested a sad paucity of inner resources. "Really, Holmes, you might have warned me."

Holmes merely smiled.

Moriarty disliked the deceit but felt too benevolent to press the point. He wouldn't admit it, but he actually felt rather splendid at the moment. He asked Watson, "Is it possible to die of an overdose of cocaine?"

"Oh yes," Watson said. "Especially an inexperienced user dosing himself with the pure drug. I've never heard of anyone dying from Peruvian wine, although I believe this formula can be addictive."

"Like wine," Holmes said, "which, in my opinion, muddies the effects."

"You would say that," Watson scolded. "But to expand on your question, Professor, one of the hazards of cocaine is that it can drastically increase the heart rate. If a person already suffers from a weak or irregular heart, too much of the drug could cause heart failure."

"That's very interesting, Doctor," Moriarty said. "Very interesting indeed. Could that effect be delayed?"

"No, it would be immediate," Watson said.

"Of course it would, that's not what I meant." Moriarty snapped his fingers several times. "I mean, wouldn't it be possible for a doctor who knew his patient had a weak heart to send her home with a tonic containing an overdose of cocaine, knowing that when she drank it later, at whatever time he had instructed her to do so, it would kill her?"

Watson took a moment to absorb the spate of speech. "Yes, that would certainly work."

"Furthermore," Moriarty said, excited about his idea, "if the family knew about the existing condition, they wouldn't be surprised. In fact, they would have been expecting the death, sooner or later."

"A clever idea, Professor," Holmes said with a shade of envy in his voice. "The cause of death would be given as heart failure and no one would investigate further."

Moriarty ignored him. "If the tonic had a label as uninformative as . . . as . . ." He plucked a bottle from the collection and barked a laugh. "As Trumbull's Electric Bitters, for rheumatism, dyspepsia, constipation, weakness, insomnia, liver troubles, and cholera. Great Scott! This will cure everything but a broken leg!"

Watson laughed. "Some of them do make extravagant claims."

Moriarty poured a small dose into his glass and drank it. "Ugh!" He made a sour face. "Tastes like bitter oranges and pine tar." It occurred to him belatedly that he was getting a little reckless; no doubt the effect of the coca wine.

"If it does anything for constipation, it probably has mercury in it," Watson said.

"Thanks for the reminder, Watson." Holmes turned his attention back to his experiment. He stirred the contents, which had visibly thickened, and removed the flask from the burner with a pair of tongs, setting it aside. "We'll let that cool for a while."

"We're back to mercury," Moriarty said. "Is that a common ingredient?"

"Very common," Watson said. "It can be beneficial in small doses. It's the essential ingredient in blue pill, for example. A time-honored remedy, although I don't prescribe it myself anymore. More roughage in the diet would be my first recommendation."

"Blue pills!" Holmes waved a finger in the air. "That's how I would do it."

The others looked at him blankly. He flicked his eyebrows in that irritating, supercilious way he had. "If I wanted to murder someone with whom I had intimate contact, like a patient or a spouse, I would use blue pill or something like it. I would take my time about it — months, to be perfectly safe. First I would encourage my victim to acquire the habit of taking some such daily medicament. Blue pill, liver pills — there are many to choose from. Everyone in the household would become accustomed to the presence of that little bottle or box beside the bed. Then, when I could be sure the pills had faded into the background like an old pair of curtains, I would introduce one pill containing a lethal dose, and let habit take its course."

"By gad, Holmes!" Watson cried. "What a mind you have!"

Moriarty had to agree. "It's brilliant. You could put whatever you liked in the odd one, assuming you could fit a sufficient quantity of poison into the same form."

Watson shook his head. "It would take some experimentation. You won't be the first man to think of that ploy, Holmes. Take mercury, for example. You can't build up a tolerance to it as you can arsenic or opium, and people have widely varying abilities to absorb the stuff. A dose that will kill one man will only make another one sick to his stomach. And if your dose is too far off, your victim will vomit it up before it can do much harm."

"Blue pills!" Moriarty cried, smacking himself on the forehead. "I forgot to report on our Torquay expedition."

"So you did," Holmes said, shaking a finger at him. "You're holding out on us, Professor."

"Not intentionally," Moriarty said. "You distracted me."

"Very well, then." Holmes poured them each another glass of Vin Mariani. "What did you learn?"

Moriarty took a sip, liking the flavor better than he had at first. He leaned against the table behind them and crossed his arms. "We were able to verify Mr. Wexcombe's story to some extent. Both Angelina and I encountered Trumbull's touts, as she termed them."

"A nice phrase," Holmes said.

"And an apt one. A fellow suggested the Clennam treatment to me one evening in the billiard room, although it wasn't the dark-haired chap Wexcombe met. This one had ginger hair. I got his name later from one of the staff: Mr. Randolph Atlee. Furthermore, Angelina learned from the old tabbies on the terrace —"

Holmes murmured, "Tabbies on the terrace and Trumbull's touts."

Moriarty scowled at the interruption. "Angelina learned that Mrs. Atlee, another member of that circle, had died several months ago, supposedly of an overdose of blue pill. The tabbies were adamant that no one could make such a stupid mistake."

"I don't know about that," Watson said. "Some elderly persons do become confused about these small daily rituals."

"Even so," Holmes said, "it's an intriguing coincidence. I propose we add Mrs. Atlee to our list of victims. Did you obtain any other names, Professor?"

"Just one — a Mrs. Winifred Delaney, who died during a fox hunt on Boxing Day last year. The verdict was heart failure, but the tabbies said she had no trouble with her heart before she entered Halcyon House."

"Ha!" Holmes said. "I knew you hadn't come up with that idea on your own, Professor. You haven't the right sort of imagination."

How could anyone refute such a charge? Moriarty contented himself with a sneer and another swallow of Peruvian wine. Holmes seemed to have forgotten about his mercury test, but it didn't matter. They couldn't exhume any of the bodies of their supposed victims anyway. Examining the labels and exploring the effects directly helped Moriarty understand how these tonics worked, both legitimately and otherwise.

He asked Watson, "Do all popular tonics contain hazardous elements like mercury and opium?"

"Not all," Watson said, "but the most effective ingredients are inevitably the most dangerous. It's a matter of proportion. You would be alarmed to hear the full list."

"You'll find me quite unshockable," Moriarty said.

"Well, then," Watson said, "antimony, usually listed as tartar emetic, is a common one. It's used to treat sick animals and melancholia." He smiled at Moriarty's skeptical frown. "I know. These lists typically include unrelated afflictions. Also strychnine, prescribed as a stimulant or for weight loss. Morphine, of course, and codeine, another opium derivative prescribed for pain or coughing. Then you have your herbal ingredients, added for flavor, but some also have mild therapeutic effects. Things like sarsaparilla, as you noted, and ginger tickle the tongue so it feels like the tonic is doing something. Hops, dandelion, gentian, tansy, chamomile, aloe, saffron, cinnamon, cloves — you're liable to find any herb you care to name in one tonic or another and, of course, alcohol so it will keep and plenty of honey or sugar to make it palatable."

"That's quite a list," Moriarty said. "I now understand how Trumbull could achieve mercury poisoning with blue pill or ruin a woman's heart with cocaine, if he is in fact doing any such thing. But I still don't see how he could give an overdose of laudanum to an experienced user such as Lady Georgia. Your contention, Holmes, is that she would know her own tolerance too well to drink too much of her tonic. Especially if the standard measure is a teaspoon. She would have her spoonful, wait a bit, feel the effects she expected to feel, and take no more."

"True," Holmes said, "unless that spoonful had been made more potent without her knowledge."

"Her tolerance level is the key to the puzzle," Watson said.

Holmes nodded, the light of a new idea in his eyes. "An overdose is caused by ingesting more than the accustomed amount. That equation can be balanced two ways, gentlemen: increasing the dose or reducing the tolerance."

"I don't follow you," Moriarty said, but Watson had started nodding too. "That's right, Holmes. And a month in a private hospital is long enough to clear the drug out of the system. Lady Georgia would be starting from scratch when she got home. Her old dose might very well kill her the first time out."

"A most ingenious method," Holmes said, "that could never be proved by chemical tests. Her tissues would merely confirm her long-standing and well-attested use."

Moriarty said, "I suppose if she didn't understand that her tolerance had been altered, she might innocently resume her old practice."

"And the servants would think nothing of it," Watson said. "Insidious."

"Would hospital staff have been aware of the doctor's program for Lady Georgia?" Moriarty asked.

"They'd remember it," Holmes said. "The process of withdrawal isn't pretty."

"Yes," Watson said. "It's quite distressing for the poor patient. They experience tremors, cold sweats, headaches, sometimes waking delusions. Whoever cared for her during this time would certainly know what was happening."

Moriarty grimaced at the description and drank off the rest of his Peruvian wine. It seemed to stimulate his whole brain, very useful in this discussion. "Another unprovable method of murder."

The other two nodded grimly. Holmes refilled their glasses.

"However," Moriarty said, "we must remember that this is pure speculation so far."

"True," Holmes said. "We learned nothing useful at the inquest, apart from the Lady Georgia's once customary dosage. I did obtain an empty bottle and testimony on that score from her maid."

"The inquest!" Outrage flooded Moriarty's chest, heating his cheeks and his bald head. The reaction surprised him, but he didn't resist it. "When were you planning to share those results with me?"

"When the topic arose." Holmes blinked like a cat who had successfully pulled the head off a mouse.

Moriarty let a silence develop in which the full measure of his dissatisfaction could be felt. Then he spoke calmly but with a crisp edge in his voice. "Bear in mind, Holmes, that you are dependent on reports from my wife to learn about Trumbull and the workings of his establishment. I expect a full *quid pro quo*. You will share what you learn or get nothing from us."

"Duly noted," Holmes said. The gleam in his eyes undermined his sincerity.

Watson, as usual, played peacemaker. "We didn't learn much. Before she started seeing Dr. Trumbull, Lady Georgia obtained a custom preparation of laudanum from her local apothecary, who testified that she was accustomed to taking six to ten drops about four times a day. No bottles of the old preparation had been kept. Trumbull declined to appear at the inquest, but he asserted in writing that his prescription had been for a lesser dose. His aim was to reduce Lady Georgia's dependence without causing her a shock. An empty bottle of Trumbull's Nerve Tonic, which is what he calls his laudanum formulation, was found beside the bed. There was evidence that the contents had been spilled, so it was impossible to determine how much she had consumed. The verdict declared a death by misadventure, but the comments included hints that suicide could not be conclusively ruled out."

Moriarty tucked his chin while he absorbed that information. Then he grunted. "Well, then, my wife and I did better than you." He spoiled the effect of that claim by producing a loud hiccough. He held his breath while swallowing another large gulp of Peruvian wine, which made his head swim. He set his glass on the table, making two attempts to avoid landing it on a pencil that had appeared out of nowhere.

Watson watched him with a wry professional eye. "One thing is certain," he said.

"That James Moriarty can't take his medicine," Holmes crowed, pointing his long finger with only a few degrees of wobble.

"That Sherlock Holmes is a drug-addle . . . addle . . . addict." Moriarty drew himself up to his full height and had to grab the table as he listed sharply to one side.

Watson pursed his lips. "No, although you're both right. What's certain is that we can't hope to produce medical proof of murder in any of these cases. We must find that disgruntled employee or those incriminating Clennam letters, assuming they've been kept."

"In short, Professor," Holmes said with an insolent smirk, "this investigation depends entirely upon your wife."

# Chapter Nine

Angelina didn't bother with itchy knickers for her next appointment with Dr. Trumbull on Tuesday morning. She had confidence in her ability to play her role without such tricks. In fact, she was looking forward to this consultation. Talking with the doctor had made her feel better in general last time, though she'd never admit that to James.

He'd asked, of course. "What did you find to talk about? Not me, I hope." He'd said it with a twinkle as if he were joking, but she knew better. She'd said, with an answering twinkle, "When I learn something useful, you'll be the first to know."

Well, he hadn't told her much about his activities either. He'd spent hours with Holmes and Watson testing tonics, for example, and had hardly told her anything of what they'd learned.

She had to smile as she remembered that evening. James had come home in an amorous mood, waltzing in the front door whistling. He'd tossed his hat at the rack and laughed when it missed, grabbing her around the waist to plant a passionate kiss on her lips. He'd sent Rolly down to tell cook to hold dinner until further notice and to bring them a bottle of wine. Then he'd carried her up the stairs to their bedroom, where he had been *most* attentive and inventive. They'd ended up taking a late supper from a tray in bed like a couple of libertines.

The next morning, he'd woken up with a sore head and a sour temper. He'd blamed her, naturally, since she was handy. "If you hadn't gotten me involved with that drug fiend Sherlock Holmes . . ."

He'd managed to crawl out of bed and dress himself and stagger down one flight of stairs, but then he'd collapsed on the sofa in the drawing room and spent the whole day there, interrupting the servants' work to demand seltzer water — no, hot tea, the stronger, the better — no, no, just a bit of dry toast, if it wasn't *too* much trouble.

It hadn't helped that Friday was the day the men came to remove that horrible red flocked wallpaper from the dining room, right below James on his bed of nails. Every bump, every "Gor blimey!" made him jump and complain to her. But these men were the best and they weren't available every day.

James had been an absolute bear. She hadn't known he had it in him. Heaven help the woman whose husband has a headache!

Saturday morning he'd been back to his usual taciturn self. Their marriage had more ups and downs than the switchback railway at Frascati Gardens in Paris. At least she could use it in her consultation today, twisting it to make James out to be a habitual drunkard and domestic tyrant. She'd mix in a little of her father, who really had been a tyrant, in his way. She'd never managed to please him either.

As her cab approached the house with the glossy blue door, she rolled her shoulders, flexed her gloved fingers, and sang the scales quietly to limber her vocal chords. Time to raise the curtain.

A different nurse opened the door today. This one was built like a Scottish farm wife — tall and stocky with red hair and a spatter of freckles across her pink cheeks. She introduced herself as Nurse Andrews in a voice that held more than a trace of Scots.

95

She said, "We'll start back here today," and led
Angelina into another small room on the ground floor.
This one lacked any softening effects. It held a narrow
table, about waist high, a pair of stiff-backed chairs, and a
curtained screen across one corner. A cabinet with jars
and instruments stood against one wall and a tall metal
scale against another. There was a washstand beside the
cabinet, furnished with a pitcher and a clean towel.

"What are you going to do me in here?" Angelina put
an honest quaver in her voice.

"There's nothing to worry about, Mrs. Moriarty.
We're going to let the doctor make a quick examination,
that's all, to make sure everything is as it should be."

"Dr. Trumbull?"

"Heavens, no. He's a *specialist*. Your physical
examination will be conducted by Dr. Oliver, a general
physician. One of the best. He trained at King's College,
you know."

Angelina's shoulders sank as she contemplated that
screen. "I suppose you want me to . . ."

"Mm-hmm. Just pop back there and strip down to
your chemise."

"I wear combinations."

"That's fine." Nurse Andrews cast a critical eye over
Angelina's fashionable visiting dress with its deep drape
of Ottoman silk at the front and the cascading flounce in
back over her bustle. She clucked her tongue. "I'll help
you with your laces."

Between the two of them, they got everything off,
draping the garments over the top of the screen. Then the
nurse led Angelina out to weigh her, a humiliating
experience.

"Don't tell me," she begged.

The nurse clucked her tongue again. "As you wish."
She recorded the dreaded number in a notebook,

however, saving it for posterity. Angelina hoped this doctor kept a close watch on his records.

Nurse Andrews took a thermometer from a drawer in the cabinet and shook it. "Open wide." When Angelina dutifully allowed the vile object to be inserted under her tongue, the nurse said, "Keep that well under now. Half a minute more. That's a good girl."

The polite forms of address seemed to have been left behind the screen with her dress.

Andrews grasped her wrist to take her pulse. "Mm-hm," she said, releasing the wrist to remove the thermometer. She nodded at the instrument and wrote down both results.

"Am I alive, then?" Angelina asked.

Nurse Andrews didn't grant that small joke an answer.

Two sharp knocks and the door opened. "Good morning," a man said, striding in with a broad smile already in place. "I'm Doctor Gideon Oliver. And how's our newest patient today? Mrs. Moriarty, isn't it?"

He presented the portrait of a jovial country doctor. Somewhere in his middle thirties, Oliver had a clean chin and wore his brown hair short and his sideburns long. He was a little taller than Angelina, with a slight paunch and a touch of sag under the chin. He wore a well-cut dark suit with a gold chain and watch fob draped across the vest. A prosperous man, too busy for sports, though he doubtless recommended exercise to his patients.

He hadn't shown a flicker of recognition at her name. Maybe James was right and poor Mr. Wexcombe had imagined the whole thing. But they had sent that letter to this address and someone had answered it. One would think they'd remember the names of their victims!

Angelina smiled shyly. "I'm fine, thank you, Doctor."

"Good, good. Don't worry. We won't poke and prod too much. But we have to make sure there's no physical

97

cause for your complaints, don't we? If we can solve your problems with a course of physic and a recipe for green salad, it would be criminal not to." He nodded at her until she nodded back.

"I suppose so." Angelina had danced across a stage in a harem costume in front of hundreds of people, but she found it miserable to sit here chatting with a fully dressed man wearing nothing but her frilly combinations.

Oliver twinkled at her. "Why don't you hop up on that table while I have a look at Nurse Andrews's notes?" He turned away without waiting for an answer.

Angelina pulled herself onto the table and sat with her legs dangling while doctor and nurse murmured, heads together.

He returned to her with a stern look on his face. "Well, Mrs. Moriarty, Nurse Andrews tells me you're lacing your corset far too tightly." He shook his finger at her. "That won't do. It won't do at all. Half the maladies known to womankind can be charged to vanity in the form of tight lacing. Loosen those laces, young lady, and get some fresh air every day. If you don't know how to get started, check yourself into Trumbull's hospital for a month. We'll put you in a sensible corset and get you plenty of exercise. We have croquet and badminton and a lovely garden to walk in. One month of that and you won't even want to go back to those bad old habits."

*Aha!* A pitch for their precious hospital. But he made it sound like a holiday resort. Badminton? She'd been expecting something nefarious, not sensible advice.

Dr. Oliver took a sort of single-lensed lorgnette from his pocket and peered into each of her ears. Then he stood in front of her and said, "Mouth open, please." He peered down her throat. "Close, please. Now open both eyes as wide as you can." He stared into them. Angelina couldn't help but notice the coarseness of the pores on his nose, though she was grateful that his breath smelled of cloves. Would a murderous doctor be so thoughtful?

Next he took a metal thing like a tiny axe with a rubber blade and rapped it sharply against her knee, making her foot swing.

"Oh!" she cried, surprised at the effect.

He chuckled and did the same to the other knee. Then he tucked the implement in his pocket and said, "Lie back now and try to think about something pleasant."

She didn't like the sound of that, but she obeyed, lying back on the hard table with her hands awkwardly at her sides. She felt horribly exposed and it got worse. The doctor pressed his palm and fingers across her belly and around to the small of her back. Then he raised her knees and put his hand through the split in her combinations. He pressed one hand against her lower belly while he probed deep inside her with the fingers of his other hand. It was quite the most appalling experience she had ever endured.

She closed her eyes, gritted her teeth, and cursed Sherlock Holmes with every oath she'd ever learned.

At least the ordeal ended. The doctor withdrew from her interior and went to wash his hands. Speaking over his shoulder, he said, "All done. You can sit up now."

Angelina struggled to a sitting position and took a deep breath, remembering why she was here. At least now she'd come through the worst of it.

Dr. Oliver dried his hands on the towel and handed it to the nurse, who had been lurking in the background with her notebook. The doctor pulled a chair up close to the table and sat down, adopting a relaxed posture. "Well, you're a healthy woman, Mrs. Moriarty, although I'd like to see you shed a few pounds. And I noticed some scarring on your cervix. Have you ever been pregnant?"

Angelina gaped at him, horrified. "You can tell that from — just from feeling?"

He smiled blandly. "That's my job. Your husband doesn't know, I take it."

Angelina pressed her lips together and shook her head. That was the worst part of the history she had kept from James.

"Well," Dr. Oliver said, catching her gaze. "He won't learn it from me. Although I don't encourage married couples to keep secrets from one another. Why don't you tell me what happened?"

She hung her head in unfeigned reluctance, gathering her thoughts. She had never expected to have to explain scars she didn't know she had. She'd have to tell the truth, more or less. She'd keep it as short and anonymous as possible.

She told him she'd met a man when she was eighteen who had promised to marry her and persuaded her to run away with him. She made him a stockbroker instead of a dissolute baron and implied that the home she'd left was the ordinary sort, not a third-class room in a seedy hotel. But the rest was true. The young man had abandoned her in Rome when she fell pregnant, leaving her with one week's rent and little else. Peg, bless her faithful heart, had managed to procure the services of a silent old woman who'd scraped her insides and given her a nasty tonic. That treatment had made her sick for weeks, but it worked. The babe was gone.

Dr. Oliver said nothing while she spoke, only nodded with a tight frown on his lips. "I am sorry. It's a common enough tale, and always a sad one. I'm afraid you will never be able to have children now though."

"That's what I've always believed."

"Hasn't your husband wondered about it?"

Angelina shrugged. "In all honesty, Doctor, I don't think he cares. He never mentions children or seems to notice them when we're out walking or in the park. You know how some people do when they're thinking that sort of thought."

"Not everyone wants them." Oliver smiled, signaling the end of the serious talk. "If he ever does, you can have a few of mine. Five and counting, I'm afraid. I don't know where they come from!"

They both laughed. The ordeal of the examination had ended.

"Now, then," he said, "I'd like to ask you a few more questions before leaving you to get dressed and go on up to see Dr. Trumbull."

Angelina nodded and folded her hands in her lap. "I'm ready."

"Good girl. You've been very brave." He accepted a sheet of paper from Nurse Andrews and glanced at it. "Do you have any history of heart trouble? Any palpitations or unusual shortness of breath?"

"Never."

The nurse stood at the cabinet shelf to take down her answers.

"Have you ever experienced night sweats? Sleeplessness?"

Angelina started to say, "Never," but remembered her role. "Sometimes I have strange dreams and have to get up to sit beside the window for a while. Fortunately, my husband sleeps like a log. He snores too."

"I see. Do you sleep with the windows open or closed?"

"Slightly open unless it's very cold."

"Any intolerance to particular foods? Shellfish, vegetable marrows . . . No? You're lucky. My wife can't eat strawberries, poor thing. They happen to be my favorite."

Angelina shrugged. She ate everything — too much, apparently. Peg had scolded her about gaining weight too. Well, she could blame that on Antoine.

"Do you have any irrational fears?"

"I don't know," she said. "I'm terrified of snakes and spiders, but that's rational, isn't it? They can bite you and they're poisonous."

"Spiders rarely bite people and you won't encounter many snakes in London." He flashed another smile. "Anything else? Bees, flying insects? Ever been stung?"

She shook her head, thinking about Mrs. Parsons. So this was how they found that out! Trumbull must read all these notes. "Not that I can remember."

"You'd remember if you'd ever had a bad reaction. Anything else that especially bothers you? Cats, dogs, postmen?"

She giggled. "I like cats and dogs, though we haven't got either one. Is anyone really afraid of postmen?"

He shrugged. "Everything frightens someone, Mrs. Moriarty. We like to know what sorts of things trouble you."

\* \* \*

Fully dressed again, with her corset loose enough to strain the seams of her snugly fitted jacket, Angelina climbed the stairs on her own to knock on the door of the consulting room.

"Enter!"

Dr. Trumbull stood beside his desk, frowning at a sheet of paper, his face hard — not the genial Father Christmas she'd met last time. Then he looked up at her and his expression changed, all warmth and welcome again. "Come in, come in!"

An interesting transformation. Which was the mask and which the man?

"Anything to drink?" Dr. Trumbull gestured at a tray with gleaming bottles and glasses.

She licked her lips without thinking, then pulled in her tongue. "No, thank you."

"Then let's get started, shall we?"

He waved her into the wide silk chair, which was just as smooth and welcoming as she remembered. Trumbull sat in an armchair turned slightly to one side so that he could listen without directly watching her. A clever technique; it made it easier to talk without always watching for that flicker of amusement or twitch of disapproval.

She could see his face if she wanted to. She ought to be monitoring his responses to make sure she was playing her role to best advantage. But with his face averted, she could speak more freely, expressing her pent-up feelings to this sympathetic audience of one.

Funny how the simple act of listening could be so seductive.

She started with an update on the home improvement project, then moved on to complaints about James's lack of cooperation. "He genuinely doesn't care about wallpaper." She was gratified to hear the faint cluck of the doctor's tongue. She'd known he would sympathize on that score. He'd probably chosen every detail in this exquisitely appointed house himself.

"He's quite the opposite of you, Dr. Trumbull, now that I think of it. You are sympathy itself and I don't think I've ever seen a handsomer room."

"Ah, well," the doctor said. "I've been in this house for many years. This room has evolved over time. It was quite ordinary when I bought it, you know. Sometimes it's better to let things develop at their own pace."

"I suppose you're right." But in truth, Angelina needed a showcase and she needed it soon. Theater people had highly developed aesthetic tastes and would judge her accordingly.

Trumbull nodded. "Every word, even the complaints, tells me how much you love your husband. Otherwise, you'd talk about something else. Let's try to remember why you married him in the first place."

More sensible advice. Would he bother if he meant to murder her in a few weeks?

But she played along. She remembered perfectly why she'd married James Moriarty. He'd saved her life and as they went on from there, she'd fallen in love with him.

She sighed. "I remember. And I still love him. And I know he loves me too, deep down. I'm just not sure we can live together." She sniffed. "He'd probably be better off without me."

"Yes, you said that last time."

Wait — did she hear a note of boredom there, or even disdain? The mask had slipped again for a moment, revealing an actor who sometimes wearied of playing the same role day after day.

He recovered quickly, speaking with a trifle more energy than usual. "It must be a sign of your deepest fear, the central concern that animates your whole nervous disposition. We'll focus on that in the weeks to come. You mentioned last time that if your husband learned the truth about you, you feared he would cease to love you. Tell me more about that. What terrible truth could a lovely young woman like you be hiding?"

He settled back into his listening posture with his chin resting on one fist and his gaze turned toward the Oriental carpet.

That was more like it. Angelina had been jolted out of her cathartic confessions when she'd felt that tremor of contempt. That was precisely what she'd come here to expose. Her mission was to prove the man a fraud, after all, not fall under his spell.

But she liked the enchantment. She looked forward to it. She wanted him to keep playing his role. She wanted to be seduced. With a flash of insight, she realized that this renowned alienist was another clever confidence trickster. Only this time, she was the mark. She knew it and she didn't mind.

Angelina nearly laughed out loud. So this was how it felt to be on the other side of the game!

\* \* \*

By the time James got home from the archives that evening, the emotional lift she'd gotten from Dr. Trumbull had sunk under the weight of her never-ending struggles at home. Today's domestic ordeal had consisted of turning the first floor inside out to accommodate the new piano, which had turned out to be far too large for the space. She'd ordered a standard grand piano, the most obvious of choices. How had the estate agent not warned her that it wouldn't fit before letting her settle on this house?

She'd had the men remove the thing at once, of course, but the furniture shop couldn't supply her with a smaller model right away. They apologized, rather tartly, in her opinion, and were unable to estimate when, or even if, they would be able to satisfy her requirements. So the mouse maids and Rolly had to put everything back where it had been, more or less, pending her complete reevaluation of the situation.

She didn't know *what* to do. No home was complete without a piano — even the wandering Archer clan had managed to absorb that bit of conventional wisdom. And one couldn't dream of entertaining theater people without a decent piano, which meant a grand piano, even if one of the smaller varieties. It was simply out of the question!

The whole ordeal had been as exhausting as if she'd lugged the hulking thing up and down the stairs herself. But she couldn't complain to James about it and be comforted because she'd have to explain why it was so important and she wasn't prepared to broach that topic yet.

So she was snippy with him. She could hear it in her voice and knew it was grossly unfair, but she couldn't stop herself. Naturally that put James's back up and made him even stuffier than usual.

After Rolly popped into the drawing room to tell them dinner was ready, James held out his elbow to lead her downstairs, saying, "Shouldn't footmen be tall?"

"I don't know. Why should they?"

"Tradition, shared values, common cultural conceptions. I fail to understand why we need a footman at all."

"Then what difference does his height make?"

James mercifully let that idiotic little argument drop. But then he watched Rolly serve the Turkish broth with such a critical eye that the poor boy fumbled the ladle and splashed a great puddle of soup on the cloth. Angelina pointedly refused to make an issue of it, merely covering the splash with a napkin and giving Rolly an extra-friendly smile to make up for James's brusqueness.

They ate in silence for a while. Angelina began to think the ill-humored interval had passed. She was rummaging her mind for a topic of conversation when James asked, "How was your visit to Trumbull today? Learn anything new?"

She'd rather bicker about the servants than tell her husband about her experiences at Harley Street that morning. She grasped at principle and answered, "Consultations with an alienist are meant to be private." It sounded more standoffish than she'd intended.

Naturally he took offense. His upper lip curled and his nose twitched in the way that meant he felt disregarded or misunderstood. "Forgive me, my dear. I had assumed you were seeing this doctor solely to assess his potential as a murderer. I must have missed the moment when you determined his innocence, on grounds you have chosen not to share, and began to treat the consultations as genuine."

"Of course I still suspect him," Angelina said. "I wouldn't go back if I didn't. But it isn't an easy role, you know. I can't reprise the whole performance."

"I see." James took another spoonful of soup. After dabbing his lips with his napkin, he said in that frosty tone he used when he was retreating into his most shuttered, uncommunicative self, "Do let me know when you uncover anything of interest."

She didn't dignify that with an answer. They got through the roast game hen with puffed potatoes and braised carrots without another word. Rolly removed the dinner plates and served the apple cake and coffee, which they took in the dining room when they didn't have guests, which, of course, they never did and probably never would if things kept on the way they were going. Angelina started mentally reviewing shops that sold pianos, wondering where she should take her business now that she'd sent the man from Pennington's home with a flea in his ear. Perhaps a boudoir piano from Broadwood would better suit that space.

"It's awfully chilly in here," James said, breaking into her thoughts.

Did he mean that literally or figuratively? Angelina rolled her eyes at her own foolishness. When was James ever anything but excruciatingly literal? "The flues don't draw well. The whole house is chilly, especially in the evenings. We'll have to have all the chimneys cleaned, but I'm told that's an *enormous* mess."

Anna Castle

"I can't imagine how anyone would notice."

"Oh, really, James. It isn't that bad."

He stirred sugar into his coffee, measuring it as if preparing a laboratory experiment. "Clogged flues would explain the unpleasant atmosphere in the drawing room, especially in the evenings."

If she didn't know him better, she would swear he'd meant that as a veiled rebuke. Well, perhaps she didn't know him as well as she imagined. Or more likely he was changing as a result of living with her, and not for the better. Most people had no idea how sensitive he was since he kept himself so tightly buttoned up. But he felt things — nuances and innuendos — sometimes deeply. He didn't always understand those feelings or know how to cope with them, but he felt them all the same.

Now, for example, he was getting stuffy and pompous because he thought she didn't trust him enough to confide in him and tell him about Dr. Oliver's examination or her session with Dr. Trumbull. But he'd gotten it exactly backward. Of course she trusted *him*. He was the most honorable man she'd ever known, from the top of his bald head to the soles of his square-toed boots.

She was the one who couldn't be trusted, with her tangled past and sordid secrets. He should not trust her and that was the heart of their problem. She didn't know how to say, "Don't trust me," without implying, "I don't love you." Or without pushing him out the door, which was exactly what she ought to do if she had an ounce of integrity.

Thinking about how much better off he would be without her and how miserable she would be without him twisted her insides and scrambled her wits so that all she could do was poke and scratch at him, like a kitten under a chair. He felt the sting of the scratches, but could not see their source.

# Chapter Ten

Moriarty hired a coach on Wednesday morning to collect Holmes and Watson for their trip to the Heffelfinger Institute of Electricity on Ludgate Hill. He hoped they might be able to extend the expedition for the better part of the day. Things had gone from bad to worse at home. He no longer had any idea how to talk to Angelina.

The latest contretemps had begun last week when he'd come home from the chemistry laboratory shamefully intoxicated. He ought to have gone to his club until the effects of that Peruvian wine wore off, but instead he had barged into his house, embarrassed the servants, and dragged Angelina upstairs like a caveman. There he had locked the bedroom door and proceeded to treat his own wife like a common prostitute.

She hadn't seemed to mind at the time, but the next day, in addition to having a wretched hangover, he'd been too ashamed of himself to look her in the face.

They'd gotten through the weekend by dint of good breeding and strategic mutual avoidance. The frost had largely thawed by Monday night and yesterday had been as normal a day as they'd had since the honeymoon ended. But when he'd tried to make a little pleasant conversation last night, asking about her visit to Dr. Trumbull, she'd bristled at him like an angry porcupine. She'd shut him out, happy to share secrets with a suspected murderer that she didn't deign to confide in her own husband. And that was proof, if proof were needed, that she didn't take this whole nerve doctor nonsense seriously. It was just a ploy to get him out of the house.

The coach pulled up to 221 Baker Street. Moriarty cleared his mind of domestic noise, looking forward to a few hours of sensible, masculine conversation. The two men climbed in, and the coach began to work its way through the dense city traffic.

Holmes said, "I suggest we let Watson take the lead today in his capacity as a general physician seeking modern treatments for the patients in his care."

"Good idea," Moriarty said. "We'll say Holmes and I came along out of curiosity and to provide test subjects if required."

"None of which will be false," Watson said. "I've read about the positive results obtained with some of these devices, especially in managing chronic pain. Some of my patients have asked me about electrotherapy, so I am genuinely curious."

"As am I," Moriarty said. "I'll confess I find everything to do with electricity fascinating."

Watson said, "It may yet surpass steam in importance to society."

Holmes looked out the window, disinterested, as usual, in social and historical developments.

The coach stopped in front of the institute and the men disembarked. The place looked impressive from the street with gleaming windows set in a polished stone facade. No bell jangled as they walked in the door. Its absence proclaimed this to be no ordinary shop.

The interior space had an equally modern ambience, being sparsely furnished and uncluttered. Posters declaring the virtues of the Heffelfinger line of products adorned the walls. The accustomed oak counter ran across the back with a display of wares that looked like undergarments constructed by a blacksmith.

A young man watched them enter, giving them a moment to absorb the initial effect of the atypical display. Then he offered them a smooth salesman's smile. "Good morning, gentlemen. How may I be of assistance?"

Watson stepped forward and introduced himself and the others. The young man said his name was Tillman. He nodded throughout Watson's explanation of his interests and responded without hesitation. "Yes, many doctors are discovering the benefits of electricity these days. I have every confidence that Heffelfinger's Electrotherapy Machines will soon be as much a part of the physician's tool kit as the stethoscope."

He reached behind him for a wooden case and opened it on the counter. "We've designed this one to be fully portable. You can easily recharge the batteries when you return to your dispensary."

The three men clustered around to inspect the offered product. The case contained three long brass canisters housing the batteries and several metal rods with spoon-shaped terminations connected to neatly coiled wires.

"Those look like telegraph wires," Holmes said.

"That's right," the salesman said, beaming as if Holmes had made something other than a mundane observation. To Watson, he said, "We also make a wall-mounted apparatus, contained in a handsome walnut cabinet. Ornamental and attractive but quite reasonable in price."

"Are those batteries galvanic or faradic?" Moriarty asked.

"Galvanic." This time Tillman looked genuinely impressed. Not everyone knew the difference. "Our doctors find that the steady, direct galvanic current gives better results for complaints such as melancholia than the alternating, asymmetric current produced by a faradic battery. Galvanic current is also highly effective for torpor, hysteria, and similar complaints."

"How much current can these batteries generate?" Moriarty asked, continuing his role as the expert in matters electrical. Holmes never learned anything that wasn't directly related to criminology and Watson always lagged a bit behind the times.

The salesman nodded at the astute question. "This particular model can produce about one volt, although we typically measure therapeutic force in milliamperes."

"One volt!" Moriarty said. "That's not even enough to power a small light bulb."

"Certainly not," the salesman said, sounding defensive. "I assure you these devices are absolutely safe. The last thing we want is for inexperienced physicians to electrocute patients accidentally."

"Does that happen often?" Holmes asked. They'd finally arrived at a topic within his limited range of interests.

"Never, to my knowledge," Tillman said. "And certainly not with a Heffelfinger product."

"Well, this is very interesting indeed," Watson said. He had no need to feign his enthusiasm. "Would it be possible to see a demonstration? My friends here have expressed their willingness to act as test subjects."

"Certainly," Tillman said. "We wouldn't expect you to buy anything that doesn't meet your requirements one hundred percent or more."

Moriarty mumbled to Holmes, "There isn't anything more than one hundred percent." Holmes acknowledged the hyperbole with a crooked smile.

Tillman led them through a curtained doorway at the back of the shop into a small room furnished with a table, a cabinet, and a few plain chairs. The cabinet held half a dozen books, toward which Moriarty moved at once. He took down one titled *Medical Electricity: A Practical Treatise* and opened it to the title page. "This is a manual," he reported over his shoulder, "by a doctor named

Bartholomew. Published in Philadelphia in 1882." He turned toward the salesman. "Aren't there any British manuals?"

"None as comprehensive at this time," Tillman answered. "Heffelfingers are writing our own, of course, but it isn't finished yet." He added for Watson's benefit, "We supply our physicians with every support in terms of literature and personal instruction. We can even send a man to your consulting room to help you learn how to use your new device in your own setting."

Watson hummed his ambivalence about that possibility with a thoughtful frown.

Holmes clapped his hands together. "So how does this device work?"

Tillman had brought the case with him. He now set it on the table and opened it up. Then he went to the cabinet and poured some liquid into a small bowl, which he brought to the table along with a towel. Moriarty caught a clean, ascetic smell rising from the bowl.

"First," Tillman said, "you should always start with a fully charged battery. There's no use driving out to a patient in the suburbs only to discover your equipment isn't up to snuff." He grinned at the mild witticism. "Second, you should wash the electrodes' sponges with soap and water after every use."

He displayed the fine sponges attached inside the cupped end of each electrode. "You moisten the sponges before applying them to the skin to improve conduction. Plain water is fine, but we add a little vinegar. Patients like the smell. It has a medicinal tang."

He showed them the controls built into the battery case — a set of sliding gauges with measurements marked on the side. "These are milliamperes," Tillman said. "This slider allows you to control the amount of current with great precision." He winked at Watson. "Some of our doctors have gotten so comfortable with these machines they test the current on their tongues. They trust their own senses more than our carefully engineered mechanics." He shook his head to show his wry amusement at the stubborn independence of the family doctor.

"What levels are used for which complaints?" Watson asked, basking in the flattery.

"It's more a matter of the individual patient than of the particular complaint," Tillman said.

He and Watson began to discuss the range of variation among patients. Moriarty and Holmes edged around them to get closer to the machine. Moriarty bent to study the sliding control. "It appears to be set at the minimum level: three milliamperes."

"Let's try it out," Holmes said. He took one of the electrodes and placed it on his tongue, flipping the switch next to the sliding control to turn the machine on. He made an odd face, flapping his tongue a little as he removed the electrode. "Well, it's a peculiar sensation, but I've gotten greater shocks from a sour pickle."

"Let me try." Moriarty held out his hand.

"No, first I want to use a stronger current." Holmes kept a grip on the electrode.

Tillman cut off his conversation with Watson when he saw what they were doing. "Please wait, gentlemen, and allow me to —"

Holmes ignored him, sliding the control to the middle of its range. He dipped the electrode into the bowl of acidulated water and flipped the switch. This time the effect made him shake his head sharply. "Ah! That's more like it."

"Give it to me." Moriarty held out his hand, twitching his fingers peremptorily.

"Gentlemen, if you don't mind," Tillman tried again.

"Holmes," Watson said in a reproving tone, "let the man do his job."

Holmes, of course, refused to cooperate. He dipped the electrode into the bowl again and reached for the slider.

Moriarty clapped a hand down to cover the whole panel of gauges. He held out the other, palm up, implacable. "Need I remind you, Holmes, that you are dependent on my wife for information vital to the pursuit of your case?"

Holmes gave him a withering look. "Oh, do give us a rest, Moriarty! We all know she's not telling you anything either."

Moriarty leveled a searing glare at him and snatched the electrode out of his hand. He placed the electrode on his tongue, holding it there for a few seconds. After he cut the current, he found himself flicking his tongue just as Holmes had done. "Well, that's dashed peculiar. Though I wouldn't say it's entirely unpleasant."

"Gentlemen, please," Tillman said. "It isn't meant to be used that way. The electrodes should be applied to the skin. Placement depends on the specific treatment, of course, but usually we'll put one on the forehead and another behind the jaw or at the nape of the neck."

"That sounds interesting," Moriarty said. He dipped his electrode into the dish and placed it under his jaw. Holmes grabbed the other one and planted it squarely in the middle of his own forehead. He slid the control all the way to the top and flipped the switch.

This time they both jumped. Moriarty could feel the current right down to his feet. Holmes's free arm swung back and forth of its own volition.

"Now that was something," Holmes said. "Let me have both of them to —"

"No, I want to try —"

"That's quite enough, you two!" Watson commanded.

He and the salesman forcibly wrested away the electrodes, packed them back into the case, and snapped shut the lid.

Tillman murmured, "Are they always so hostile toward one another?"

Watson made a dismissive noise. "This is what they're like when they're getting along. Ordinarily they're each other's worst enemy."

\* \* \*

After they left the shop, Moriarty invited the other two men to join him as his guests for lunch at Simpson's-in-the-Strand. "I've heard it's quite good."

"It's my favorite," Holmes said. "We accept with pleasure."

They hailed a passing coach, though it might have been faster to walk. On the way, Holmes smiled at Moriarty and said, "Have you learned anything useful during your week in the newspaper archives?"

Moriarty recognized the favorite game as a sort of peace offering, so he willingly offered the expected next move. "How the devil could you know that?"

Watson chuckled.

Holmes said, "Elementary, my dear Professor. That notebook peeking out of your pocket has rain spots on it, but it hasn't rained since Monday. And nearly two-thirds of the pages have been used, judging by their rumpled edges, suggesting you've compiled several days' worth of notes."

"What identifies newspaper archives specifically? I might be looking up records at Somerset House, for all you know."

"That yellow wrapper you stuffed into your left pocket and carelessly forgot about. I recognize the paper. It's from the herring stand across from the British

Museum. I doubt you've taken a sudden urgent interest in Egyptian antiquities."

"Very clever," Moriarty said, as if praising one of his undergraduates who had finally managed to grasp a simple algebraic equation.

Holmes smiled thinly. "Bloater wrappers are frightfully greasy — impossible to get the stains out, especially if left overnight. You might think about adding a valet to your domestic staff, Professor. Surely your wife knows a second-story man with an eye for fashion."

So much for the peace offering.

The maître d'hôtel at Simpson's led them to a table in the middle of the dining room. Moriarty inhaled the savory aromas with pleasure augmented by his appreciation for the masculine tone of the decor. Oak-paneled walls were soothing and quiet. Not gloomy and oppressive, as Angelina insisted. She wanted tiny flowers on everything — the walls, the windows, the carpets — a delirious profusion of distracting designs that made him dizzy.

They were seated at a linen-draped table near the wall and gave their full attention to the menu. They decided to share a dish of smoked mackerel and watercress salad to start. For the main course, Moriarty chose chicken with sausage and bacon — a classic English dish unobtainable in his own home. Watson chose the Dover sole, obliging them to order two different bottles of wine. Holmes, ever the traditionalist in matters of personal comfort, ordered the Scottish beef with potatoes and Savoy cabbage.

They spoke little during the meal, conversing in short spurts about the food and other inconsequential topics. The servings were generous, but they managed to squeeze in the house's special treacle for pudding. It wasn't quite as good as Antoine's. After that, the waiter brought coffee and brandy and the conversation turned to the problem of the murdering alienist.

"We ruled out hydrotherapy as a method," Moriarty said. "After this morning's outing, I would rule out electrotherapy as well. Those devices don't generate enough electricity to kill a hummingbird and I can't see any potential for inducing a delayed effect."

Watson nodded. "I agree with that assessment, with one caveat. We raised the question of victims with weak hearts. It might be possible to adjust the force of the current and the placement of the electrodes to exacerbate an arrhythmic heart. It wouldn't be a very predictable method, but the victim would die as soon as she overexerted herself. Riding too fast, lifting something heavy, running upstairs . . . Anything might add enough strain on the heart to stop it."

"Very good, Watson!" Holmes raised his coffee cup in a toast. "We'll make a criminologist of you yet."

"It isn't often that your cases cross into my domain of expertise." Watson looked pleased at the rare praise.

"Have we missed any likely methods?" Moriarty asked. "What else do they do in private hospitals for women with nervous disorders?"

Watson said, "I've heard of the use of hypnosis for treating irrational fears and suchlike. They probably employ that technique at Halcyon House. I'm sure they also have lots of water-based therapies, but I can't think of any way to induce a delayed death by drowning."

"Nor can I," Holmes said, "and I've been thinking about it. We've experimented a little with hypnosis ourselves, haven't we, Watson?"

"You mean I have. You are completely unsusceptible."

Holmes smiled as if that were some sort of achievement. "Regardless, one cannot instruct the subject to harm him or herself, so again, I don't see an application."

118

Moriarty wondered about Mrs. Parsons and her fear of insects. Could she be hypnotized not to fear something that was genuinely a threat to her, and thereby put herself in harm's way? That seemed like an exceptionally convoluted and unreliable method. He decided to keep it to himself. Besides, Mrs. Parsons had been alive and well, despite her many fears, the last time they'd seen her.

"Well," Moriarty said, "We've come up with at least three methods for committing murder that would be well within the scope of a skilled physician. But I'll be damned if I can think of a way for us to prove any of them."

"That is our problem in a nutshell," Holmes said. "We need witnesses — ones who are willing to testify. More victims would also help us. Sooner or later, all criminals make a mistake. That's when we catch them."

"Agreed," Moriarty said. "I'll confess I haven't found anything in the archives yet. That is to say, I haven't yet identified another patient of Dr. Trumbull's who died unexpectedly in the last two years. But I have developed a topography, if you will allow the word, of the archived information in this city, at least as it pertains to records of unexplained deaths. I'm confident things will go faster from here out."

"A scholarly approach," Holmes said. His tone was not complimentary. "I have my own methods as well."

Watson grimaced apologetically. "I'm afraid I'll have to leave you to it for a while. I have patients who need my attention."

"Just you and me, then, Professor," Holmes said. "Shall we place a little wager to add zest to the pursuit? We can meet in two weeks to compare notes and see which of us has come up with the most compelling evidence."

"By all means," Moriarty said. "With the proviso that we're as likely to conclude that no crimes have been committed."

"Agreed," Holmes said.

Moriarty looked about the pleasant dining room filled with well-dressed people enjoying good food and drink. A busy place, yet so smoothly managed that each individual felt pampered. The way a man's home ought to be. "I have just the prize. The loser treats the whole team to dinner here at Simpson's."

"A capital idea." Holmes raised his brandy glass. "Let the games begin!"

# Chapter Eleven

"Good morning, Dr. Trumbull," Angelina sang as she entered the consulting room, happy to be back in this serene sanctuary.

"Good morning, Mrs. Moriarty. You're looking well. Our little talks must be having an effect."

"I think they are."

"Good, good. And the corset's a little looser too, I see."

"Doctor!"

He chuckled. "There, there. Strictly *entre nous*. You look as stylish as ever." He waved at her favorite chair. "Shall we get started?"

Angelina sank into the plump cushions with pleasure, lifting her feet onto the little stool. She stroked the silk, appreciating the luxurious fabric. "I love this color."

"It suits you."

James used to love her in purple. He never noticed what she wore anymore. She decided to start with that classic womanly lament. From there, she moved naturally on to complaints about the house, how hard it was to get anything done right, how her nerves were simply *frazzled* by the effort of accomplishing the simplest little thing. And did James help her? Did he sympathize? Did he appreciate the results of her labors?

He did none of those things, even though they both knew she was doing it all for him. She slid a sidelong glance at Trumbull as she uttered that last lie. James could be happy in a three-room cottage with a diet of mashed potatoes and kidney pie as long as he had her and something to do. She was the one who couldn't live in such straitened circumstances.

The doctor didn't seem to notice the lie, or if he did, he hid it well. He let her ramble on until the clock on the mantel chimed the half hour. Then he asked, "Is the house really the root of your problems with your husband? Or might there be something deeper?"

She hesitated. She had no intention of revealing the true extent of her deceptions — her lower-class origins, the assumed names, the love affairs, that wretched abortion. Besides, this was about the present and how hard James was to live with.

"I don't know, Doctor," she said, "I think in some ways it is the house. The longer we live in it, the stuffier James becomes. We had a long honeymoon, you know, touring the Continent, living in spas and fine hotels."

She remembered her supposed role and added, "At my expense, of course. But we never had to make do with just each other, facing one another across the table morning, noon, and night. There are always other people in the dining room, you know. Someone else manages the staff. Dirty laundry disappears and magically comes back clean. Now, living together in the conventional way in a conventional house on a conventional street, James grows more rigid and conventionally middle class by the day. After all, he knew I was an actress when he married me."

"Were you? I don't believe you've mentioned that."

"Haven't I?" Had she just unmasked herself? She was playing an heiress with a nervous disorder, not a former actress with a burning desire to get back on the stage. But a stodgy old stick-in-the-mud might decide to murder his wife to keep her from going on the stage and embarrassing him beyond redemption.

She decided to play on. "That was before I married, of course. In fact, that's how we met. He fell in love me from the audience. I was quite the Somebody in my day."

"You must miss it."

"Well, I do sometimes. Just between you and me, Doctor, I'd like to go back once the house is all settled and I've had time to catch my breath."

"Not many men would approve that step. Have you discussed it with your husband?"

"I haven't gotten up the courage yet. But I think he suspects something. He's grown so impatient with me. And he's acting rather strange. One day he's as amorous as a newlywed and the next he can hardly bear to look at me."

"Hmm," Trumbull said. "You know, I have a tonic for male vigor. That might be all he needs. But you might consider finding a more acceptable outlet for your creative impulses."

She sniffed, pretending to accept his advice. "I'm sure it's just an idle dream."

"How did you get started acting? That's an uncommon activity for a young woman of your background."

Angelina laughed, letting a touch of genuine bitterness color the sound. "*Au contraire*, Doctor. 'Twas Mummy gave me my start."

"Did she? Tell me about that."

They relaxed again into their usual postures. She wove a tale about an ambitious parent pushing a five-year-old girl in front of an audience, only in this version the parent was a social-climbing mother, not Archie Buddle, chairman of the East End music halls. She set her imaginary stage in the town hall during the Christmas pantomime, not the back room of a tavern, and the audience consisted of sober parishioners, not a crowd of rowdy drinking men.

Her imaginary Mummy thirsted for the fame reflected from a talented child. Archie liked that too, but not half

123

as much as he liked the sound of coins falling into his hat. With Archie, profits always came first.

"That must have made you feel terribly unloved," Trumbull said. "As if you had to perform in order to earn your mother's affection."

"Well, I did, didn't I?"

She'd been terrified the first time but soon got used to singing across a noisy barroom. Before long, she'd learned to love the applause. By the time she turned twelve, she could gather her audience into her palm within minutes. Nothing else in her life worked like that. Offstage, she was either ignored or criticized, but onstage — ah, onstage she was Lovely Little Lina, the Darling of the Halls.

After talking for a while without pause, her throat felt parched. She still wouldn't accept a drink poured by the doctor, but perhaps that pitcher on the sideboard held plain water. She got up and walked across to the drinks tray, saying, "Do you mind if I have a glass of water?" She lifted the glass pitcher and sniffed at it. It smelled like nothing, as water should.

"By all means," Trumbull said. "That's the finest water in the London area. I have it specially brought from Hampstead."

Hampstead, where he had his hospital. Angelina decided to risk a glass. She took a tentative sip and tasted nothing out of place, so she swallowed a healthy draught, soothing her throat. She carried the glass over to the window, feeling the need to move around a bit after her lengthy semi-fictional autobiography. She felt a little light-headed, as if she'd been wearing an unwieldy hat all day and had finally gotten a chance to remove the blighted thing.

She stood gazing down at the traffic in the street, musing over the doctor's remark. After a moment, she turned back to him. "I didn't begin to feel unloved until the twins —" She caught the slip just in time. "Until the twins moved in next door. Their papa was a solicitor or some such thing. The family jumped right into the social whirl, taking part in everything, including school plays and the Christmas pantomime. Only their mummy and daddy applauded everything they did, all of them the same, as proud as you please, even when the little darlings forgot their cues or sang off-key. It opened my eyes."

"I imagine it did."

She'd never thought of it that way before, but she could feel the truth of it in her heart. She hadn't known any better. How could she? Archie had made sure she never had time for friends and her mother had no influence. Angelina barely remembered her. She died giving birth to Viola and Sebastian, when Angelina was six years old. Peg had joined the family troupe by then as a dresser and child-minder. The two of them had taken charge of the little mites, doing the best they could to keep them warm and clean and fed.

She had grown to love them with a power that surprised her. Archie had ignored them until they learned to walk and started lisping childish songs. Then he'd treated them the way he'd treated her, training them to perform, pushing them out in front of the crowd, teaching them to beg for tips and pick pockets between performances.

That's when Angelina had learned the difference between love and exploitation.

"Is that why you fear losing your husband's love?"

"Why I what? Oh, I beg your pardon, Doctor. My mind wandered a bit."

"It's good to bring these old memories out into the light of day. Expose them for what they are. Then they lose their power."

"I'm sure you're right." Angelina sipped her water and glanced out of the window again, ready to return to

125

her seat, but stopped cold to stare down at a scene unfolding below.

Lord Brockaway was stepping out of a black coach. He reached inside to help Viola climb out, gripping her arm as if to compel her obedience. The poor girl looked paler than ever and seemed almost too weak to walk. A nurse appeared and took her other arm. A footman carried a large portmanteau toward the house. After only a few minutes, Lord Brockaway and the footman returned, got back into the coach, and drove off.

Angelina swallowed down the fear rising in her throat and turned away from the window. She replayed the little scene in her head, knowing full well what it meant. The bag, Viola's pale face, and the grim set of Badger's jaw could only mean one thing — her darling baby sister was in terrible, terrible danger.

This was it. This was what she'd feared, what she'd come here to prevent. She'd failed, letting herself be seduced by that old scoundrel, sitting there with that sympathetic smile on his kindly face, waiting for the time to lock her up in her turn.

Well, why wait?

Angelina went back to her chair and set her glass on a table. She did not sink into her usual talking pose, but kept to the edge of the seat, her hands clasped before her. "Tell me about this hospital of yours, Dr. Trumbull. Is it very nice?"

He blinked, but to his credit as an actor, only once. "Very nice indeed. We make every effort. Some patients tell me they like it better than the Grand Hotel in Paris."

"It must be frightfully exclusive."

"Oh yes. We accept only the very best sort, I assure you."

"Would I have to wait a long time to be admitted?"

He smiled at her slowly, as if savoring a victory. "No need to worry on that score, Mrs. Moriarty. We can always make room for a special patient."

# Chapter Twelve

Moriarty checked his watch against the clock in the lobby of the British Museum. Two minutes to nine — perfect. Punctuality was one of the foundations of success; a truth he was utterly unable to convey to his wife. Take the clocks in their house as an example. He hated the cacophony of five clocks chiming out of tempo every quarter hour. She, on the other hand, found their music pleasing. That could be argued either way, but it was beside the point. Clocks were tools for the regulation of the household. The aesthetic qualities of their chimes were mere decorations, like embossing the leather cover of a book.

He bounded up the marble steps to the reading room with an eager spring in his step. Holmes was right; a wager did add zest to a pursuit. Everything about the British Museum swelled Moriarty's heart with British pride, from the stately columns at the entrance to the unparalleled collections of art and artifacts from around the globe inside.

The reading room made his scholarly heart beat even faster. The room had been erected only ten years ago, specially built to accommodate the numbers of people desiring to study the museum's collections. Its soaring dome was ringed with arched windows admitting an abundance of natural light. Beneath these stood two tiers of stacks loaded with bound volumes. The floor of the vast room held five long tables with shelves built down the middle to afford some privacy to each pair of readers, one on either side. Many chairs were filled already this morning with a couple dozen men and three or four women, all absorbed in their research.

Moriarty had prepared his slip in advance. He handed it across the counter to his favorite clerk, Mr. Lester Quick, who had been helping him since the beginning. The clerk greeted him with a greater than usual sparkle in his eyes.

"If you'll forgive the liberty, Professor Moriarty, I've already brought down a few volumes that I believe will interest you."

Moriarty had asked Quick to watch out for obituaries or articles with the names of Trumbull, Oliver, Fairchild, or Halcyon House.

"That's kind of you, Mr. Quick, and very helpful. You save me a great deal of time with your sharp eyes. You know this archive better than anybody."

Pink spots flared on the young man's cheeks at the praise. "I've been admiring the methodical way you work, Professor, if you don't mind my saying it."

"Not at all."

"A man needs a system," Mr. Quick said. "That's my watchword. I suppose that's what drew me to this line of work."

"A logical connection."

Mr. Quick glanced left and right and then leaned over the counter to speak with a lowered voice. "You're investigating unusual deaths, aren't you, Professor? Are you working for the police?"

"Not at the moment," Moriarty hedged. "If I'm successful, naturally I'll inform the authorities." He hadn't thought that far ahead. He'd assumed Holmes would take everything into his hands once they obtained some indictable evidence.

Mr. Quick's wide smile practically split his narrow face in half, showing rows of crooked teeth. "Have you ever heard of this fellow?" He showed Moriarty a recent issue of *The Illustrated Police News*, one of Peg's favorites. They specialized in stories about sensational crimes and clever detectives.

The page in question contained an article about some arcane puzzle in Scotland last month, solved by none other than Mr. Sherlock Holmes. The newspaper had included a sketch of the famous detective, showing his distinctive profile under what looked like some sort of Scottish hunting cap.

*Sleuth hound, eh? More like a publicity hound!*

But Mr. Quick's interest in crime-solving could prove useful, given his position in this storehouse of all English newspapers.

"I happen to know Mr. Holmes rather well." Moriarty glanced from side to side, then shot his new ally a wink. "And never fear. I won't forget to give credit where credit is due."

Mr. Quick blushed to the tips of his ears. "I'll keep looking during my off moments, Professor, never you fear."

Moriarty took the volumes Quick had reserved for him and found a seat at one of the long tables. He set his hat on top of the divider and drew his notebook and pen case from his pocket. After several minutes of focused skimming, his eyes caught the name "Parsons."

"Oh my stars."

There was no doubt about it. This obituary concerned the same Mrs. Elizabeth Parsons he and Angelina had met in Torquay less than a fortnight ago. She had died only a few days after returning from the Beaumont Hotel. She had been sitting in her bedroom on the ground floor of her house, in a favorite seat near the garden window, when she had been attacked by a swarm of wasps.

Moriarty had to read that passage three times, it seemed so incredible. Angelina had said the poor woman suffered from a fear of flying insects, having reacted badly to their stings in the past. But the obituary said the cause of death had been determined by her own physician, who lived nearby. Mrs. Parsons was survived by her husband, Alfred Parsons, who sadly was away from home at the time of the incident.

The timing of Mrs. Parsons's death was suggestive, but no one could engineer a wasp attack. Could they? The event was recent enough to pursue if he could come up with an excuse to visit the house or question the servants. How did the wasps get into the room?

Moriarty turned to the next newspaper in his stack. Mr. Quick had marked the relevant page with a long piece of string. Moriarty read a brief report of the inquest, which had been held last Monday at a tavern in Highgate. A verdict of unlawful killing had been delivered and the maid, Flora Semple, had been arrested and committed to Newgate Prison until the trial. Angelina had met that maid and liked her, commenting on how devoted the girl had been to her mistress.

The article offered few details. The doctor testified that the victim's face and throat were swollen, her skin was flushed all over, and she was covered in hives. He concluded that the immediate cause of death would have been suffocation caused by the swelling of the throat.

Crucial testimony had been given by the gardener, who happened to see Miss Semple standing at the window, waving her arms as if driving the angry wasps in toward her mistress. Wasps were attracted at this time of year to the fallen apples lying around the ground outside the window. Mrs. Parsons's intolerance for insect bites was well known among the staff and those windows were supposed to be kept closed during this season.

Further evidence against Miss Semple was given by the doctor, who said he found a box of Turkish delight in the victim's lap, which had apparently been opened by Miss Semple immediately prior to driving in the wasps.

Her motive was presumed to be a fifty-pound note found in a drawer of Mrs. Parsons's dressing table, although Miss Semple did not have the money on her person at the time of her arrest.

Her fiancé, a Mr. August Norton of the Hampstead Fire Brigade, raised noisy objections from the audience in the Angel Inn, where the inquest was held, causing the coroner to have him ejected.

Moriarty made notes of the pertinent facts, then sat with his chin cupped in his hand while he considered this strange tale. Assuming the local doctor knew his business, the cause of death had been wasp stings, not poison or an overdose of medicine. Wasps were normally inoffensive creatures, as he knew from his childhood in a Gloucestershire village. If you left them alone, they would return the favor. But aggravate one and you'd have the whole swarm after you. They liked sweets and red things and could be very dangerous, especially to people who were unusually susceptible to their venom.

As a murder method, however, it seemed bizarre. Unreliable. Unless —

Unless the wasps had been *inside* the box of sweets. Was that possible? How could he find out?

If Trumbull possessed the ingenuity to murder a woman by withdrawing a drug, he might have the imagination to plot a death by wasp attack. He would know about Mrs. Parsons's intolerance for the venom and her fear of the insects. One could have anything delivered in a matter of hours in the London area; presumably the creatures could survive that long with a sugared treat to feed on. If they had flown out of the box, poor Miss Semple might have been trying to shoo them away from her mistress.

That plan was far too sophisticated for the humble maid Angelina had described. Miss Semple had become another victim of Trumbull's greed — and Mr. Parsons's.

Clever — devilishly clever, if true. Moriarty didn't how he could prove this wild theory, but he looked forward to the attempt.

\* \* \*

Moriarty strode into the house with a nod at Rolly as he shed his hat and coat. He called out, "Good news!" from the stairs before even reaching the drawing room. He could hardly wait to share his discovery with his wife. At last, they had their own fresh trail to follow, one that Sherlock Holmes knew nothing about.

He found Angelina at the back of their long drawing room, standing beside the fireplace staring at a figurine of a Greek maiden, one of the bits and pieces that had come with the house. She gazed at it as if deciding whether to throw it out with the other outdated bric-a-brac. He hoped she'd keep that one. He rather liked the thing. It reminded him of Viola, before she'd become afflicted with her current malaise. It didn't look like her, but it had that golden quality she and her brother shared.

He watched her for a moment, attempting to gauge her mood. She'd been as unpredictable as their drafty chimneys ever since she'd started seeing that nerve specialist. Whatever else he might be, this Trumbull was evidently not very good at his job.

"Why are you lurking out there?" Angelina's voice held an unusual note.

"I'm not lurking. I just got home."

"You're early."

"You make it sound like an accusation."

She clucked her tongue. "You throw the whole household out of order when you drop in and out, James. This isn't a hotel, you know."

"No, hotels are more welcoming." What brought this on? He took a few steps into the room and tried again.

133

"Caught on the horns of another decorating dilemma? A woman's work is never done, they say." He smiled to show his appreciation of her wifely efforts. "Perhaps I can distract you over lunch with a bit of real news."

"Real news?" She arched an imperious eyebrow. "Unlike any news that I might have, one supposes."

"I didn't mean that. I only meant —" He broke off with a loud sigh. Another fit of womanish temper to cope with. How any man survived marriage was a mystery to him. "I found a notice in the newspaper in the reading room. Your friend Mrs. Parsons died, only last week. You'll never believe this, but she was apparently attacked by a swarm of wasps in her own bedroom."

"That's ghastly!" Angelina gaped at him in horror — horror aimed at him, as if he had somehow caused this thing. "*That's* what you call good news?"

"I didn't mean 'good news' in the sense that the occurrence was fortuitous."

"Oh, stop being so insufferably pompous! You use that professorial whitter-whatter to cover up your utter heartlessness."

"Heartlessness! Whitter-whatter!" That cut him to the quick. He spoke judiciously, choosing his words with precision for maximum clarity. "Really, Angelina, I must protest! What's gotten into you? Did something happen at your consultation this morning?"

"Now he asks." She addressed that sarcastic comment to the figurine. "Well, yes, James, if you can stop rejoicing about poor Mrs. Parsons's death for a moment, something did happen this morning. I saw Badger deliver Viola to Harley Street with a portmanteau."

Moriarty frowned at her while he put those pieces together in his mind. "Ah. And from that you conclude that she intends to enter Halcyon House for a month of much-needed medical care."

"Care? *Care!*" Her voice took on that ringing theatrical tone he'd learned to loathe. It resonated through this sound box of a house from attic to basement. "How can you possibly refer to what goes on in that hospital as *care?*"

"We don't know what goes on in that hospital, Angelina, other than that no one, to the best of our ability to discover after two weeks of concerted effort, has ever lodged any sort of complaint about either the place or the person who owns it."

"Lack of evidence does not indicate an absence of crime," she retorted. It sounded like a quote, but who would say such a ridiculous thing? "I believe, with every ounce of intuition I possess, that my beloved sister is being sent into that closed institution for the purpose of having her killed." She patted her bosom with one hand as she spoke, as if decrying some outrage perpetrated against all womankind.

"Now, my dear, let us —"

"I'm going in with her." She spoke right over him, meeting his pacifying gesture with a defiant glare. "I want you to come with me to Harley Street to sign the committal form so that I can be admitted without delay."

"Committal form? Great Scott, Angelina! You can't be serious."

"I'm perfectly serious. I mean to go tomorrow, as early as possible. I can't allow them to give her any drugs, James, not after what you and Holmes have learned."

"It's out of the question, Angelina. What earthly good could you do there? Our best plan is to continue as we have begun, seeking information about Trumbull and his patients. We still have no idea if anything untoward has happened. As far as I can see thus far, the whole idea of a murder-for-hire scheme is a melodramatic fantasy concocted by persons with overactive imaginations and too little occupation."

"*Melodramatic?* Is that what you think of me?" Her contralto voice spiraled up, gaining volume as it rose. She shook the figurine at him as if she wanted to strike him with it. "Oh yes, the little woman can make sixteen impossible decisions every morning running this *monster* household, but she can't be trusted to find her way down the street once she steps outside the door or understand the least little thing without an explanation from her all-knowing husband."

Moriarty took three steps back, putting some distance between them, and sniffed to show his disdain. "I won't dignify that histrionic hyperbole with an answer."

She regarded him with a cold eye. "Will you come with me to sign that form?"

"I will not."

"Even though my own dear sister is presently in terrible danger?"

"Since I do not grant the premise, I can hardly validate the conclusion."

Her eyes narrowed. "Then there is nothing more to be said."

"Clearly there is not." Moriarty returned her glare with equal frostiness. "Other than that I have decided to have lunch at my club. Perhaps by the time I return, you will have calmed down enough to listen to the voice of reason."

"If you walk out that door, James Moriarty, don't bother to come back tonight."

"An ultimatum, Madame?" In point of fact, he would welcome the peace of the Pythagoras Club, which did not allow women, even as guests in the dining room. He had never fully appreciated the wisdom of that policy until now. "Perhaps you'll send me a note when you feel capable of engaging in a rational discussion."

He turned on his heel and walked out the door, ignoring Rolly, who pretended not to have heard every word of that ugly dispute. Moriarty and Angelina had somehow managed to turn each other into people no one in their household would recognize in a matter of minutes.

As Moriarty pressed his hat onto his head, he heard a shriek loud enough to rattle the windows, then a loud crash as a brittle object smashed against the wall or, more likely, the lintel of the door through which he had just passed.

Moriarty grabbed his coat and hastened out into the safety of the public road.

# Chapter Thirteen

Angelina read the note from Holmes over a cup of tea, ignoring the toast and boiled egg Antoine had provided for her breakfast. She had risen and dressed a short while earlier, also ignoring the undented pillow on the other side of the bed.

"Not one word, Peg, I beg you," she'd said when her dresser had opened her mouth to ask the obvious question. Peg had clapped her lips together and gone about her work in silence.

Angelina had written to Holmes almost immediately after her traitor husband had disappeared from view around the corner. Confound these men and their obstructive condescension! A woman ought to be able to fling herself into danger when she decided it needed to be done without having to dispute all the whys and wherefores.

But Sherlock Holmes had his own internal compass, not guided by the same worn-out, middle-class, conventional claptrap that afflicted James Moriarty. Holmes made his own rules; furthermore, he honestly wanted to solve this case, unlike James, who seemed to want nothing more than an opportunity to lean in the doorway casting little stones of logic and skepticism.

*Calm down and think rationally!* All very well if sitting and thinking was your only goal. But if a loved one was in danger, what then?

Holmes had known from the start that she would have to enter Trumbull's hospital. She had known it too. Both of them possessed a full measure of human intuition, which had told them both from the outset that such a drastic step would be required to get the proof they needed to catch their rat and put the rope around his neck.

That image confused her for a moment. She shook it off and finished her letters, one for James and one for Peg. Then she packed a small valise with a plain dress, a change of linen, and a few other necessities. She tucked James's letter into the edge of the mirror over her dressing table and slipped into the adjoining room to leave Peg's on top of the sewing basket, where she'd see it when she came up from her morning gossip with Antoine.

She started down the stairs with her valise as the clocks began to chime — a lovely cascade of tinkling music flowing from room to room. If James had his way, they'd tick in strict conformity, one single sound throughout the house, bounded by his will and his almighty pocket watch, set to the rhythm of Britain Herself.

Her renewed anger carried down the stairs and across the hall to the front door. As she shrugged on her coat and settled her hat, she met her own eyes in the mirror. Her reflection begged her to reconsider, but it was too late for that. Viola needed her and Holmes was waiting.

The die had been cast.

\* \* \*

The detective greeted her briefly as he joined her in the hansom cab but had the sense not to attempt a conversation. They reached Harley Street in short order and descended. Holmes took the valise. Angelina rang the bell.

The pretty nurse admitted them and heard their request. "Dr. Oliver is here. He will be happy to assist you."

She led them to the middle drawing room in which Fairchild had interviewed Angelina on her first day. That now felt like something that had happened months ago, at some other period of her life, when she was embarking on some swindle for a lark. The nurse remained in the room with them.

Dr. Oliver rose to shake Holmes's hand. "A pleasure to meet you, Mr. Moriarty."

"Professor," Holmes corrected with a straight face.

"My apologies, Professor. It isn't often we get to meet the husbands, you know. Not for any unseemly reasons, mind you! Confidentiality is essential in the treatment of the delicate and elusive mental disturbances that are Dr. Trumbull's specialty."

"I understand," Holmes said. "I've done my part and haven't pried, have I, dearest?" He smiled fondly at Angelina as he took her hand and gave it a squeeze.

She squeezed back hard, batting her lashes to say, *Don't overplay it!*

Holmes turned his amiable grin back toward the doctor. "Now she wants a month of rest, or so she says. I understand there's something I need to sign?"

"I have the form Dr. Trumbull gave me," Angelina said. "I filled out as much as I could."

"I'm not sure I understand the need for this," Holmes said in a cutting imitation of James at his most pompous.

"It's just a formality," Dr. Oliver said. "One of Dr. Trumbull's rules, and a wise one, I believe. We can't plan a successful course of treatment unless we can be certain it will be carried all the way through. Some parts of our regimen are stressful for some women, especially those who have grown accustomed to rich diets and little exercise. We don't want them changing their minds in a fit of pique and thereby missing out on the full benefit."

"I see," Holmes said, stroking his chin. "The form is an expression of the patient's willingness to do what must be done in order to get well. A little guidance and some well-defined boundaries are precisely what most women need, if you ask my opinion."

Angelina widened her eyes and nodded, as if receiving valuable instruction for her own good. Dr. Oliver nodded, satisfied. Holmes nodded too, raising and lowering his chin with just a touch more energy than was required.

"Shall we sign?" he prompted.

"Of course." Dr. Oliver twitched his fingers at the nurse, who came over to observe the proceedings. He took the document from Angelina and spread it on the desk. He took a fountain pen from his pocket, unscrewed the top, and handed it to Holmes. Holmes read through it, humming under his breath, and finally signed it with a flourish. He returned the pen to the doctor, who turned the document and signed as well. Finally the nurse added her neat signature on the line for the second witness.

Holmes bent his head to kiss Angelina on the cheek. "I'll see you in one month, then, darling."

She allowed the kiss, feeling a sudden longing for her beloved James and his warm scent of bay rum and cigar smoke. She faced the doctor, squaring her shoulders and lifting her chin. "I'm ready to go now, Doctor."

"I'll take you myself," Oliver said. "I was on my way out. If you'll wait one minute, I'll send for the coach."

He ushered Holmes through the door and closed it, shutting her inside alone.

# Chapter Fourteen

James Moriarty pounded on the blue double doors at Number 153 Harley Street. "Open this door! I demand to see the doctor!"

A pretty young nurse opened the door partway. "I'm sorry, but the doctor is —"

Moriarty pushed past her into the marble-floored entry and strode toward the carpeted stairs. The nurse grabbed at his coat sleeve in a futile effort to stop him.

"Doctor! Doctor!" she cried.

"What's going on here?" a plummy voice boomed from the top of the stairs.

Moriarty looked up at a stout man with an impressive pair of side whiskers. This must be Trumbull. "I demand that you return my wife!" Moriarty shouted.

"Now calm down," the doctor said, descending the stairs. He took each step with such stately confidence he managed to press Moriarty back down by sheer force of character. Once they reached the bottom and stood together on the chequered floor, Trumbull said, "We haven't any wives here at the moment, I can assure you, Mr. . . ."

"Moriarty. And of course I know she's not here. She's been committed to your hospital." He practically spat the last word. He could hear the near-hysterical quaver of his voice and took a deep breath, forcing himself to calmness. Irrational agitation would not help his cause. He drew himself to his full height, forcing the paunchy older man to tilt back his head.

It didn't discommode him in the slightest. Fitting that a nerve specialist should be utterly nerveless. "Ah, Mrs. Moriarty," the doctor said. "Yes, you signed the form for her here, this very morning, as my nurse here informed me. Dr. Oliver witnessed the signature."

"That wasn't me!"

The doctor chuckled. "Yes, we often feel that way when we regret a past decision. It's a form of buyer's remorse. In my considered opinion, however, you made a wise decision. Never fear, my good man. The month will go by in a flash and you'll get your wife back again in better health. You'll both be happier for having this little break from one another."

"I'm telling you, man. That was not me this morning. That was an impostor."

The nurse murmured, "The one this morning did have a much bigger nose, Doctor."

"Don't be absurd!" Trumbull scowled at her. "This man has a perfectly ordinary nose." He smiled up at Moriarty, man to man. "She mixed up a baroness and a soprano only last week. Worse, she put them into the same waiting room. You can imagine the furor that created!"

Moriarty rejected the attempt at levity with a curled lip. "You can't keep my wife captive against my will, Trumbull. I demand that you send for her at once, or better, authorize me to go collect her myself." He clenched his fists and let his full wrath show.

Trumbull regarded him with a cool gaze, then tilted his head toward his assistant. "Nurse, why don't you pop out and see if you can spot a constable? Try the pub on the corner of Marylebone Road."

She edged around Moriarty and hurried out the door.

Trumbull turned back to Moriarty, shaking his head and smiling, as if dealing with a stubborn child. He spoke in a soothing tone. "You know as well as I do that no one is being kept captive. It is of vital importance that the therapeutic program be allowed to run its course. My twenty-five years of experience have taught me that the best results are obtained by completely removing the patient from her old environment. She must be free to concentrate on getting well. Visits and letters from family members can be quite detrimental. This is why we insist on having both the husband and the wife agree in writing before witnesses, so all parties understand the conditions."

"I never signed that form," Moriarty said through clenched teeth.

Trumbull shot a glance at the mahogany wall clock. "Lady, ah — My next patient will be here in a few minutes. I'm afraid I must ask you to leave now."

"What about my wife?" Moriarty could hear the desperation in his voice and didn't care.

"Your wife is in the best of hands, receiving the treatment she deserves. Treatment you yourself requested for her."

The door opened and a burly man in a blue coat with two rows of brass buttons loomed upon the threshold. "Is this man causing you any trouble, Doctor?"

"Not at all," Trumbull said. "He was just leaving."

"This isn't over," Moriarty said. "I know what you're up to and I'll stop you any way I can."

Trumbull smiled up at him, altogether unruffled. "You asked for this treatment for your wife, Mr. Moriarty. You signed a contract. Now you'll have to let the treatment run its course."

* * *

Moriarty strode up Harley Street to Marylebone Road, feeling the constable's eyes on his back. Anger boiled in his chest. He needed something to strike at or tear apart,

144

but there was nothing on this city street but iron railings and polished facades. Frustration gnawed at his heart. He clenched his fists and must have growled out loud, judging by the alarmed look on the face of a passing gentleman.

He passed Madame Tussaud's with its Chamber of Horrors. Would Dr. Trumbull's whiskered face be given a place of honor there one day? He reached the corner of Baker Street and thought of an even more suitable target for his wrath.

Moriarty pushed past the boy who opened the door at 221B and bounded up the stairs, taking them two at a time. He pounded his fist on the door of the first-floor flat, which swung open almost the moment his skin touched wood. The face of Sherlock Holmes filled Moriarty's field of vision. He drew his fist back and threw a punch, but Holmes was too quick. The blow grazed past angular cheekbones, doing no real harm.

Moriarty adjusted his stance, ready to try again. This time Holmes caught his wrist in a viselike grip. "Enough, Professor. You've made your point." The detective stood back, opening the door wide. "You might as well come in."

Moriarty stalked into the cluttered room, still fuming but no longer hot enough for fisticuffs. He rubbed the bruised knuckles of his right hand and observed the red mark blooming on Holmes's cheek with some satisfaction. "You were ready for me. How?"

Holmes rubbed his offended cheek. "I'm waiting for a cab. I looked out the window and saw you striding toward my house, your intentions written on your face as plainly as the letters on a billboard. People cleared a path to avoid you." He chuckled. "And I must confess, I've been expecting a visit all morning."

"Then you know why I'm here. Your deception this morning went well beyond the bounds of decent behavior, Holmes. I consider it a personal affront. What do you have to say for yourself?"

Holmes crossed to the mantel and lit a cigarette before answering. He blew out a great stream of smoke, then said, "I make no apology." He held up his hand. "No, don't bristle at me again! Your wife is a most determined woman. If I had refused her request, she would simply have found someone else. She has many friends among the acting tribe, as you should know."

Moriarty grunted. "Her brother's friends, you mean." Sebastian's cronies would have seen it as a lark, knowing nothing about the hidden dangers.

Holmes chuckled, an ironic twist to his mouth. "Your wife has an excellent mind, Professor. You should know that too. Her intuition told her from the first that this case would require her full commitment."

"Intuition! That's just wishful thinking dressed up as some sort of supernatural insight. I'm surprised you should credit it. We're men of reason, you and I."

"The one does not preclude the other. Quite the contrary. Intuition has nothing to do with the supernatural, Professor. It's a form of extreme mental alertness, a fluid, nearly instantaneous compilation of minute observations. It's not a trick — far from it. It's a talent honed into a skill by diligent practice. Your wife chooses to call it intuition, but it is exactly the same art which I practice and label acute observation."

Moriarty grunted again, pursing his lips. He couldn't argue with that, although every fiber of his being wanted to reject it purely for having taken his wife away from him. But he was a man of reason, rational to the core. He prided himself on it. And reason recognized the truth in Holmes's words.

Holmes smoked patiently, waiting for the relaxed posture that signaled a cooling temper. Then he smiled and said, "I would further advise you not to attempt to extract Mrs. Moriarty from the hospital before she signals that she is ready to leave. She is capable as well as determined and will no doubt have some scheme in play even as we speak."

"I hope you're right," Moriarty said.

"So do I. She is best placed to obtain the concrete evidence we require to lay charges against Trumbull and his confederates. Meanwhile, you and I have our respective investigations to conduct. I suggest we embark upon them without delay. You must trust your wife's intuition and ingenuity now, Professor, if you hope to achieve our goals."

\* \* \*

Moriarty returned to the empty house on Bellenden Crescent. Now he sat beside the front windows in the drawing room, reading and rereading Angelina's letter, Holmes's bitter lesson echoing in his ears. He recognized the truth of that lesson but couldn't stop berating himself for a stubborn fool. If he'd gone to Harley Street first thing in the morning, he could have prevented this whole calamity.

Instead, he had dithered and dawdled, torn between crawling home with his tail between his legs to beg forgiveness and clinging to his crumbling patch of moral high ground. He'd spent a miserable night at the Pythagoras Club, lingered over breakfast longer than was decent, then sat in the library turning the pages of newspapers, his mind trapped in an endless circle of debate. Go home and surrender, or wait for Angelina to send a note begging him to forgive her?

Lunchtime came. He'd returned to his table in the dining room, where he'd cut up his chop, rearranging the pieces until he threw down his fork, pushed the plate away, and called for a whiskey and soda.

The drink had stopped the whirling of his mind. What was pride compared to Angelina?

He'd bounded up and raced home, forgetting to sign his bill, his torpor replaced by an overwhelming desire to see, hear, and touch his beloved wife. He would apologize for his stiff-necked obstinacy, although of course he wouldn't sign that blasted form. They'd think of another way, together.

But she had already gone, leaving nothing but the scent of gardenia and this inadequate letter.

*My darling James,*

*I know this hurts you. I know you'll see it as a betrayal, but it isn't. I beg you to believe me and know how much I love and respect you. But I cannot let my sister go into that dangerous place without so much as a warning. Try not to worry about me! I am not afraid. They won't hurt us during our month as patients; they'll wait until after we leave, but then we'll be wary, we'll be ready, and we'll be safe at home with you to protect us.*

*Holmes has agreed to go with me to sign the form, pretending to be you. They've never seen you there. They won't know the difference. You must see that this is a necessary step. We can't stop these monsters without proof, and we can't get proof any other way. At least not in time to help Viola. Now I can watch over her while I search for something damning.*

*I must do this, darling. I hope you can understand and forgive me.*

*With all my love,*

*Angelina*

The clocks in the house began to chime, each distinct tune joining in the round in its turn. He sat transfixed as the gentle rain of sound washed over him, its meaning forgotten. He started to read the letter again when Peg's voice roused him.

"You got one too, eh?"

Moriarty nodded mutely, gesturing at the other chair, which she accepted.

Lady's maids in conventional homes didn't normally sit down with the master, but this was hardly a conventional home and Peg was more than a mere servant. She'd been with Angelina since they were children. As Moriarty understood the story, she'd joined the family as a dressmaker when Angelina was performing as child star in Christmas pantomimes. When Angelina grew up and become the leading soprano in an opera company, Peg stayed with her, traveling throughout the Continent and even to America. Although not of the same social class, Peg had become as much a companion as a maid; naturally enough, given the unsettled life of performers.

After so many years of faithful service, the woman could hardly be set aside. So now she had the second-best bedroom and spent her evenings as she pleased. She didn't dine with them, although she sometimes joined them for tea. The *modus vivendi* continued to evolve. If not for her appalling Cockney accent, she might almost pass for an eccentric aunt.

She peered at the letter Moriarty held. "Yours is longer than mine."

"What is?"

"Your letter." She sniffed. "It's longer."

"Oh. Be my guest." Moriarty handed it to her. She gave him hers in exchange.

*Peg, darling,*

*I'm sorry to sneak out like this, but I can't endure another argument. You know more than anyone that I can't abandon my sweet angel, not again. I simply must go. But chin up, ducky. I'll be back in a month, so fit and trim you'll have to take in all my gowns.*

*Love,*

*Lina*

They stared at each other's letters in silence for a while. The mouse maids slipped in with a tray loaded with a teapot and cups, which they set on the table. When they'd gone, Peg asked, "Pour you a cup?"

Moriarty regarded the teapot sourly. "I'd rather have a whiskey."

"I wouldn't mind one myself."

He got up to fix them each a substantial drink. He handed her a glass and sat down again. "What am I going to do, Peg?"

"Get her out of there, of course. Both of them."

"I tried, and failed. The renowned doctor reminded me in no uncertain terms that a contract was a contract and summoned a constable to show me out."

"Too bad."

Moriarty shot her a wry glance. "Then I went to punch Sherlock Holmes in the nose."

"Did you?" Peg's brown eyes danced. "I hope you mashed it flat."

"Alas, I did no real harm." Moriarty took a large swallow, relishing the burn of strong spirits in his throat. This whiskey deserved to be sipped, but he wasn't in a sipping mood. "He informed me that my wife had a will of her own."

Peg snorted. "I could have told you that, ducky." She shook her head. "She's always had a mind of her own, our Lina. We should have known she'd never be content with half measures, not where one of her little angels was concerned."

Moriarty smiled at her form of address. She'd never called him "ducky" before. "I know you're right. And that insufferable Holmes is right. I want to get them both out of that place. But how? What can I do, alone?"

The whiskey seemed to have revived Peg's innate Cockney optimism. "Well, you ain't alone now, are you? You've got plenty of friends who would come and help at the snap of a finger."

"I do? Who?"

"Captain Sandy, for one. Have you forgotten about him? He's a useful man in a pinch, is he, and he'd do anything for our girls."

"Captain Sandy," Moriarty whispered. The mere thought of the valiant cabman revived his spirits.

Gabriel Sandy had been born into an aristocratic family. After being sent down from Cambridge for a bit of rambunctious horseplay, he'd joined the 13th Duke of Connaught's Lancers and distinguished himself in Afghanistan, rising to the rank of captain. Then his luck had turned again and he'd been made a scapegoat by an embezzling major and cashiered for irregularities in the mess accounts. After kicking around the globe for a while, he'd ended up in London with his own hackney cab.

While his troop had been stationed in London, Sandy had become an ardent admirer of Angelina and her Little Angels. He'd carried one of their photograph cards with him when his troop was sent abroad. He credited that card for saving his life when he'd stooped to pick it up, just missing a bullet from a sniper's rifle. When he'd learned of the Archer family's troubles last spring, he'd sworn his undying devotion.

"I'll write to him at once," Moriarty said. "He can reconnoiter the hospital grounds in Hampstead. I can't go, now that I've made a spectacle of myself." He went to the writing table and scribbled a short letter, folded it into an envelope, and sealed it.

He got up to ring the bell, then turned back to Peg with a grim look. "I'm not sure what good that will do. The place is probably surrounded by a brick wall."

"It's a start, ducky. It's a start."

Rolly, their irregular footman, came in with a letter on a silver tray. "The three o'clock post, Professor."

"Thank you." Moriarty traded his letter for the one on the tray. "Hop down to the box and mail this one right away, please."

"Wery good, sir." Rolly bowed, head to knee, then bounded out of the room.

Moriarty inspected the envelope. "No return address. Sent late this morning." He took up a slim knife and slit it open. He skimmed the letter and cursed out loud. "Pardon me."

Peg shrugged that off. "What is it?"

He passed it to her. "It's the instructions for paying the thousand pounds, for the 'Clennam treatment.' By gad, Peg! They mean to go through with it, even after my protest this morning. Confound the bastards!"

"Don't pay it," she said.

"I won't. But I'm not sure that will be enough." Moriarty began to pace back and forth across the room, hands clasped behind his back. "I've got to do more. I've got to bring these villains to book, the sooner the better."

Peg pursed her lips and watched him pace. After a few minutes of nothing whatsoever, a thought emerged. He stopped in front of her chair and said, "I will pay that thousand pounds."

"No, Professor! You mustn't."

He held up a hand. "Hear me out, Peg. Angelina is right. They won't do anything until after she comes home. We need a bold move; well, this is bold. If I pay it, with Sandy's help, I can follow whoever collects the money to the bank."

Peg made a dismissive noise. "Who'd put that kind of lolly in a bank? They'll spend it. And he — or they, however many there are — they'll have to divvy it up, won't they?"

Moriarty's feeble idea sank. "I suppose you're right." But another rose up in its wake. "Let's look at the other side of this coin. The other clients must have drawn their payments out of a bank. Nobody keeps that much money sitting around the house. I have the names of four putative victims. I can easily identify the heirs from the records at Somerset House. Follow the money — a time-honored strategy. I must find out which banks these clients used . . ." His enthusiasm subsided as he recognized the flaws in his plan. He shook his head, defeated. "It's useless. How could I persuade a bank to give me any information about another man's accounts?" He returned to his chair, shoulders slumped.

"Don't give up yet, Professor. You might be on to something. What's the name of that woman?" Peg started snapping her fingers. "Your old landlady. Wasn't she a banker's widow? And didn't you and Lina buy her house for her with the swag you took off that rascal in May? By my reckoning, she owes you a favor."

"Mrs. Peacock. By gad, you're right, Peg! All of her friends are bankers' wives and widows. She might know someone who knows someone who could get a peek into those accounts. A servant in the house would know which bank. We could find a way to ask without tipping our hand." Moriarty jumped up and started pacing again, this time with a spring in his step. "Yes. Yes. This is good. This is something. We'll have to connect the pieces . . . It'd be best if we could get our hands on the other clients' letters, the ones requesting the Clennam treatment in the first place. We'll want to connect the whole chain, from requesting the treatment to paying the thousand pounds."

"That could take forever," Peg said. "We want something faster than that, don't we?"

Moriarty wagged his finger at her. "We build a solid case brick by brick, Peg. Brick by brick. It will take all of us working toward the same goal to get it done. I'll write to Mrs. Peacock at once and Captain Sandy. There's no time to waste."

"Now you're talking." Peg poured the last of her whiskey into a teacup and added tea and sugar to it. "And don't forget the rest of the gang. They're bound to come in handy somehow or other."

"What gang?"

"Our gang here. Antoine and Rolly."

"Of course." Moriarty smiled. "I'm sure the whole staff will do whatever they can to support our efforts."

Peg rolled her eyes, shaking her head at the ceiling. "Whatever they can, he says. Professor, don't you know who's livin' in your own house? You've got a first-class forger down in the kitchen and one of London's slipperiest pickpockets hopping back from the post box this very minute."

"I do? They are?" Moriarty stopped in his tracks, frowning as he considered the possibilities. Then he shook his head. "No, no. We can't employ criminal tactics."

"Can't we? Not even to save our girls?"

Moriarty met her eyes. For that? Maybe they could.

# Chapter Fifteen

Angelina pulled back the curtain to examine the view she'd be enjoying for the next month. Her room was situated at the far end of what they called the new wing, a two-story extension built on to the original four-story Georgian building they called the main house. They'd snugged a stone terrace into the angle formed by the two buildings. Between the terrace and the nine-foot wall that circled the whole estate lay a broad green lawn dotted with fruit trees and flower beds. Hampstead Road ran past the hospital's tall iron gates. Beyond the road spread the wilderness of Hampstead Heath, wafting its wholesome breezes over the troubled residents of Halcyon House.

Her personal attendant, a brawny, flat-faced woman named Jenks, had met her in the reception room at the front of the main house. She led Angelina up the central staircase and through a series of corridors, trailed by an orderly carrying her valise. Their short parade traversed the distance in silence, thanks to the plush carpets. Trumbull's decorators had mimicked the style of the great European hotels, with lots of potted palms and paintings of soothing landscapes everywhere.

Cozy groups of upholstered chairs dotted the long corridors, many of them occupied by patients, most of whom had some sort of handiwork in their laps. Some stared blankly at a half-finished needlepoint canvas or napped over an open book. One woman knitted at a furious pace, muttering to herself while her scarf spilled onto the floor like a vine possessed by demons.

The walls were embellished with oak wainscoting about four feet up. Above that ran a painted stripe that changed colors at several points along their route. Angelina realized after a few minutes that the patients wore dresses in the same range of colors. A clever idea; it would help the attendants return wandering women to their proper rooms.

"If you'll just change into this, Madame," Jenks said.

Angelina turned away from the window. Jenks was holding up a shapeless cotton gown in the most appalling shade of apple green. That color would make any woman look like a lunatic! These people really *were* evil.

* * *

Angelina saw Viola every day during that first week. They could hardly avoid one another since their rooms were directly across the hall. Viola wore the same hideous dress — they seemed to be the only two in the green section — but on her, it looked stylish. Her spun-gold hair worked with any color while the bilious shade made the warm highlights in Angelina's chestnut hair stand out like livid stripes of aniline dye.

They'd had one short, heated, whispered conversation on the first day.

"What are you doing here?" Viola had demanded.

Angelina had grabbed her arm and pulled her away from their attendants. "I'm here to protect you."

Viola had rolled her eyes and refused to listen. "I don't need you hovering over me every minute of my life. I'm *resting*. Go find someone else to smother!"

"Sorry, ducky. You're stuck with me for a whole month."

Viola must really have been resting because Angelina had eaten alone at her assigned table all week. The staff followed their color scheme even at meals, sitting patients from the same section together. If it weren't for the obviously institutional garments, the dining room would fit right into the Grand Hotel in Paris. The women sat at linen-draped tables for two or four decorated with small vases holding sprays of flowers or pretty leaves from the garden. They dined from real china with silver-plated knives and forks and ordered their meals from handwritten menu cards set at each place. The food was excellent, if far less rich than Antoine's.

Tonight Angelina sat in her accustomed place, gazing as usual around the room, pretending that she sat alone because she preferred to do so. She doubted anyone thought twice about it. Only half the seats were filled on any given night since patients could dine in their rooms if they wanted. A man played the piano in the corner near the main entrance.

She hadn't turned up anything even remotely sinister yet, although she'd been pampered within an inch of her life. She'd had herbal baths and long massages. She'd dozed under an apple tree in the late afternoon and played a few rounds of badminton on a grassy court. Dr. Oliver had weighed and measured her almost to the point of counting the hairs on her head. Dr. Fairchild had asked her a raft of questions, too many to remember what she'd said. She used sweet Mrs. Parsons as her model and pretended to be afraid of everything, especially her husband. She'd added the touch of a weak memory, hoping that would cover any inconsistencies in her answers.

All in all, it had been an uneventful week. She had to keep reminding herself why she had locked herself into this silk-lined prison. She also missed James, more than she'd ever missed anyone. They weren't allowed visitors, not ever, nor letters from anyone. She hadn't expected that. She'd have to think of a way to communicate with James one of these days. A laundry maid, a waiter . . .

Something would turn up by the time she had something to tell him.

A familiar figure at the garden doors caught her attention. "Well, well, well. The star finally grants us an appearance."

Viola entered the dining room, walking with her old confident strut, looking around her with interest. Her attendant guided her to the green table and held her chair.

"So kind of you to join us at last," Angelina said. "I've been sitting her for a week, the only woman in a green gown. The pinks and lilacs have been laughing at me behind their hands."

Viola wrinkled her nose at her as she sat down. "I told you I've been resting. It's done me a world of good."

She did look much better. The roses had returned to her cheeks and the mischievous sparkle to her eyes, although her waistline had expanded more than the loose-corset-lacing rule could account for.

Angelina waited until had attendant had joined the others along the rear wall. "I'm glad you're feeling better. But I must warn you about this place, darling. You must be on your guard."

"On my guard against what? That piano player? I'll admit he is terrible. He's missed two notes already."

"This is serious, Viola. Deadly serious. Listen to me." Angelina bent her head toward her sister and lowered her voice. "Your dear Dr. Trumbull uses this hospital to murder select patients for money — lots of money. I'm afraid Badger may have sent you here to get rid of you without being suspected."

Viola stared at her in silence, her blue eyes as hard as stones. "I cannot believe you would say such a horrible thing, Lina. Not even as a joke. My beloved Badger would never hurt me. Never."

"Oh, darling, I know it's hard to believe." Angelina tried to take her hand, but Viola snatched it back.

"He brought me here to help me. This is the best care in London — possibly the best in all of England."

"For everyone except the special few. Have you heard your attendant say anything about Mrs. Clennam?"

"What are you babbling about? You'd better watch out, ducky. Lunacy might be catching."

"Very funny," Angelina said, but the point was well taken.

"If you must know," Viola said, "we had a long talk before we decided *together* that I should try this place. Badger would do anything to help me. Anything at all. He's even hired a firm to remodel my flat while I'm here from floor to ceiling. He's afraid the wallpaper might be making me sick."

"Really?" Angelina frowned, distracted. She wished she'd thought of that. Heaven only knew what state her house would be in after a month of James living alone with their untrained servants.

"I don't know how you could come up with such a cruel idea, Lina, I really don't."

"All right. I'm sorry. I won't say another word about Badger — for now. But please just hear me out." She gripped her sister's hand and held on to it while she told her the whole story as quickly and quietly as she could. Told like this, all at once in a hoarse whisper, sitting in this room filled with nervous women in hospital gowns, the story sounded absolutely barmy.

Viola listened without interrupting. At the end, she laid her hand on Angelina's cheek, worry darkening her eyes. "I'm appalled that you could sit here speaking such nonsense, Lina, and even more horrified that you actually seem to believe it."

Angelina met her sister's worried gaze, struggling for some convincing proof. "Peg believes it," she finally managed.

Anna Castle

Viola rolled her eyes. "Peg believes in Spring-heeled Jack."

"All right. But James believes it too, and you've never met a more rational man."

"Except when it comes to you. He'd believe chalk was cheese if you wanted him to."

Angelina glared at the stubborn minx. How could she make her understand? She gave it her last shot. "Sherlock Holmes believes it."

Viola yelped a laugh, then clapped a hand over her mouth. "Oh yes, that does it. Sherlock Holmes, the man who spent weeks of his life convinced that your scholarly, retiring husband was a criminal mastermind."

Angelina had nothing else. She'd just have to turn up some real evidence. Dr. Fairchild had interviewed her in his office on the ground floor, which he apparently shared with Dr. Oliver. Both worked in other hospitals, but they were public ones. Not even Dr. Trumbull's house was as secure as this guarded fortress. She'd bet the letters from the other special clients were hidden somewhere at Halcyon House.

Also, these people took notes on everything. The nurses, the attendants, the doctors — they all carried clipboards and pencils. The notes must be intended for the doctors to analyze or compile or whatever they did with such things. They must keep them and where better than their private office? Perhaps those notes included a record of Lady Georgia's cruel treatment — the month-long withholding of the drug she needed to prepare her for her final overdose.

Angelina gave it one last try. "Please be careful what you eat and drink, Viola."

"I intend to eat whatever appeals to me and follow Nurse Andrews's instructions to the letter. She's taking *such* good care of me. Maybe you're jealous that you're not getting the same attention, have you thought of that?"

160

An attendant in a gray uniform came to take their orders. They always offered a few choices, maintaining the illusion of a luxury hotel. Viola studied her menu with relish, then said, "I'll have the cream soup, the beef bourguignon, and the trifle for pudding." She batted her lashes at the attendant. "Are we allowed to have seconds of pudding?"

The attendant beamed at her the way everyone beamed at the twins when they chose to turn on the full power of their natural charm. "If you eat all your vegetables like a good girl, I think we might manage a *little* extra, just for you."

Angelina's appetite had decreased over the past week. Too much sleep, probably. Jenks gave her a large spoonful of some syrupy tonic every night before bed. She slept like a log, if a log could have elaborate dreams. "I'll have the clear soup, please, and the fish. And no pudding. I would love a cup of coffee if there is any."

The attendant clucked her tongue. "You know very well that coffee and wine are against the rules, Mrs. Moriarty. I'll bring you a nice fresh lemonade instead." She collected the menus and moved on to another table.

Angelina smiled as if that fresh lemon had been squeezed between her teeth.

# Chapter Sixteen

"They're here!"

Moriarty frowned at the excessive exuberance of his young footman but hastened to the window to watch Captain Gabriel Sandy draw up to the pavement in his hansom cab. Sandy climbed down from his perch at the back while Zeke, a street urchin who had attached himself to the cabman by making himself indispensable, tied the horse's reins to the post.

Moriarty jogged down the stairs, unable to remain sedately in the drawing room waiting for the guests to be announced. They'd been obliged to wait a week already because Sandy and his sidekick had gone down to Brighton for a respite from the city smoke. Cabmen enjoyed the odd holiday as much as anyone else.

Rolly opened the door and Zeke bounded inside. The boys punched each other in the shoulder, then stood back to give each other a thorough inspection. Zeke's face was as brown as a boatman's, incongruous under his battered top hat. But Rolly's transformation was the more astonishing. Zeke pursed his lips, whistling under his breath as he surveyed his old pal from the neatly oiled hair to the gleaming buckles on his polished shoes.

"Well, ain't you the perfect swell!" he finally said.

"Lookin' the part and livin' the life." Rolly struck a pose, chin high. "I've got my own room."

"Nor you don't!" Zeke pushed him hard enough to stagger him back a few steps.

"That's enough," Sandy said, and they subsided at once. Every boy and girl on the London streets adored the former Lancer. Something about his ginger moustache and his freckled face, or the shadow in the depths of his hazel eyes that spoke of past troubles, made folks trust him at first meeting. The space between the freckles hadn't gotten any browner at the seaside, but there did seem to be more of them.

Moriarty extended a hand. "Man, it's good to see you! I feel better knowing you're with us."

"Always." Sandy took the proffered hand and shook it heartily. "I'm sorry I didn't get your letter sooner. But we'll get this sorted out, James. I have every confidence." He shrugged off two overcoats and slung them over Rolly's outstretched arms, adding his weather-beaten top hat to the stack.

"Let's go upstairs," Moriarty said. "I have a rather nice whiskey to chase away the chill." He shot a glance at the two boys. "I believe Antoine has made apple cake for tea."

Cheers met that remark. Moriarty ushered Sandy up the stairs while the boys clattered down to the kitchen.

Moriarty went straight to the drinks table. Sandy strolled around the room murmuring vague compliments about the decor until Moriarty handed him his glass, saying, "You might as well save it. I wouldn't know a valuable antique from an old chamber pot and I believe Angelina's going to change out the whole lot when —" The fear that he would never get her back rose in his chest and choked off the words. He had now spent six sleepless nights without her.

"When she comes back," Sandy finished. "We'll put our heads together and roust out my gang of boys. If there's proof, we'll find it, and if we can't? By that time, you'll have found a way to get her out of that house if we have to drag her over the wall on a rope in the dead of night."

163

Moriarty chuckled, the knot in his chest breaking up. "We'll keep that in mind. Though I doubt she'd thank us for it."

"Angelina does have her own mind. So does Viola." Sandy sat in one of the rococo armchairs. He took a sip of the whiskey and made an odd face. "I've grown so used to drinking gin I'd almost forgotten what whiskey tastes like."

That touched a chord of guilt. Moriarty never knew quite how to treat his unorthodox friend. He had trouble reconciling the Etonian accent with the tradesman's rough hands. Sandy had fallen far below his station by society's standards, but he seemed indifferent to the supposed loss. Moriarty didn't know if he would offend, flatter, or please the man by sending him a bottle of good whiskey now and then.

Sandy chuckled. "I see that furrowed brow, James. It isn't necessary, not on my account. A glass of hot gin hits the spot like nothing else after a cold day in the dirty streets. I like the life I've made for myself. I've got honest work that provides for me and that little scamp I've more or less adopted. Enough for a family — if I ever meet the right woman. And yes, I'm still bitter about what was done to me in Afghanistan, but only when I think about it, which isn't often. Best of all, I've got good friends, true ones, better than I've ever had."

He raised his glass toward Moriarty, who raised his in reply. They drank to friendship.

"I'm glad to hear it," Moriarty said. "I'll endeavor to stop furrowing. No promises on that score — I'm told it's something I tend to do."

"It can't be easy, living with a woman who can read your mind from every little slip and twitch."

"You have no idea." Moriarty blinked away a touch of moisture in his eyes. "I want her back, Sandy."

"Then let's get to it."

Moriarty took his customary chair by the window. "You must have questions. I know our story sounds like something out of one of Peg's penny dreadfuls, with evil doctors concocting undetectable murder methods."

"No questions whatsoever. I trust your judgment and Angelina's intuition, especially when they point in the same direction." Sandy set his glass on a side table and placed his fists on his thighs, sitting up straight in a military posture. "The first thing I'd like to do is reconnoiter the territory around that hospital."

"I'm not sure what we can expect to find."

"That's why we look. We can't strategize without information." He chewed the fringe of his long moustache, nodding while he thought. "Hampstead is very hilly. Lines of sight are limited, as are avenues of access. As I recall, there's only one straight road in the whole village — the high road."

"I've looked at the map," Moriarty said. "Halcyon House is one of the larger estates bordering the heath." He picked up the map from the floor beside his chair. He'd done more than look at it. He'd stared at it for hours, studying each street, each plot of land, as if he could peer through the lines of ink into Angelina's window and see her face.

Sandy took the map and spread it across his knees. "It's essential to get properly oriented. Zeke and I will drive up this evening, try to get a general sense of the place. I don't get up that way often."

"Perhaps you could give me a ride," Moriarty said. "I'm meeting a man at a pub in Highgate at six o'clock." He told Sandy what little he knew of Mrs. Parsons's death. August Norton, the maid's fiancé, had responded to his note by return mail, heartened to discover an unexpected ally and eager to help.

"That's a good start." Sandy rolled up the map and set it on the table at his elbow.

165

"I hope so. He attended the inquest, so he might be able give me the details of Mrs. Parsons's death and some insight into why they arrested the maid servant. I grew up in a small village, you know, in Gloucestershire. There are apple trees everywhere, irresistible to hungry boys. I don't remember ever having a conflict with wasps."

"Nor do I," Sandy said. "The newspaper must have garbled the account."

Moriarty nodded, calmed and heartened by having an intelligent and knowledgeable friend to discuss the matter with. Far better than pacing around the dining table table scolding himself for being a heartless, obstinate buffoon.

"You mentioned letters," Sandy said. "Would you mind if I had a look at them?"

"Not at all." Moriarty got up to take them from the drawer in the writing desk. He'd folded them together into one large envelope for safekeeping. He handed them to Sandy, saying, "I've had an idea about how we might use these to our advantage."

Sandy nodded as his eyes skimmed the three pages. "You've had two demands for the thousand pounds. I take it you haven't paid, then."

"Not yet. Peg can't abide the idea, and I'm worried that receipt of payment might initiate whatever plan they have for Angelina."

"Although presumably Viola's program is already underway," Sandy said. "I must say, these are disturbing. That second demand for money reads like a threat, even though it makes no mention of specific services to be rendered."

"Yes, it seems to imply that they'll go forward in order to force me to pay. 'A contract is a contract.' The same words Trumbull used when I confronted him." Moriarty's mouth twisted at that bitter memory. "If I do pay, it might give me a chance to follow the money through the doctors' bank accounts." He held up a hand to forestall the obvious objection. "*If* they deposit the cash in a bank and *if* Mrs. Peacock's friend's son can identify the accounts. Both events are unlikely. However, it occurred to me that if payments are distributed among conspirators, presumably employees of the hospital, some of them might spend it on some visible luxury, like a watch or a new hat."

"You're thinking of the ones down the chain, like cleaners and orderlies."

"Yes. There must be at least a few people other than the doctors who know what's going on, especially the ones who attend personally on the Clennam patients."

"I agree," Sandy said. "I'll post a few boys up there to keep an eye on hospital staff as they come and go. They'll notice anything that looks shiny and new." He grinned. "They can keep their eyes peeled for what Zeke calls that 'money-for-nuffink smile.'"

"Excellent." Moriarty finished his whiskey and got up to pour them each another round. "I had another idea about these letters. They're all written in the same hand, did you notice?"

Sandy shook his head and fanned the pages out like cards. "Well, so they are! An educated hand, to my eye, with the same little flourish on each crossed *T*."

"We don't yet know if Trumbull is working alone," Moriarty said, "or if one or both of the other doctors — Oliver and Fairchild — are working this scheme without his knowledge. But whoever wrote these letters is definitely involved. If we could get a sample of his writing on a page with his signature, like a letter, we would at least know one name for certain."

"That's brilliant, James. Absolutely brilliant. Not only would we know who to focus on, we'd have something concrete to show a judge."

"It wouldn't be enough to charge a gentleman with deaths that have already been judged natural or accidental."

"No," Sandy said, "but it's a brick in the wall. A good, solid one. How do you plan to get those writing samples?"

"They're well-known doctors who have published articles in widely read journals. I thought I'd write to each one asking a few questions about their areas of expertise with reference to my own wife. Not Angelina, of course. I'll invent someone with the relevant symptoms. There's one catch, however."

"Whoever this is," Sandy said, shaking the letters for emphasis, "has seen your handwriting as well."

"Precisely." Moriarty grinned at his friend. "But now that you're here, perhaps you could write them."

"I could write one," Sandy said, "if you'll draft the content. I don't know anything about nervous disorders."

Moriarty laughed at that idea. A man who could sit atop a hansom cab in all weather driving a horse through London traffic must be possessed of nerves of steel. "It would be better to have each of the three letters written in a different hand. But Peg's writing is like chicken scratches. They'd never believe the author had ever read a medical journal." He frowned, tapping his foot. "How hard is it to change the way you write?"

"I don't know," Sandy said, "but the boys tell me you have a famous French forger in your kitchen. They could be exaggerating."

Moriarty slapped his knee. "I don't believe they are! Peg told me the same thing. I suppose a forger could produce three different styles of writing easily enough."

"I should think so." Sandy chuckled. "Your wife's unusual hiring practices have their advantages."

"I'll draft the letters tonight," Moriarty said, grinning. The prospect of doing something tangible energized him.

"We'll bring food in from the public house until Antoine crafts his three versions."

"Speaking of letters," Sandy said, "the next thing I'd like to do is establish a means of communicating with Angelina, or Viola, if necessary."

"I've been going around in circles on that one." Moriarty said. "They're not allowed letters or visitors. It interferes with their treatment, I was told, which would sound reasonable if I didn't think what I thought about that damned doctor." He took a healthy swig of his whiskey.

Sandy studied the map, moving his finger along the marked roads. "We need someone who can get in and out without question, like a maid or an orderly."

"I thought of that, but it would take time to cultivate such a person. Too much time, I think."

"You're probably right, but if my boys are watching for women in new hats, they might spot someone. Those rascals have a rare eye for the corruptible."

Moriarty nodded. "We can hope. Mr. Norton, the fellow I'm meeting this evening, is a Hampstead fireman. He might know someone who works at the hospital."

"The more, the merrier."

The two men sipped and thought for a while. Then Moriarty shot an uncertain glance at his friend. "At the risk of sounding corruptible . . . I keep asking myself, what would Sherlock Holmes do?"

Sandy laughed. "I don't believe he's corrupt — just unconventional. And unreliable, from our perspective."

"To say the least. If you remember last May, he interrogated my landlady's housemaid by getting himself up as a local tradesman. He had the poor girl believing he had a genuine liking for her."

"I do remember. He has a reputation for being able to blend in anywhere, apart from that nose."

"Thank God for that nose," Moriarty said. "So, if Sherlock Holmes wanted to get inside a private hospital, how would he do it?"

"Ah," Sandy said. "I see where you're going. Well, he wouldn't pretend to be a doctor. There can't be very many of them and everyone would know them by sight."

"The patients are all women, which means most of the attendants must be as well. That would make the few male orderlies and garden staff equally distinctive."

"What about salesmen?" Sandy asked. "Don't they buy supplies? Drugs, medical instruments, that sort of thing. They must accept deliveries."

"By gad, Sandy, you're a genius!" Moriarty slapped his hand on his knee again. "That's it! I know exactly how I can do it. These doctors pride themselves on their up-to-date treatments. The one I met couched everything he told me in electrical analogies. Well, I happen to be acquainted with a salesman offering the top of the line in modern electrotherapeutic devices."

\* \* \*

Sandy dropped Moriarty off at the Angel Inn at the top of the hill in Highgate, a pleasant village lying directly across the heath from Hampstead. He assumed Norton had chosen to meet here because this was where the inquest had been held.

A noisy crowd of men stood around the bar in the public room, but Moriarty found an empty table in a quiet corner and ordered a mug of ale. He had pinned a black silk bow to his top hat as an identifier, but now he doubted it would be visible across the room.

He needn't have worried. He had barely wet his lips when a substantial young man loomed up beside him. "Mr. Moriarty?" He rose to shake the proffered hand.

Moriarty stood an inch over six feet tall and took daily exercise at the London Athletic Club in Chelsea. Rowing was his sport of choice and he had the shoulders to prove it. He considered himself fitter than average, but next to August Norton, he felt like one of those sorry weaklings lampooned in advertisements for muscle-building tonics. The fireman might be a few inches shorter, but those inches had clearly gone into his chest and biceps.

"Please sit down," Moriarty said, resuming his own chair and flicking his finger at the barmaid. "What I can offer you?"

"Ale, thanks. They've got a good one here." When his mug arrived, Norton took a deep draught, finishing with a satisfied sigh. "Long day."

"I appreciate your taking the time to meet with me."

"I'd swim the Channel to meet the man who can get my Flora out of jail." He gave Moriarty a curious look. "What's your interest, if you don't mind my asking?"

"I believe it's possible that your Miss Semple has been falsely accused, perhaps deliberately. It is possible that Mrs. Parsons was murdered by her doctor at the request of her husband, for a considerable fee."

Norton stared blankly at him for a long moment with his mouth half open. Then he started shaking his head. "That can't be, Mr. Moriarty. Her doctor wasn't nowhere near the place."

"I know how strange it sounds, but I am investigating another case that is only slightly less bizarre. Please, Mr. Norton, bear with me while I explain."

Moriarty told him about Lady Georgia's death and outlined the conclusions he and the others had reached after their week of experimentation. He sketched a few of the methods they'd identified for inducing delayed deaths, emphasizing the intimate knowledge and daring imagination required to implement such methods.

Norton's initial disbelief gradually faded, replaced by a dawning light of hope.

"Well, I can't say I like any part of your idea. The whole thing is just plain nasty. But I'll go along with anything that might prove my Flora's innocence." He scratched his brushy side whiskers and gave Moriarty a wry smile. "I can add one piece to your puzzle. You can mail bees in a box. My granddad keeps hives on his farm in Kent. He started 'em with a queen and some drones he bought from some honey producer in Dorset. You can put bees to sleep with smoke and then tuck 'em into a box with a bit of honeycomb to keep 'em happy."

"That's very interesting," Moriarty said. "I suppose wasps would be similar. Thank you for that confirmation."

Norton drank off half of his pint. "Well, it might sound stark raving mad, but it makes more sense than their story. My Flora never killed nobody, much less Mrs. Parsons. She liked the lady and it was a good job. A step up from working at that hospital."

"Have you spoken to Miss Semple? She's in Newgate, the article said."

"They won't let me see her. They only allow family and friends, once every three months and only after the trial. Police detectives go in and out as they please with their warrant cards. And people say lawyers roam around in there looking for business."

"I'm sorry to hear that," Moriarty said. "What more can you tell me? Did you attend the inquest?"

"I did. Two days off without pay, but at least she could see me and know I stand by her."

Moriarty said, "The paper wasn't clear on the sequence of events. How did Mrs. Parsons happen to have that box of Turkish delight in her lap at the moment Miss Semple opened the windows?"

"The box came in the post. That's what caused it all, Flora said, but they didn't believe her. She said the wasps came out of the box, not through the window."

"That was my hypothesis. Then she must have opened the window to get rid of them."

Norton shook his square head. "She couldn't say why she went to the window. That's the strangest thing of all. Flora said that when she saw the missus open that red box, she just walked over to the window and unlatched it. Like she was in a dream, she said. That's why they wouldn't listen. They thought she was making up excuses after being caught red-handed."

*Like she was in a dream.* Watson had said some nerve doctors used hypnosis to treat patients with irrational fears. Could that induce a dreamlike state?

Moriarty asked, "Can you tell me anything about the witness against her? That gardener?"

"Not much," Norton said, but then he looked out the window and waved at someone. "But here comes one who can. I hope you don't mind, sir. I asked Beatrice, the downstairs maid at the Parsons' house, to come along and talk to you too. It's her half day."

He went to greet a slim young woman wearing a cloth coat and a perky hat trimmed with flowers. Norton guided her to the table and held her chair. "This here's the gentleman I told you about, Bea. This here's Beatrice Wrenn, Mr. Moriarty. She can tell you more about that day than anybody, shy of my Flora."

"What can I offer you to drink, Miss Wrenn?"

Miss Wrenn hesitated, looking around the room as if wondering who might see her. "Perhaps a glass of ginger beer?"

Moriarty summoned the barmaid, asking for another round for himself and Norton. The young persons chatted about mutual acquaintances until the drinks arrived. Then they turned their attention to Moriarty, ready for questions.

He asked the housemaid, "Did you know Flora Semple well?"

"Well enough to know she never murdered nobody. She'd only been with us for a week, but we hit it off right away, we two. She's about my age and we both have our young men. My Phillip's a groom at Kenwood House."

"Tell him about the red box," Norton said. "You're the one that brought it in to Mrs. Parsons, aren't you?"

"That's one of my jobs, bringing her mail to her. That box came in the ten o'clock post, wrapped in pretty red paper and tied with plain string. No return address — they asked me about that." She leaned forward, lowering her voice. "But I'll tell you something I didn't tell them. They scolded us for not sticking to the questions and they didn't ask it, so I kept it to myself. But I remember that box shivered in my hands as I was taking it upstairs. Like this." She held out both hands, about ten inches apart, and shook them as if she were being electrified.

Moriarty frowned. "That's a very important observation, Miss Wrenn. Would you swear to it in court if you were asked?"

"Of course I would. It's the truth, ain't it?"

Moriarty and Norton traded smiles.

"Was that box kept?" Moriarty asked.

She frowned, turning her gaze toward the smoky ceiling. "I don't know, now that you mention it. I didn't keep it."

"They didn't present it at the inquest," Norton said.

Moriarty said, "Look for it, Miss Wrenn, if you please. And let me know at once if you find it." He took one of his calling cards out of his notecase and handed it to her. She slipped it into her coat pocket.

Norton said, "Tell him about the gardener, Bea."

She puffed out a dismissive breath. "That superstitious old goat! Who ever heard of anyone summoning wasps, like they was demons or imps or something? Nobody, because no such thing ever happened. He's the one who should be in jail, if you ask me. Leaving those apples lyin' beneath the window to rot when everyone knew how scared the missus was of bees and stinging insects. If it weren't for him, there wouldn't've been any wasps in the first place."

Norton asked, "Is it his job to keep the garden clean?" The fireman was an able interviewer, keeping his subject to the point and asking all the questions Moriarty would have. Doing a better job of it too, since he knew more about the Parson household. This young man might make a fine police constable one day if he ever had a mind to change jobs.

Miss Wrenn was happy to heap coals on the gardener's head. "Of course it's his job, the lazy sot. Master's favorite is what he is. I asked him that very question that very night at supper. He says, well, he's only one man, ain't he, and besides, the master told him to get the flower beds mulched first."

"Where was the master?" Moriarty asked.

"When he said to do the mulch?"

"On the day of Mrs. Parsons's death. He wasn't home, was he?"

"Nor he wasn't," Miss Wrenn said. "He was sunning himself at that place in Torquay he likes so much. He pops down there the way you or I might pop round to the pub. He came home two days after, all shocked and sad, not that we believed any of it."

"Tell me about him," Moriarty said. "Did they have a happy marriage?"

She trilled a laugh, startling everyone in earshot. Then she lowered her voice and said, "I've been there two years and I never saw a kiss or hardly a friendly word.

175

Sometimes he'd be downright rude. Then we'd try to make it up a bit, in our little ways. We all liked her. She was kind to us. She paid fair wages and always spoke so polite. If you ask me, he married her for her money. He was always short and, oh, how he hated it whenever she bought something nice for herself!"

"Did he have a job?" Norton asked.

Miss Wrenn shrugged, her meaning plain before she answered. "Not so's you'd notice." She gave Moriarty a curious look. "But he wasn't home, was he? And even Flora says she's the one opened that window."

"I know. I have a theory about that."

Miss Wrenn frowned at the word "theory," but she said, "If it saves Flora from hanging, I'll be glad. I chose her to be my maid of honor." She glanced out the window, the third time in the past minute or so.

"Don't choose another one yet," Moriarty said. "Do you know why Mrs. Parsons chose to sleep on the ground floor? Most people prefer an upstairs room."

"She used to have the best bedroom, at the back of the house on the first floor. But then she took a nasty tumble down the stairs last June. All over bruises she was, poor thing. It left her with an awful fear of heights. And stairs."

"I hadn't heard that," Norton said. He traded dark glances with Moriarty. "Was Mr. Parsons home when that happened?"

"Oh yes, he was right there. He's the one carried her back up to her room."

Moriarty nodded. Another piece of the puzzle — the impatient heir. Mr. Parsons might have made other attempts that went unremarked at the time. It wasn't easy to do away with one's spouse, not without exposing oneself to suspicion. Hence the special service at Halcyon House.

"One last question, Miss Wrenn," he said. "Where did Mr. and Mrs. Parsons bank, do you know?"

"Where they kept their money, you mean? At the Central Bank of London, I think. Leastways, they both got letters from there. I remember because the envelopes are so creamy; they feel expensive."

Miss Wrenn waved at someone outside, then asked, "Can I go now? There's my Phillip."

Moriarty said, "Of course."

"I'll walk out with you." She rose, but Norton paused. "If there's anything I can do, Mr. Moriarty, day or night, you send word to me at the firehouse and I'll be there in a heartbeat."

"I'll remember that."

He thanked them again and watched them go, lingering over his pint. He liked the detail of the shivering box. If wasps were like bees and could be put to sleep with smoke, it wouldn't be difficult to put a nest in a box with a supply of food. And they were likely to be angry when they awoke, from the shaking they'd endured en route. They would fly up when the box was open and strike out at the first offender they encountered.

If that ploy didn't work — if the wasps died or behaved peacefully — the doctor could simply try again another day. Patience was his most insidious resource.

Norton and Wrenn had filled in several gaps tonight. The facts added up to a coherent, if highly unusual, story. Moriarty doubted they would be enough to convince a sober judge and jury. He needed more.

How long had Flora Semple worked at Halcyon House? If she had been Mrs. Parsons's personal attendant during the past month, she must have been there while Lady Georgia was undergoing her harsh treatment. She might have seen or heard something whose importance she hadn't understood at the time.

177

He must arrange to visit her as soon as he could. Norton had said only lawyers and policemen with warrant cards were allowed inside the prison. He polished off his drink and smiled to himself. An official Metropolitan Police warrant card, eh? That should not pose an insuperable barrier for a man with a talented forger in his kitchen.

# Chapter Seventeen

Angelina woke up when someone lifted her arm and let it drop. A voice at her side said, "She's dead to the world."

A low, rumbling chuckle sounded from a few feet away. "You might choose a better phrase, considering the circumstances."

*Where am I?*

The shape and texture of the mattress beneath her back told her it was her own bed in her private room. She could feel the warmth of the sun on her cheeks. Her attendant usually woke her much earlier to dress for breakfast. Had she eaten breakfast? She vaguely remembered a boiled egg and toast, but that could have been yesterday or the day before. The days tended to run together here.

*I should get up.*

Her body failed to answer the thought, as deaf to her will as if it belonged to someone else. Her limbs lay slack, like a rag doll dropped in a corner. Even her eyelids were too heavy to lift.

The voices — one male, one female — sounded echoey, as if underwater. The woman said, "What are we going to do with her?"

"I don't know yet," the man said, "beyond keeping a close eye on her. Good thing I spotted that confounded Sherlock Holmes in *The Illustrated Police News*. He certainly had us fooled."

"So did she, the artful wench. Dr. Trumbull is quite taken with her."

The man said, "She must be an actress Holmes hired to spy on us. But how did he get onto our little scheme?"

"It's that woman. She gossips too much. I've said it before."

"Without Mrs. Northwood, Nurse, we wouldn't have any special patients. She's done an admirable job of recruiting this year."

The woman grunted. "True enough. You could at least suggest she be more discreet. And I must say, Doctor, I don't like doing two at once. It doubles the risk."

"You worry too much. The last two went beautifully. One lived in Highgate, the other in Richmond. Different social circles, different newspapers. Impossible to connect."

"They were both here at the same time."

"Along with twenty other women now happily getting on with their lives. Or unhappily, given our pathetic clientele. I tell you, nobody misses these useless hags."

"Someone did and told Sherlock Holmes about it."

"He might be guessing, based on some stray coincidence in the papers. He could be fishing for clients." The man barked a short laugh. "Once we silence his spy, he'll have nothing. Besides, I need money rather badly at the moment. You won't complain so much once you've been paid."

"Surely you don't expect Holmes to pay our fee?"

"He already has," the man said. "Or someone has. The handwriting matches the first letter signed 'James Moriarty.' One thousand pounds, which I'll distribute this evening when I finish my rounds."

*James paid? Could that be right?*

Something muddled Angelina wits, making it hard for her to follow the conversation. James couldn't have paid to have her killed. He loved her — as much as Badger loved Viola?

*What are they going to do with me?*

The woman spoke the words she couldn't. "How will we manage this one? We can't have her die here, not with Sherlock Holmes watching."

"I don't know yet," the man said. "I've been working on her tonics, getting her habituated. Next week I'll start experimenting with her heart. I can induce an irregular beat with the right combination of drugs and electrotherapy. It's preferable for her to die before she talks to Holmes, but not essential. There won't be any evidence, never fear. Meanwhile, I want you to reduce her morphine today, then increase it on Sunday. Another week or two of that and she'll be panting for her daily dose. But get her out of bed by lunch today, will you? Use the hydro if you must. It's a badminton day. If she's not outside, someone will notice."

*Dear God, they're turning me into an addict!*

The man's voice continued, "As for the other one, I think we should induce a miscarriage as soon as she gets home. It would be quite plausible for her to die a week or so after that. Pregnancy's a risky business, as everyone knows."

"If you say so, Doctor." The woman's voice sounded flat. The "other one" must be Viola. But she wasn't pregnant. She was just fat and moody and . . . *Oh my stars!*

Angelina concentrated and managed to wiggle her toes and twitch her finger. But unless she could spring up and fight like fury, these two would inject more poison into her body to subdue her. Then she might never wake up.

Papers rustled and feet shuffled. Then another male voice, much heartier, said, "Here you are! You're wanted in the examination room."

The first man said, "Is it ten o'clock already?"

More shuffling sounds were followed by the soft thump of the door closing. The new man said, "I wanted

181

to get Mrs. Moriarty's vital signs while I'm upstairs. What's this? Still asleep? At this hour?"

Fingers pressed against the inside of her wrist. Then one of her eyelids was lifted, blinding her in the sudden light.

"Why, this woman's unconscious! What's happened here?" Papers rustled. The man said, "Look here, Nurse Andrews. You've given this patient three times as much morphine as I prescribed. That's beyond mere carelessness. What do you have to say for yourself?"

"That's impossible, Doctor." More papers rustled. The woman coughed, a disgusted sound. "They must have made a mistake in the dispensary. I assumed she was faking it. You know how lazy some of these women get, especially their first week away from home."

"Well, see that it doesn't happen again. I'm putting a note in my records about this incident. We're trying to make our patients better, not worse."

"Yes, Doctor."

Firm hands lifted Angelina's arm and rolled up her sleeve. A needle stung her, then the sleeve was rolled down and the arm dropped. Feet shushed across the floor and the door thumped shut. Silence fell and lasted.

Life stirred in Angelina's veins. She wiggled her toes and fingers and almost managed to lift her head. She must get up, warn Viola, do something to save them both. But the sun warmed her cheeks and the mattress held her in its comfortable embrace. She fell asleep again.

# Chapter Eighteen

It had been ten nights since James Moriarty last slept with his wife.

On Monday morning at half past nine, Moriarty stood outside the iron gates of Halcyon House waiting for an attendant to escort him to the electrotherapy room. He had chosen this day and time deliberately, even though it meant waiting a week, in order to avoid the one member of the Trumbull gang who could identify him: Dr. Alan Fairchild.

Peg had assured him that no one could see through one of her disguises, but Moriarty was new at this game and wanted to hedge his bets. She had decked him out like an up-and-coming salesman in a checked suit. She'd made him comb his moustache down instead of waxing it into tight curls. Now it tickled his upper lip mercilessly. She'd even tugged a short wig over his bare scalp and pushed a pair of tinted spectacles onto his nose.

He had a small trunk set on casters that he'd filled from the shelves at the Heffelfinger Institute. He'd spend the weekend studying instruction manuals, practicing on himself and Rolly. Antoine had supplied him with a few visiting cards. Moriarty had wanted to invent a fictitious company, preferring not to involve Heffelfinger in this charade, but the others had voted him down on the grounds that the doctors would be familiar with all the manufacturers.

A woman in a gray dress approached and the guard opened the gate at last. These people certainly kept a strict control over access.

"If you'll follow me, Mr. Watson?" He'd chosen that name entirely at random.

Moriarty followed the woman down a long drive to the main house and through a corridor muffled by a thick carpet and plush furnishings, then down a central staircase into the basement of the main house. They went through a door marked "Electrotherapeutic Treatment." The room was lit by high windows and by gas lamps attached to the walls. They hadn't advanced to electrical lighting yet here, even in the electro room. Their devices must run on batteries.

A big wooden chair outfitted with metal plates and electrical connectors stood in the center of the stone floor. A sink with a pump had been installed in one corner with a few bowls and basins stacked neatly nearby. Some treatments required the patient to immerse her feet in water to achieve full transmission of the electrical current to both limbs.

"You can set your models out on the table, Mr. Watson," the attendant said. "The doctor will be with you momentarily." She left, closing the door behind her.

Moriarty opened his trunk and took out a belt, a corset, and the portable unit he and Holmes had experimented with. He spread a few books at one end, opening one to a table of electrical equivalencies in case he got his measures mixed up in the heat of performance. This fluttering in his stomach must be a familiar condition for actors, although Angelina never betrayed so much as a flicker, even when fabricating a story out of whole cloth on the spot. Perhaps it got easier with practice.

The door opened and a man in a white coat with long brown sideburns entered. He held out his hand with a smile. "You must be Mr. Watson, the Heffelfinger man. I'm Dr. Oliver."

"Thank you for giving up some of your valuable time to see me," Moriarty said. "I'll try not to waste it."

After giving Moriarty's hand a hearty shake, the doctor rubbed his together and moved eagerly toward the new equipment. "I must say I do enjoy these marvelous devices."

"That's music to my ears," Moriarty said. "I hope I can tempt you with some of our new products."

Peg and Rolly had coached him in keeping an image of the person he was emulating in his mind to help him come up with the right words and gestures. He'd encouraged Mr. Tillman to talk at length when he'd gone back to buy out the shop, so he had plenty of examples at the ready. "I brought an assortment of our latest devices, including some that are more appropriate for home use. But I thought you might recommend a continuation of treatment after a patient is discharged."

"Certainly," Oliver said. "We don't forget about our ladies when they walk out the gate. Quite the contrary." He selected an electric belt and wrapped it around his own torso, lifting the skirt of his coat. It fell short by several inches.

Moriarty smiled. "We make a full range of sizes. Although I believe I can demonstrate this equipment more effectively with a more appropriate subject. Would it be possible to call in one of your patients?"

"Of course." Oliver scratched his chin. "Let's see, should it be a smallish person?"

"Size doesn't matter. I would recommend someone new, or at least new to electrotherapeutics. That way you'll get a less contaminated — if you'll pardon the word — reaction."

Oliver snapped his fingers. "Good suggestion. I know just the one." He poked his head out the door and said, "Nurse, would you bring Mrs. Moriarty down? Go ahead and interrupt whatever she's doing."

Moriarty stroked his brushy moustache to stop himself from smiling. This was what he'd hoped for — the reason for the whole elaborate charade — but until this moment he hadn't believed it would work. He'd gambled on either Angelina or Viola being the newest patients in spite of the week-long delay.

He cleared a bit of moisture from his throat and said, "I couldn't help noticing the beautiful grounds on my way in. Those lawns look ideal for croquet. Do you include outdoor exercise as part of the treatment?"

Sandy had told him that he'd seen women in colored gowns outdoors playing games during his survey of the hospital and its environs. He'd suggested Moriarty find out who was allowed to participate and when. They might find a way to pass messages over the wall or through it using the loose brick in the wall where they'd left the envelope with the thousand pounds as instructed. But for that, they'd have to find a way to tell the women where to look.

Oliver said, "Fresh air and outdoor activity are essential for good health, in my opinion. Combined with a healthy diet, they form the centerpiece of my therapeutic regimen."

*My* regimen — not *ours.* Revealing of his true position in this establishment? Or it could be ordinary self-aggrandizement. Doctors weren't known for their self-effacing natures.

"But I seldom allow croquet here," Oliver went on. "I prefer badminton. It requires more engagement of the upper limbs as well as brisker movements overall. And frankly our patients aren't very good at it, which tends to suppress the competitive aspect. That isn't healthy'for women, as you must know."

Moriarty grunted a low chuckle, implying that he knew only too well the trouble that could cause. "I admire your modern views on medicine, Doctor."

Oliver accepted the flattery with a smug smile. "As a matter of fact, I'm finding badminton to be a most effective component of the therapeutic program. I'm writing a monograph on the subject."

"I'd like to read it," Moriarty said with as much sincerity as he could muster. "I like to keep up with developments in the medical field as best I can. We at Heffelfinger's consider ourselves your partners, in our humble way. Do your patients play every day?"

"No, no. Mustn't overdo. Some can't manage it at all, especially not at first. But for those who can, I find three days a week to be ideal. We're doing Tuesdays, Thursdays, and Saturdays at present."

"Morning is best, I suppose."

"No, we do examinations and craft activities in the morning, when they're at their sharpest. I find that a good outdoor game before tea relieves the buildup of nervous tensions and gets them ready for a quiet evening."

"Very sensible," Moriarty said. He'd just had an idea for a means of regular communication, at least those three afternoons. It might not work, but it carried little risk if it failed. The last thing he wanted to do was bring punishment down on his wife or her sister. Or foil whatever Angelina might have in play. She wouldn't forgive him for that!

The nurse returned with Angelina at her side. Moriarty's heart turned over at the sight of her. Her amber eyes sparked when she saw him, but her face remained calm, without a trace of the surprise she must be feeling. Her self-possession inspired and heartened him.

"I'm Mr. Watson from the Heffelfinger Institute," he said. "I'm demonstrating some new devices and the doctor thought you might enjoy helping us out."

"Mr. Watson." She held out limp hand for the briefest contact. "I'm happy to follow Dr. Oliver's advice." She simpered at the doctor, sounding a trifle meek. Well played!

"Well, then," Moriarty said, clapping his hands together. "Why don't we sit you down right here since it's convenient?" He pointed at the chair with the electrical fittings. He added to Oliver, "We have a newer model, by the way. It's not much different, I'll confess, but it supports two additional electrodes and has clearer indicators on the controls."

The nurse led Angelina to the chair and had her sit with each arm resting on one of its wide, flat arms.

The doctor glanced at his pocket watch. "I should warn you I only have about fifteen minutes. I'm consulting at Colney Hatch today."

"Oh, you are?" Moriarty tried to sound like a man discovering a lucrative new opportunity. "You might find Heffelfinger's devices useful there as well. Our chair, for example. The price is very reasonable. But I'm demonstrating our portable unit today. This handy device allows you to treat patients in their rooms. Useful for bedridden cases, I should imagine."

"Yes, I can see that. Getting some of them down here can be a problem." A light glittered in Oliver's brown eyes as he contemplated Angelina in the chair. "Mrs. Moriarty hasn't had a chance to try electro yet, so she'll be able to give us an unbiased report, won't you?"

"I'll try," Angelina said, keeping her eyes on her lap.

"Good, good, good," Moriarty said, struggling to stay in character. He had a powerful desire to lift her into his arms and bear her bodily out of this luxurious prison. But he couldn't do it. They would stop him and Viola would be left behind. They'd lose all chance of getting any kind of evidence from inside the hospital. Worst of all, Angelina would be furious.

So he fought down the urge by saying, "Good, good, good." He must sound like an absolute idiot.

He positioned a small table so he could stand between Angelina and the others. He opened his case and unrolled two electrodes. "This won't hurt at all, Mrs. Moriarty." He stumbled a little on the name. Then he spoke to the nurse over his shoulder. "Could I have a small dish of water?"

She filled a bowl at the sink and brought to him. He dipped the sponge coverings of the electrodes into the water, just a touch. "I assume you're familiar with the advantage of a slightly moistened electrode, Dr. Oliver."

"Of course. I usually add a splash of vinegar to improve conduction."

"Good, good." While Moriarty attached the nodes to Angelina's temple and throat, he whispered almost soundlessly into her ear, "We're doing all we can."

She blinked slowly, once. An acknowledgement. "I have every confidence in you, Mr. Watson."

Dr. Oliver strolled closer to the table. "What setting will you start with?"

Moriarty explained the levels of current supplied by the machine. He repeated as much as he could remember of Tillman's patter about different settings for different maladies. Oliver asked some questions that revealed knowledge surpassing Moriarty's. Lucky they only had fifteen minutes.

"Are we ready?" Moriarty turned his back to the doctor, met Angelina's eyes, and mouthed the words, *I love you.*

She nodded and said, "Me too."

He flipped the switch, let the current run for a few seconds, then switched it off. "How did that feel?"

"Like nothing." She shook her head, bemused. "I expected it to hurt."

"Heavens, no," Moriarty said. "I wouldn't hurt you — or any patient — for the world."

"If it hurt, it wouldn't be therapeutic, now would it?" Dr. Oliver asked. "But that's not a particularly illuminating test. I only use three milliamperes for elderly or very frail patients. This robust young woman can hardly feel such a weak current. Let's try it again at ten. And then I'm afraid that will have to be enough for today."

Ten seemed high to Moriarty, but he wasn't sure enough of his facts to contradict the doctor. He made a bit of a fuss replacing the sponges at the ends of the electrodes and stroking Angelina's temple and throat with a soft cloth. While he performed these tender tasks, he said, "The doctor tells me you play badminton here. I'll bet you're quite the athlete."

"I love it," Angelina said, playing along as he'd hoped she would. "I never miss a game."

"Good, good," Moriarty said. "There's nothing like a little fresh air. As long as you don't bat your shuttlecock over the wall." He chuckled inanely as he adjusted an electrode below her jaw. Under cover of straightening the wire running from it, he slipped a note under the collar of her dress.

Dr. Oliver said, "I see a third electrode in this case. Let's put that on the other temple."

"Certainly." Moriarty uncoiled it, feeling like Dr. Frankenstein preparing a deranged form of torture. He simply hadn't been able to devise any other way to see her. Every second playing the part of a passionless salesman cost him greater effort. His hands were trembling with the strain. He had to find a way to get through these last few minutes.

He found it in a memory of an argument that had wounded him at the time. He and Angelina had been having one of their short, hot spats, which now seemed as inconsequential as a bit of mud splashed on his trousers by an omnibus. She'd accused him of being stubborn and

190

inflexible, too middle class to adjust to their irregular household. Or that's the way he'd heard it. She'd said he was so predictable, he had no surprises left for her. "No mystery," she'd said. "No magic."

That novel requirement baffled him. Who wanted mystery in their own home? He'd said fewer surprises would suit him a great better and she'd stomped away in huff.

He still didn't understand. He liked stability, knowing that tomorrow would be much like yesterday. But he would enjoy revisiting the topic, once they got through this crisis.

He caught her gaze, pretending to straighten a twisted wire and filled his eyes with all the love he had. "You may find this hard to believe, Mrs. Moriarty, but I am about to give you something of a shock."

His reward was a flash of delight in her amber eyes. He winked at her and flipped the switch.

# Chapter Nineteen

Angelina lingered in the lavatory, the one place in this hospital where she could steal a moment of privacy. She drew the precious note from the high neck of her dress and unrolled it to read the short lines in James's bold hand.

"Sandy and the rest are with us. I have a fresh case and a possible witness. Don't yet know how, but watch for more notes. Be careful! I miss you. Your loving husband."

She read it again, blinking back tears, then tore it up and flushed it away. She was surprised and touched that he trusted her enough to leave her here and let her do her part instead of finding some judge to demand her release, leaving Viola behind and abandoning who knew how many vulnerable women to be murdered. She wouldn't leave this place until she could put these wicked doctors in jail. And Nurse Andrews, whom she had come to loathe with a special fury.

Things were worse than she'd expected. She hadn't realized how hard it would be to resist their potions and tonics and pills. But she was still holding her own and had a pretty good idea of where she might find those client letters. She might even manage to make friends with sour-faced Jenks one of these days and turn her into a witness.

She loved James more than ever for believing in her strength. She just wasn't sure how much of it she had left.

* * *

That afternoon Angelina and Viola stood on the lawn near the wall watching four other patients play badminton. Or attempting to — they missed the shuttlecock more often than they struck it. But they all enjoyed the game, even those who had trouble remembering what the net was for. They were out-of-doors and moving around freely instead of sitting as they waited for treatment or pretended to do the needlework the attendants endlessly pressed upon them. Even better, their watchdogs let them bumble about as they pleased, keeping only half an eye on the games while they stood near the terrace gossiping about the doctors — an evergreen topic.

It was a lovely autumn day too, the sky as blue as Viola's eyes and dotted with pretty white puffs. The green lawn spread like a carpet from the wall to the terrace. Even the nine-foot wall that made this place a prison had a comforting aspect. It reflected the warmth of the late September sun, blocked the noise of rattling carts and the peering eyes of passersby. It even supported a thick vine, whose last lingering blossoms tempted late-season bees.

Angelina turned her face into the light breeze, savoring its gentle touch. She also enjoyed the chance to spend a little peaceful time with her sister. "You know, I don't think I saw a blue sky more than half a dozen times when we were little. The city was so dirty, worse than it is now. Nothing but gray smoke and yellow fog."

"I remember," Viola said. "We never saw the sky until we started playing theaters in the West End. I thought blue skies were a fantasy, something in songs, because 'blue' is so easy to rhyme. Until you started taking us to the park." She trilled a musical laugh. "I have a vivid memory of one day in particular. You and Peg dragged us to Hyde Park after a matinee. Sebastian and I must not have been more than four because I remember sitting down and howling that I wouldn't go. You picked me up

193

and kept on marching. Peg gripped Sebastian's arm like a bobby delivering a prisoner to the Old Bailey. Someone had told you children needed fresh air and you were determined that we would frolic on green grass if you had to stake us out like horses to get it done."

"Oh, I remember that day!" Angelina's laugher sluffed off some of the muzziness that had clouded her mind since she'd gotten out of bed. "But we took a cab, you silly chit. We were flush with cash. That was when the Little Angels really started filling the theaters. You were six and you both loved it. It was all we could do to keep Sebastian out of the pond."

"It was the most peculiar thing I'd ever seen, that bright green grass. It didn't make any sense to me. Why was it there? Why wasn't it hard and gray, like proper pavement?"

"You ate enough of it. Fortunately, grass doesn't seem to do children any harm."

"You always looked out for us." Viola regarded her with a fond smile. "It can't have been easy."

"I wish I'd been better at it. Peg and I had to make it all up as we went along."

"Maybe that's how you got so good at improvisation."

Was that meant as compliment or criticism? Viola had a knack for combining the two.

Angelina's tummy twisted. For all her forewarning and wary intentions, she had no control over what they put in her food and drink. If she refused to take her tonic, two attendants would hold her arms while another pinched her nose and forced the spoon between her lips. They'd given her something in the past couple days that gave her slight cramps.

Viola, on the other hand, grew healthier and more chipper every day. Angelina said as much. Viola answered, "I feel so much better. I'm *so* grateful to

Badger for insisting that I come here. I'm sleeping like a baby and my appetite is back to normal. I'm not losing my breakfast every morning like I was for a while. Nurse Andrews supervises my attendant, you know. She takes *such* lovely care of me."

Angelina's stomach roiled again. "Ugh! I don't like that woman one bit and I definitely don't trust her. I'm certain she was standing by my bed one morning a few days ago when I woke up late. She was giving me the oddest look, as if she thought I was malingering." That was the worst accusation they had around here — pretending to be sicker to avoid craft time or hydrotherapy or whatever it was they wanted you to do.

Another memory swam into her mind. "Do you know, Viola, I dreamed the other night that you were pregnant."

"Me? How odd." Viola tossed her head, but she looked like the cat who ate the cream.

"Oh, darling! I'm so pleased for you!" Angelina beamed at her baby sister, happy, but realizing that now she had an extra little person to rescue somehow.

Viola accepted the warm response with a smile of pure sunshine. But then she tossed her head again and sniffed. "I suppose you think Badger knew, even if I didn't. I suppose you think that's why he would want to have me killed, according to your horribly fantasy."

"Oh, Viola, don't be absurd!" But as she spoke the words, she knew pregnancy only gave his lordship another compelling motive to dispose of an unwanted courtesan.

She could never say such a beastly thing out loud, so she painted a bland expression on her face and pretended to watch the game. She'd played badminton when staying in people's country houses, although she liked croquet better. Men and women could play that one together. Why would James take precious seconds of their brief time together to mention this game in particular? It must mean something to him. But what?

"Ow!" Viola rubbed her head. "Where did that come from?" She pointed at a shuttlecock bouncing to a halt at her feet.

Not from the court — that one was still in play. Angelina shot a glance at the attendants to make sure they were still gossiping away, then bent to scoop it up. "Odd little birdie, why are you here?" She examined it, flicking at the stiff feathers and pressing the cork head. She turned it up, peered inside, and laughed. "Oh, my darling James, you *are* the cleverest of men!"

She teased out a rolled-up slip of paper and said, "Hide me."

Viola rolled her eyes but moved to block Angelina from the attendant's view while she unrolled the note and read the words out loud. "If you get this, throw it back. More next time. Sandy."

The mere thought that stalwart Gabriel Sandy was nearby lifted her spirits. She tucked the note back into the cork head of the shuttlecock and hurled it over the wall.

Viola watched her, a thoughtful crease marring her smooth forehead. "I would have thought Sandy would have more sense than to fall in with your silly dramas."

"Come with me tonight." Angelina put a challenge in her tone. "If we don't find anything in the doctors' office, I'll concede your point."

Viola wrinkled her pert nose and pursed her cherubic lips. "All right, then. I could use a spot of adventure. But I still think you're making it all up."

\* \* \*

That evening another woman in a green dress appeared at the main entrance to the dining room shortly after the soup was served. Her dress was a darker, more flattering green and fit her much better than the others. She had brown hair streaked with silver and styled by an expert hand. She sashayed through the room with a proprietary tilt to her chin. As she approached their table, Angelina recognized her — Mrs. Northwood, the woman who'd been talking up Dr. Trumbull in Torquay.

"That's her," she hissed at Viola. "The tout!"

"The what?"

"The tout. The woman who solicits patients for Dr. Trumbull at convalescent hotels. Act like you don't know her!"

Viola rolled her eyes. "That should be easy enough since I've never seen her before."

Angelina pretended to be absorbed in her soup until the newcomer reached their table. She looked up with bland interest, changing to surprised recognition as the attendant seated the older woman and took her order for dinner. Then she smiled and said, "Haven't we met? Weren't you in Torquay a few weeks ago?"

"I was. You do look familiar. It's Mrs. . . . ."

"Moriarty. Angelina Moriarty. And this is Miss Viola Archer. Viola, this is . . ." Angelina wiggled her fingers in the air as if summoning the memory. "You know, I'm not sure I caught your name. There were *so* many women on that lovely terrace, all of us bundled to the noses in scarves and shawls."

"I'm Mrs. Julia Northwood." She tilted her head toward Viola with the condescension of a duchess. "Pleased to make your acquaintance. I hope you're enjoying your stay at Halcyon House. It's one of my favorite retreats."

"It's lovely," Viola said. "This is my first time in such a place. Have you visited many of these health resorts?"

"Oh yes," Mrs. Northwood said, unfolding her napkin. She moved like a woman who expected her every gesture to be noticed — the star of her own little drama.

Angelina had met several women like her during her months pretending to be a wealthy American widow in London for the Season. She disliked them immensely, not for the dramatic flourishes — she enjoyed flamboyant personalities — but for the unfounded arrogance. If you were going to turn your nose up at everyone else, you'd better have a damned good reason.

The attendant brought the main courses Viola and Angelina had ordered and a dish of poached eggs in a butter sauce for Mrs. Northwood, which had not been on the menu. Special treatment, eh?

The older woman picked at her food while entertaining the others with stories about the fabulous spas she'd visited and the famous people she'd met. She spent her year on the convalescent circuit and knew the names and qualities of nurses, bathing masters, and masseuses from Sicily to Stockholm. Viola played the eager listener, asking pert questions now and then and expressing awed admiration when appropriate.

Angelina was grateful. She didn't feel up to playing a close game these days. And she didn't like having that woman at their table one bit.

Why was she here? She must know that her tablemates were marked for murder. She'd helped arrange it. She entertained Viola with the amused yet predatory air of a notorious rake making polite conversation with a debutante he intended to ruin to win a bet.

"Those are lovely earrings," Viola said after the pudding was served.

"Do you like them?" Mrs. Northwood turned her head from side to side to show off a pair of diamond baubles. "A little treat I gave myself."

Quite an expensive little treat. How big a slice of the Clennam payments went into Mrs. Northwood's beaded purse?

The woman went on to tell a snobbish story about having tea with the lovely Lady Brockaway in the south of France, practically licking her lips as she smiled at her latest victim. Angelina watched her prattle merrily away, disgust souring the chicken-and-rice croquettes in her stomach.

This dreadful woman hadn't come downstairs to brag about her worldly experiences. She'd come to gloat over her latest victims.

# Chapter Twenty

It had been eleven nights since James Moriarty last slept with his wife.

He sat at the octagonal dining table on Wednesday after lunch. He spent all his waking hours at this table now, apart from rare ventures outside to pursue some slender lead. He watched at the window for each hour's post, sinking disappointedly back into his chair if nothing came. That had to serve for exercise these days.

The mouse maids tended him with constant, unobtrusive attention. They had little else to do since he only left this room to sleep and wore the same clothes every day. There was no point lighting fires in unused rooms or dusting objects no one admired. So they tended him instead, sliding cups of hot tea beside his elbow, removing cups that had gone cold. After the third day, he started finding a glass of whiskey in place of the tea after five o'clock.

Even the cook had adapted to the new regimen. At first he'd sent up artful dishes with delicate sauces and pretty sprinklings of herbs. Then Rolly must have told him the master forgot to eat as often as not, remembering an hour later and shoveling the cold cuisine into his mouth without any interest in its qualities.

So Antoine had changed course. Now lunch consisted of sandwiches of beef or ham on thick bread with pungent mustard. Supper, served at the unfashionable hour of six o'clock, brought hearty English dishes like sausages with mashed potatoes. The familiar aromas worked their magic. Moriarty ate every scrap as soon as it arrived.

Although heartened by the support from his friends and servants, Moriarty was still oppressed by the knowledge that he had failed in a man's centermost duty — to protect his wife from harm. If he'd listened instead of throwing up a wall of obstinate logic, if he'd given her a chance to share her fears, to work through them together instead of cutting her off with a wave of his mighty hand, he might have kept her home, safe, by his side.

He had once bemoaned his lack of employment; well, he had a job now. A dour one, but it kept him occupied. He spent his days studying reports from his confederates. Mrs. Peacock wrote every day, mainly to express her continued determination to find something incriminating for him. She had turned up one friend whose son was a bank examiner. His access to London's banks had limits, but after hearing the tale of the murdering doctors, he had promised to do his utmost to peer into the accounts of their suspect heirs.

Today Moriarty awaited a call from Mr. Cosmatos, a hypnotist one of Peg's theater friends had recommended. He wanted to review his theory about Mrs. Parsons's murder with an expert.

"'E's 'ere," Rolly said, poking his head around the doorway.

"Well, let him in, then." Moriarty checked to be sure the red box he'd prepared hadn't been tidied away, then straightened his tie out of habit. He rose to greet a round-bellied man with a well-waxed moustache and a dark, pointed beard. "Mr. Cosmatos, I presume. I'm James Moriarty."

"Henri Cosmatos, at your service." The little man bowed, showing a full head of black hair liberally slicked down with Macassar oil. Both his accent and his olive complexion revealed his Greek origins.

"Do sit down," Moriarty said, gesturing vaguely. He wasn't used to entertaining or to having so many rooms to do it in. That was Angelina's job.

Cosmatos took a chair at the dining table without comment. He smiled, his pink lips curving in a small bow. "I understood from your letter that you have questions about hypnotism. I will endeavor to answer them for you. Although I may earn my bread and butter in doing small performances to amuse and entertain, I consider myself a professional man rather than merely an *artiste*. Hypnosis can be of great therapeutic benefit, you know."

Moriarty took his chair again. "That is one of the aspects that interests me. I've read one paper on the subject, but it contained few details. Is it true that hypnosis is chiefly used in the treatment of nervous complaints?"

"But of course." Cosmatos chuckled. "You cannot cure a disease like malaria with the mind, my friend. No, no. Hypnosis induces a state of calm, which can in itself be beneficial for persons suffering from agitation or oversensitive nerves. The hypnotist then plants suggestions to sustain that sense of calm. Allow me to give you a simple example. Imagine a nervous woman, one who is easily overwhelmed by the daily routines of life. She may be distressed by finding too many letters on the tray or confounded by the simple task of choosing a dress for lunch. I make to her the simple suggestion that when she opens the door of her wardrobe, she feels a great sense of calm and easiness, knowing that any decision she makes will be a good one."

"I see," Moriarty said. "That's very interesting. You can use hypnosis to effect a sort of mental retraining."

"Precisely so! Hypnosis can be used to help a person give up a harmful habit, like drinking or gambling."

"Or worse." Moriarty wondered if hypnosis had played any role in Lady Georgia's treatment. "Could you use hypnosis to cause a person to drink too much or risk too much at the gaming table?"

Cosmatos wagged his finger at him. "Only a most unscrupulous hypnotist would attempt such a thing. And it would not work, in any case. It is not possible to induce a person to harm themselves."

"I see. Then I suppose it would not be possible to instruct your patient to commit a crime — murder, for example."

"Not even to squash a bug, Professor, if so small an act of violence was not in his usual repertoire. I can only suggest actions you would normally and willingly undertake."

"That's reassuring," Moriarty said. Then again, if that were possible, he would expect to find several of Trumbull's clients' servants in prison on murder charges.

Cosmatos nodded, his black eyes glittering. "I have never met a fellow practitioner who did not regard his abilities as a gift intended to serve and to heal, but a man determined to do harm would find this method most unhelpful."

"That relieves my mind," Moriarty said. "Is it possible to remove the suggestions once planted?"

"Certainly," Cosmatos said. "We simply return the patient to the hypnotic state and suggest that the triggers now have no importance."

"Triggers," Moriarty said. "Is that what you call the suggestion?"

"No, that is the word or event that provokes the suggested behavior. Would you like a demonstration?"

"Yes, I would." Moriarty got up and retrieved the small hat box Peg had provided, along with the red scarf serving as wrapping paper. He put them on the table. "I have a specific test in mind." He explained that he wanted to see if hypnosis could cause someone to get up and open a window at the sight of a red box being unwrapped.

"That is very simple," Cosmatos said. "Are you to be the subject?"

"No, I would like to observe the whole procedure. I thought we might ask my footman to perform that role. Let me call him in." He tucked the box out of sight again and went into the hall.

Rolly sat at his usual post at the foot of the stairs, practicing sleight of hand tricks with a deck of cards. He stuffed them into his pocket as Moriarty approached and asked, "Shall I bring tea, Perfessor?"

"Not yet, Rolly. Would you join us for a moment? Mr. Cosmatos has offered to show me how hypnosis works and we need a subject."

"Me?" Rolly got to his feet and peered toward the dining room doubtfully. "I don't know, Perfessor. 'E won't make me bark like a dog or dance jigs when I see a man in a hat or nuffink like that, will 'e?"

"Not at all."

Rolly lowered his voice. "'E can't turn me into a rabbit or nuffink, can 'e?"

"Of course not. I wouldn't allow it." Moriarty looked down at his young footman and said gravely, "When you live under my roof, Rolly, you are under my protection. You understand that, don't you?"

"Yes, sir!" Rolly grinned from ear to ear, his moment of doubt replaced by his Cockney irrepressibility. "'Course I do. I ain't no dully."

Moriarty ushered him into the dining room and introduced him to the hypnotist, who asked him to pull a chair over to face him and sit down. "Now don't be afraid. Nothing will harm you."

"I ain't afraid," Rolly said, but he looked very stiff and uncomfortable sitting in the unaccustomed chair with two men facing him attentively.

Cosmatos pulled a silver watch from his pocket and dangled it by the chain, holding it at Rolly's eye level. "Focus on the watch, if you please. Let your thoughts break apart, gently, gently, like shifting masses of fluffy clouds, and scatter, falling away, drifting apart."

He spoke in a low voice and a rhythmic monotone, his accent giving the sound something of the quality of a Latin chant performed during evensong. After a minute or two, Cosmatos put the watch back in his pocket. "Very good. Can you hear me, Rolly?" His voice was still gentle but had regained its normal pitch and cadence.

"Yes, sir."

"Are you feeling calm and relaxed?" Cosmatos asked.

"Yes, sir." Rolly sounded like a child being tucked into bed.

"Good. I'm going to make a little suggestion, nothing strange or frightening." Cosmatos gestured at Moriarty to fetch the red box and set it in his lap where Rolly could see it.

The hypnotist turned back to his subject. "Do you see that red box, Rolly?"

Rolly nodded.

"It's nice, isn't it? Such a pretty color. There must be something pleasant inside it, don't you think?"

Rolly nodded again, his eyes softly focused on the box.

Cosmatos said, "Now, Rolly, listen very carefully. When Professor Moriarty removes the red wrapping and opens the box, I want you to get up and go open the window. Open it wide and wave down at the street. Do you understand?"

"Yes, sir."

"That's a good boy. I'm going to wake you up. When I do, you will feel relaxed and refreshed, as if you've had a good night's sleep." Cosmatos waited a few seconds, then snapped his fingers. "Wake up!"

The boy blinked a few times and then cocked his head at the hypnotist. "When are we going to start?"

Cosmatos smiled and flicked his eyebrows at Moriarty, who recognized the cue. He unwrapped the red scarf from around the hat box and opened it, trying to perform the ordinary task at an ordinary pace.

Rolly watched him until the lid was off the box. Then without a word or flicker of emotion, he got up and went to the front window. He unlatched it and heaved up the bottom sash. Then he leaned halfway out and waved his hand.

"Impressive," Moriarty said to the hypnotist.

At the sound of his voice, Rolly turned away from the window, put his hands on his hips, and frowned at the two gentlemen seated at the table. "Now why'd I go and hopen the bleedin' winder? Hit's freezin' out!"

* * *

After Mr. Cosmatos left, Moriarty sent Rolly down the kitchen for a piece of cake as his reward. He sat in his chair and jotted a few notes about hypnosis for future reference. The process had been so simple. It took less than a minute to put the boy into that curious waking sleep. And the result had seemed so natural. Any observer would have believed the boy had gone to the window from some impulse of his own.

Poor Miss Semple! If she had been subjected to hypnosis, she would have had no control over her behavior. Nor would any observer have considered the suggestion harmful in any way. A flawless plan — and utterly insidious.

Moriarty coughed a small laugh as he realized that he now believed without a shred of doubt that Mrs. Parsons had been murdered with a box of wasps, an idea he had found preposterous a week ago. His skepticism had flown out the window when Angelina walked out the door.

Rolly bounced into the room, wiping his chin on his sleeve. "Yer card is ready, Perfessor."

Peg and the maids kept trying to get the boy to walk with more decorum, as befit a footman in a fine house. Moriarty didn't care if he hopped around on one foot as long as he brought the mail up on time. He'd grown to like the lad. Rolly was quick-witted, plucky, and utterly without scruples. Such niceties as scruples were luxuries — or perhaps consolation prizes — for men who married conventional women.

"Let's have a look." Moriarty took the folded leather case and opened it. The card looked quite proper. Antoine had written "Metropolitan Police Certificate of Identity" next to an amazing facsimile of the official symbol. He'd listed Moriarty's age, height, and eye color down the middle and given him the rank of detective. Antoine had signed "Sir Charles Warren, Commissioner of the Metropolitan Police" at the bottom.

"This is beautiful," Moriarty said. "Look, he's even aged the leather case, as if I'd been using it for months."

"'E's a true hartist, our cook." Rolly beamed with pride. He deserved thanks as well since he had nicked the original from a rozzer's pocket in a public house down the road from Scotland Yard. Moriarty hadn't fully understood what a rozzer was until this moment. He hoped the fellow wouldn't get in too much trouble, but his loss would facilitate the righting of a great wrong.

"I thank you both heartily," Moriarty said. "And now I'm ready to go. Pop out and whistle up a cab for me, won't you?" Today he would visit Flora Semple in Newgate.

"Right ho!" Rolly touched the fingers of his hand to his forehead in the flat-handed salute Sandy taught his boys.

Moriarty donned the bowler hat he'd worn to impersonate a Heffelfinger salesman. It had worked so well that time that he considered it a lucky talisman. Otherwise, his costume today was unremarkable. Peg had made a few judicious choices from his wardrobe and pressed a shine onto the knees of his oldest trousers. He'd scuffed a small valise to match the wear and tear of the rest of his appearance, stocking it with his notebook, pens, ink, and one other item.

Peg gave him a final inspection in the entry hall and nodded, satisfied. "You'll do, ducky. You'll do. Just remember you're a copper and don't be too polite."

* * *

Moriarty's nerves tingled as he handed his credentials to the guard at Newgate. What was the penalty for impersonating a police officer? He couldn't afford to spend time in jail, not now. He tilted back his hat and tried to look bored, then repressed a grin when the card was returned to him with a gruff, "The guard will take you up to the cell."

Extra Christmas bonuses all around this year! But why wait? The day Angelina came home would be declared a household holiday, to be celebrated annually forevermore.

Newgate Prison had been half burned ten years ago and then substantially rebuilt, so it wasn't nearly as foul as legend had it. It was still a gloomy place, however, with long shadows and unwholesome odors leaking out from under doors.

Semple's cell was on the third floor of the women's wing. The guard let Moriarty in, saying, "More questions for you, Semple," then closed the weighty door, shutting them both inside.

He spoke quietly. "I'm Professor James Moriarty. I'm here to help you."

The poor girl gasped a sob, smothering it with a trembling hand. She was probably a pretty creature under normal circumstances, but here she looked thin and tired. Stringy blond hair straggled out of a clumsy knot at the nape of her neck and she still wore the maid's uniform she must have had on when she was arrested.

"Did Gus send you?" she asked, gulping down her tears.

"Not exactly. But I have spoken with him and he stands ready to do whatever he can. I know you are innocent, Miss Semple, although I do not yet have proof."

"It's enough to know that someone out there believes me."

Moriarty summoned a smile, although her plight was sorrowful. Her cell was clean enough, if dank, but barren of all but the minimum comfort — a cot with one blanket, a plain shelf that served for her table, and two stools. He gestured at one of them. "Please sit, Miss Semple. I have a few questions."

"I don't know anything," she moaned, but she sat.

He moved the other stool closer to the shelf, laid out his notebook and pen, and set his valise at his feet. He put a hand into it and said, "First, allow me to try a little experiment."

He pulled out the box wrapped in the red scarf. Semple grew very still, staring at it unblinking. Moriarty opened the wrapping and removed the lid. Semple got up from her stool and walked the few feet to the rear wall, where a high window let in the gray light of the city.

She touched the bricks, then turned back to Moriarty with a puzzled frown. "What am I doing here?" She pointed at the hat box. "What is that? There's something I don't like about it."

Moriarty tucked the red scarf back into his case out of sight. He opened the box to show her. "Empty, you see? Quite harmless. Please sit down again and I'll explain."

Her eyebrows still furled with suspicion, but she resumed her seat. "A box like that came right before my missus was killed."

"I know. I believe it was the instrument of her death."

"I didn't do nothing!"

"I know." Moriarty berated himself for his unsympathetic manner. Angelina would have found a gentler way to conduct this test. "I know you are innocent, Miss Semple. I suspect you were hypnotized by the doctor at Halcyon House and given the suggestion to open the windows at the sight of a red box being unwrapped, to disguise the fact that the wasps issued from the box itself."

She breathed in a long gasp, then stared at him with her mouth open. Finally she asked in a whisper, "Who would do such a wicked thing?"

"I believe one or more of the doctors affiliated with Halcyon House have devised several insidious methods for effecting the untimely demise of select patients for a substantial remuneration."

Semple frowned. "What's me-you-neration?"

"Forgive me. Pomposity is an old and bad habit. I think some of those doctors have cooked up a bunch of clever tricks for murdering women with greedy husbands and children for a fat fee."

"Why, that's horrible!" Semple worked her face into a deep scowl. "That's just plain wicked is what that is! And to leave me to hang for it makes it all the worse."

"I agree." Moriarty gave her a minute to collect herself, but his pocket watch told him he didn't have time to waste. "If you can bear it, Miss Semple, I would like to ask you several questions. I'm not sure how much time we have."

She gulped, folded her hands in her lap, and nodded. "I'm ready."

"Did you undergo hypnosis while attending upon Mrs. Parsons at Halcyon House?"

"Yes. Funny you should know that! It didn't work on her, so the doctor said, 'Let's try it on Semple here to make sure you're doing it right.'"

"Didn't the doctor do it himself?"

"No, they hire a specialist. They have specialists for everything at that place."

"Do you remember the hypnotist's name?"

She stuck her tongue between her lips to stimulate her memory. "Mr. Sprat — no, Mr. Spring. Mr. Springborn! That's it. I'm sure of it."

Moriarty made a note. Mr. Cosmatos might know the man, and he might be willing to testify to his part in the strange story.

"That's very helpful. Did the doctors ask Mrs. Parsons questions about her house? How could they know there was an apple tree outside her window?"

"Oh, they ask everything, sooner or later. The doctors say they can't know exactly what's troubling a person without a complete portrait of their everyday lives."

"I see. Can you remember any details about the contents of that box?"

"Like it's painted on the inside of my eyelids," Semple said. "Little squares of Turkish delight, the missus's favorites. Yellow, pink, and green, dusted with white sugar. All crumbly, like they'd been nibbled on, but the box was closed up tight."

"Did you see a nest inside the box, like a paper honeycomb?"

"I said there was!" She clenched her fists and shook them. "I said it was a nest! I said those horrible things flew out of that box, not in from the window, but nobody believed me."

"I believe you," Moriarty said. "I believe you were heartlessly used to distract attention from a very clever murder."

Semple bit her lip, ducking her head to hide the tears that sprang into her eyes. Then she sniffed, recovered, and asked, "What's next?"

"It would help me to learn something about how things are done at Halcyon House. How long did you work there?"

"Two years. I started as a cleaner, but the patients liked me so well they made me an attendant. At twice the pay." Semple lifted her chin, proud of that achievement. "They need a lot of attendants. They watch the patients all the time, everywhere they go. Then each patient gets a personal one because they're not allowed to bring their own maids. Ordinary lady's maids don't know how to get them ready for their baths or fix their medicine, you see. Mrs. Parsons and I got along so well that she stole me away from them when she left."

"You didn't give any notice?"

"Of course we did. I'm not a sneak. Mrs. Parsons had to bargain with them for me."

"How often does Dr. Trumbull visit the patients?"

"Him? He never comes there unless there's a titled lady. Then everybody has to polish everything from top to bottom and stand up straight and not speak a word until he goes, which isn't long, thankfully."

Could Trumbull design these carefully individualized methods from his Harley Street house? Perhaps that's what all the note-taking was for. "Did you know a nurse named Andrews? Does she spend much time at the hospital?"

"She's the head nurse. She was there most of the time." Flora wrinkled her nose. "She's not a nice woman.

We were all afraid of her, but nobody'd breathe a word, would they? They'd lose their jobs. That place pays well; I have to give them that. They expect complete loyalty in return. Of course, they don't show us any when trouble comes, do they?"

"They do not," Moriarty said. They treated these young women like cheap tools, to be discarded when no longer needed. "Is Nurse Andrews in charge of training the attendants, or does a doctor do that?"

"She does it, and she has two other nurses. We ignorant servants didn't have much to do with the doctors. They're too grand for the likes of us and they weren't there all the time. They only came to do their rounds and personal examinations. Nurse Andrews and her best two were there every minute, watching and taking their notes."

They ran a tight ship at Halcyon House. They couldn't risk their employees telling tales out of school.

"You've been very helpful, Miss Semple. I have one more question. Did you ever meet or hear of a patient named Lady Georgia Estbury?"

"Lady Georgia? Oh yes. She was a lovely woman, poor thing."

"Why poor?"

"Well, she was so miserable, wasn't she? She came to the hospital to get free of the opium. That's what we were told. Nurse Andrews got us into the servants' hall one evening to instruct us. 'No medicine whatsoever, no matter how much she might beg for it. She's got to persevere if she wants to be healthy again.' It's good she warned us because the poor thing was simply frantic by her second week. I bumped into her in the green corridor one day and she clutched my arm, weeping and begging and offering me money for one little dram of laudanum. I had to grit my teeth and bring her back to her own attendant."

"What's the green corridor?"

"Oh, didn't I say? They put the patients in different colored dresses to match the corridor they're in. It's quite clever, really. Some of the poor dears have trouble finding their way around, and the colors make it easy to bring them back to their rooms."

Angelina had been wearing a green dress, definitely not one of her own. Green might be the color of the patients who were receiving the Clennam treatment. "Was Mrs. Parsons on the green corridor?"

"Well, yes. That's why I kept running into Lady Georgia." She blinked at him. "Do you think her ladyship was one of the — one of those . . ." She couldn't speak the words.

"One of the special patients," Moriarty said. "The victims. Yes, I believe she was. Where is the green corridor in relation to the main house and the front gates?"

"It's clear to the other end from the gates," Semple said. "At the back of the new wing in the farthest corner inside the walls, on the first floor."

"Thank you." Moriarty made a note. That must be where Angelina and Viola were housed. "Do you remember Lady Georgia's attendant's name?"

"Shirley Frost."

"Very good."

Moriarty jotted down a few more notes, then packed up his utensils and rose. Semple watched him, her animation subsiding into the weary resignation he'd seen when he arrived. He felt like a brute, leaving her here alone, with the light fading beyond her little window.

There was no good time to be in prison, but autumn must surely be the worst, sitting in a cold cell that grew colder by the day, watching the days grow shorter as your future slipped away.

214

He looked down at the girl, so young and innocent, with fear pinching her hollow cheeks. "Be brave, Miss Semple. I will do everything in my power to prove your innocence and free you from this place."

"Thank you."

He pounded on the door to summon the guard. As the lock clicked, she added in a very small voice, "Please hurry."

# Chapter Twenty-One

"Lina!" Viola whispered. "This is it." She stood beside a partly opened door on the ground floor of the main house. The sconces lining the corridor, with the gas turned down low, cast an eerie yellow light, distorting proportions and lengthening shadows.

Angelina ran toward her on tiptoes. They both slipped inside and shut the door carefully. They had slithered through the dim hallways from their rooms at the end of the new wing to the doctors' private office on the ground floor of the main building. The luxurious furnishings made it fairly easy to sneak around at night. The hospital was well secured from the outside, but the doctors trusted their drugs to keep patients in their beds at night. Angelina had managed to pour her tonic into a potted plant at bedtime by screaming at an imagined face outside her first-floor window, distracting her attendant for a few seconds.

Now she felt her way to a flat surface, took a candle from her pocket, and struck a match to light it. Viola lit hers from that one. The soft glow illuminated a large library furnished on the same luxurious scale as the rest of the main house. Bookcases with gleaming glass doors, a thick Aubusson carpet, and deep leather chairs created an environment meant to impress visitors and express the doctors' aspirations. When open, the brocade drapes would look out toward the wall rather than in toward the terrace where the patients lounged and strolled.

"Let's start with the desks," Angelina said, "and then the shelves behind them."

"What are we looking for? Whips? Manacles? Recipes for poisoned tea?" Viola had agreed to come out of a sense of family obligation, nothing more.

Angelina ignored the sarcasm. "Look for a small bundle of letters tucked out of the way. Beyond that, I don't know. Recipes for packets of poison tea would not surprise me."

Angelina moved to the desk on the far side of the commodious space. She sat in the chair and began opening drawers with a sense of familiarity. She'd spent many a midnight hour rifling gentlemen's desks last spring.

"This must be Fairchild's desk. Here's a drawer full of letters addressed to him." She remembered an important detail. "Don't forget to feel underneath the drawers. People sometimes attach envelopes or bundles there."

"Aren't we the accomplished burglar?" Viola loved to grouse, but once engaged, she was no shirker. "This one must be Dr. Oliver's, then." She started opening drawers, grunting whenever she bent over to peer at their undersides.

She pressed her hand into the small of her back to stretch and turned her attention to the shelf at shoulder height behind the desk. She pulled out the largest volume — a good candidate for a hollowed-out hiding place — and opened it. "Eew!" She tilted the book so Angelina could see the full-page drawing of a woman with a grotesque deformity of the midsection.

"Ugh! Put it back," Angelina said. "I am so glad this isn't *that* sort of hospital. Our fellow patients look perfectly normal from the outside."

"Appearances can be deceiving." Viola put that book back and took out another one. She clapped that one shut after the briefest peek. "I must say, I am glad Badger went in for finance instead of medicine. I couldn't bear to have these pictures in my house."

217

Anna Castle

Angelina had finished her desk and moved on to the shelves. She had a method of tilting each book forward just enough to see if anything had been stuck between the pages, making quick work of a long row. She paused to watch her sister opening books, making faces at them, and shoving them back into place and smiled, maternal affection welling in her breast.

"I hope you're braced for whatever we might find here tonight."

Viola gave her a weary look from under her corn silk eyebrows. "*Do* give me a rest, Lina. I wouldn't believe Badger meant to hurt me if he were sharpening an axe blade on my bedpost, muttering about ridding himself of a vile pest."

"Must be nice to have such blind faith."

"It isn't blindness. It's experience. I know him and I trust him." Viola turned back to her search.

Angelina returned to her task as well, although her energy flagged. She'd expected to find something in Fairchild's desk. She only saw him twice a week, but he seemed like a different man each time. Joking like Dr. Oliver on some days, practically growling at her on others. She started on the next row of books, the highest row she could reach without a footstool.

Viola half turned to look over her shoulder. "You can trust yours too, you know."

"My what?"

"Your husband, of course. James. You should just sit down with him one afternoon and tell him your whole history from start to finish. The public houses, the trouser roles — all the names and dates and places. Then pop down to the nearest license office and make it all proper and legal."

Angelina shuddered at the thought. She couldn't even tell her whole story to Peg, who had been there for most of it. "Impossible. It's too long a story with too many ugly little vignettes."

"Nonsense. James is not an infant. He knows how the world works. And he loves you absolutely. It lights him up every time he looks at you. He won't think less of you because you danced on a few tables or had love affairs with a few fake Italian counts."

Angelina shook her head. "Maybe in a few years. He'll be getting tired of me by then and be grateful for the excuse to walk away."

"What a coward you are! If you respected him, you'd tell him the truth."

"It isn't James I don't respect," Angelina muttered as she turned back to the shelves.

She tilted forward a fat medical dictionary and observed that it had been cut in half width-wise. Two inches across the front, but only four from front to back. Behind it sat three brown bottles and a thin leather case.

"What do we have here?" She put the half-book on the desk and took out a bottle, moving closer to her candle to read the label. "Cocaine hydrochloride, seven percent solution. Oh my stars." She held it up for Viola to see. "Look what I found. This explains a thing or two, doesn't it?"

Viola came over to read the label and drew in a long gasp. "That old rascal! I knew I didn't like him for a reason."

Angelina opened the leather case, revealing two hypodermic syringes. She replaced the case, the bottles, and the half-book. Then she considered what they meant, tapping her nose with one finger. "Well, it isn't good and it is a secret, but it doesn't prove he's murdering his patients."

"Hmm," Viola said, pretending to consider the problem. "Could that be because nobody's doing anything of the sort? Maybe Oliver's a drug user too."

Angelina clucked her tongue. She knew in her bones that Mr. Wexcombe and the old tabbies were right about this place. "Keep looking. We won't get another chance." She scanned a few more shelves within arm's reach of the desk, then decided to try a different tack and started pacing the floor, pressing down at each step.

"What on earth are you doing?" Viola asked. In spite of her doubts, she was still working doggedly through her assigned area.

"I'm testing for loose floorboards. That's where they hide things in Edgar Allan Poe's stories."

"Oh, Lina! Is that where all this is coming from?"

A section of the floor near Oliver's desk flexed beneath Angelina's foot. She got down on her knees to turn up the rug and press the oak boards with her palms. One of them tilted up, revealing a narrow hole. "Aha! What did I tell you?" She reached in and pulled out a bundle of letters tied with flat brown tape.

Viola must not have heard. She trilled a short laugh and said, "Now here's a useful book — *Dietary Regimens for Bedridden Patients,* published in 1796. I wonder if this is what they use to plan our menus?"

Angelina replaced the strip of flooring and folded the rug back over it. She brought the letters over to the desk to look at in the pool of candlelight. She'd already spotted James's handwriting on the topmost envelope, so she knew what she'd found. "I do hope I'm wrong about Badger, darling. But it's better to know, don't you think?"

"Oh, you found your letters." Viola's voice sounded oddly detached. "Good for you. But I'm afraid this will trump them." She walked toward Angelina holding a thin notebook open in both hands, as if offering a sacrament. "Look, Lina. Look at what he does."

Angelina took the notebook and skimmed the first page. "Oh dear!"

Dr. Oliver had designed and performed experiments with the deliberate intention of discovering ways of murdering his patients after they left his care, keeping careful notes about what had worked and what hadn't. The second page had Lady Georgia's name on it in several places. The third one had detailed notes about using a combination of cocaine and electrotherapy to worsen a patient's heart, with reference to Mrs. Winifred Delaney, one of the women the tabbies at Torquay had mentioned.

"This is it," she said. "This is the proof we need."

"And here's me," Viola said. She'd started opening envelopes to peek at the letters. "This one's about me."

"Oh, my darling, I am so sorry." Angelina reached for her, but Viola sidestepped the embrace, shaking the letter and grinning with delight.

"It's not from Badger. I *told* you he would never hurt me. It's from his wife, that horse-faced, envious bitch." She squealed a laugh. "He could divorce her for this. It's the best thing that's ever happened to us. Well, the second best."

"Keep your voice down," Angelina warned. She took the letter back and restored it to its envelope, then bundled them back together and tucked the bundle inside the pasteboard cover of the notebook. She clutched the precious evidence, pursing her lips while she considered her options. "I'm not sure I can hide these for two weeks. Let's think of a way to wrap them up and throw them over the wall next badminton day. In the meantime, you'd better take them. Nurse Andrews likes you and your attendant isn't as keen as mine."

"Mine's an idiot." Viola unbuttoned the front of her dress and stuffed the notebook into her corset. "I could carry them around all day like this. I've gotten so fat, no one would notice." She laughed again and danced on her toes, delighted to prove her protector's innocence.

"Shh!" Angelina hissed. "We've been in here too long. Put that big book back and make sure everything looks the way it was when we came in. Then let's go."

Too late. The door swung wide and Nurse Andrews stalked in, followed by two male orderlies. "What are you doing in here?"

Viola gasped, throwing up her hands as if caught with her hands in the till.

Angelina said, "Nothing," stupidly, scrambling for an excuse. Then she found one. Not good, but better than the truth. "We wanted to see what Dr. Fairchild writes about us in those monographs he's always talking about. I don't want everyone in London to know what's wrong with me."

"Me neither," Viola said, picking up the cue. "I'd die of embarrassment. And what would my dear old father think?"

Nurse Andrews scowled at them, hands on hips, then turned her gimlet gaze to survey the room. The only thing out of place was the book about dietary regimens on Dr. Oliver's desk, which didn't seem to ring any alarm bells for her. It would for him, but then he'd miss his nasty book the next time he wanted to add to it. Maybe he only did that once a week. They could be gone by then if they could get a message across the wall.

Andrews turned to Viola. "Scurry straight back to your room, Missy, and breathe not one single word, if you know what's good for you! If the doctor finds out you've been snooping in his desk, I won't be able to protect you anymore."

"What about my — Mrs. Moriarty?"

"I'll deal with her. You run along now and tuck yourself back into bed. Quick as a bunny! Hop, hop!"

With a helpless grimace at Angelina, Viola slipped around the orderlies and ran out of the room.

"I promise not to say anything either," Angelina said. "I couldn't understand anything in here anyway." She edged toward the door. "I haven't been sleeping well and I wanted a bit of a lark. I'm sorry. It won't happen again."

"It certainly won't. That stupid girl." She must mean Angelina's attendant, who slept like a log and snored like a steam engine rumbling through a tunnel. "Trouble sleeping, eh?" The nurse said, narrowing her eyes. "We can fix that." She spoke to the orderlies. "Take her down to hydro."

The two men gripped Angelina's arms and marched her to the basement. She didn't struggle. She loved the warm herbal baths that were one of Halcyon's specialties. Apart from the murderous side line, this hospital was really a lovely place to recoup and refresh.

But a soothing bath wasn't what Nurse Andrews had in store for her tonight. She directed the orderlies to seat Angelina in a wooden chair over the drain under the shower. Warm showers were supposed to be good for nervousness. She'd had them before, but never fully clothed.

"A bath would work better to help me sleep," she said, hope fading.

Andrews hissed at her sharply, shocking her. The words she spat out scared her more. "I don't care if you never sleep again, you lying, prying, sneaking little whore. Don't think we don't know what you're up to, Mrs. Moriarty — if that's your real name, which I very much doubt. It sounds made-up to me."

She jerked her chin at one of the orderlies. "Strap her down." He bound Angelina to the chair with wide canvas straps.

"No, please," she begged, trying to catch his eyes. "I'll be good. I promise."

"You don't know what the word means," Andrews said. "But you'll learn to obey the rules. I'll see to that." She said to the other man, "Start the pump."

He went to the sink in the corner and fitted a thick hose, like a fire hose, to the faucet. Then he began to work the pump while the first man started blasting Angelina with icy water, striking her face, freezing her scalp, and piercing the thin cotton gown like sharp needles.

She screamed and shouted for help, struggling to protect her face.

"Scream all you want," Nurse Andrews said. "Why do you think this room is down here, so far from everyone else?"

# Chapter Twenty-Two

It had been twelve nights since James Moriarty last slept with his wife.

Her absence unbalanced his life like the loss of a leg. She'd packed his very soul into her brown valise and carried it out the door with her.

Until last May, he had lived the comfortable life of a confirmed bachelor. His parents had sent him to Rugby at the age of eleven. Good at sports and better at maths, he'd found his place in the hierarchy of boys and managed to hold his own. Eleven years under his father's regime had made him impervious to bullying.

From public school, he'd gone straight on to Cambridge, an equally masculine society, but one focused on the life of the mind. There he had flourished, winning first-class honors in mathematics. He even made a few friends. Every now and then one of them would introduce him to a sister or a cousin. One read novels; another painted watercolors. Mostly they talked about clothes and houses and the people they knew. Moriarty would soon lose interest and his mind would wander back to statistical anomalies.

The University of Durham offered him a chair before he even finished his degree at Cambridge. His bachelor life continued, with a few more comforts. He rowed, he taught, he studied. Twice a year he went abroad to a conference. Once a week he visited a clean house on a quiet street beyond the marketplace. He'd thought he'd found his place in the world and would live that way forever.

Then everything fell apart. He was cast out — blameless, but irretrievable. He found his way to London like all of Britain's lost souls and began to build another solitary burrow to creep into. He ventured out once — just once — and met Angelina, the most extraordinary woman on this earth. She'd turned his life upside down and his heart inside out, changing him from a pasteboard scholar into a whole man.

He could never go back to the old life. He couldn't live without her. He wasn't sure he could even survive to the end of this cursed month.

He pushed away the plate of cold kidney pie and poured himself another glass of whiskey. He'd had two already in lieu of lunch and hadn't done much else that morning. He'd risen with a sense of aching futility in spite of the small success in getting to speak with Flora Semple. Her information rounded out the story of Mrs. Parsons's murder, but supplied nothing in the way of actual proof. He had nothing solid. No evidence, no case, no wife.

She wouldn't have gone if it weren't for Lord Brockaway, that intemperate viscount, unable to keep state secrets from his mistress. He lived in a grand house in Mayfair. Couldn't he entertain his unofficial visitors there? Why should he drag Moriarty's relatives into his underhanded games?

Moriarty poured another shot of whiskey into his glass, fueling his disgruntlement. It felt good to have a target other than his own stubborn self for a change.

The clocks began to chime, their out-of-tempo tunes filling the house. Moriarty checked his pocket watch. Half past noon.

His watch, always correct, divided time into indivisible moments, each distinct from the last, moving inexorably from past to future. For Angelina and her syncopated clocks, time was something more elastic. A moment had extent, a span. Time enough to knot a tie or tuck a curl behind the ear. To finish a sentence. To steal a kiss.

He finally heard the music and understood its nature. Too late.

Moriarty tossed back his whiskey. "I'll be damned if it is!" He marched out into the hall.

Rolly jumped to his feet. "Goin' out, Perfessor? Want me to come wif you?"

"Not today."

Moriarty grabbed his hat and coat and found a cab to carry him the short distance to Lord Brockaway's house in Mayfair. He elbowed past the footman who opened the front door, striding implacably through a gleaming blur of mahogany and marble. He spotted a wall of bookcases through an open door and entered his lordship's library without a pause.

"Brockaway, I demand satisfaction!"

Two tall footmen grabbed his arms and started to drag him out.

"What's all this?" Brockaway looked up from his cluttered desk. He frowned at the intrusion but said, "Let him go. He's a friend. I think."

Moriarty shook off the restraining hands and straightened his coat, listing slightly to one side. He might be a shade drunker than he'd thought. He steadied himself and raised an accusatory finger. "This is your fault, Brockaway. If you hadn't been indiscreet with your mistress, I wouldn't be forced to live without my wife."

"What on earth are you babbling about?" Brockaway walked around his desk to face Moriarty, disgust written across his patrician features. "Good gad, man. Are you drunk?"

"I am. But that's not why I'm here." Moriarty considered the untruth. "All right, it is. I wouldn't be here if I weren't drunk. But the fact remains that your desire to

227

murder your mistress — my sister-in-law — is the reason my wife has placed herself in harm's way."

Brockaway grabbed Moriarty by the lapels, hauled him onto his toes, and scowled right into his face. "Are you telling me Viola's in danger? What have you done to her?"

"Nothing." This wasn't the response Moriarty had expected. Now that he was here, two inches from his suspect's wrathful countenance, he couldn't remember what exactly he had expected. But surely a guilty man would be more evasive than furious. "I haven't done anything. You're the one who brought her to that villainous villain. That murdering doctor."

"Doctor? Do you mean Robert Trumbull?" Brockaway shook his head, perplexed. "I'm told he's the best in his line." He pushed Moriarty into a chair and towered over him, hands on hips. "You had damned well better explain yourself."

Moriarty did the best he could. The story didn't sound any less insane for having been told before. But as the implausible plot unfolded, Brockaway's scowl transformed to puzzlement and then to offense.

"And you think I would do such a foul, underhanded thing to Viola?" He patted his chest. "*My* Viola. That woman is the light of my life."

"You brought her to Trumbull's office. Angelina saw you."

"Why wouldn't I? She needed help." Brockaway clutched his forehead as if holding it in place, staring down at Moriarty. "You honestly believe this."

"I do."

"I thought you were a rational man, a man of science and logic."

"I am."

Brockaway's gaze turned inward as he considered what he had been told. Then he rubbed his hand across his mouth as if wiping away a bitter taste. "I'm going to give you the benefit of the doubt, Moriarty, at least until I can learn something substantial. If it's true, the one who made the special contract would be Emily — my wife. This sounds like something she would do, if someone dangled the opportunity before her. She thinks the mere fact of Viola humiliates her, but she accomplished that herself years ago by refusing to live with me."

"Has she ever visited one of the spas favored by Trumbull's clients?" Moriarty asked.

Brockaway blew out a disgusted breath. "She practically lives in them. She spends the whole year on the convalescent circuit." He whirled around to go back to his desk, where he pulled out a telegraph form and began scribbling a message. "If Viola's in the slightest danger, I'll bring her home at once."

"They don't allow letters or visitors," Moriarty said. "You must have signed a committal contract agreeing to those terms when you brought her to Harley Street."

"Damn their committal contract!" Brockaway signed the form with a flourish. "Rank has its privileges. They'll let her out if I want her out. Don't worry. I've included Angelina."

He reached behind him and touched the bell. The footman reappeared, casting a wary glance at Moriarty. "My lord?"

"Send this right away. And bring the coach. And have Montgomery prepare the guest room."

"Very good, my lord." The footman walked forward to accept the slip of paper.

Moriarty's heart leapt with longing as he watched the man take the telegram from Brockaway's hand. He wanted that message to be sent. He wanted the guards to summon the doctors at Halcyon House to read it and submit to the viscount's demand. He wanted his wife to come home.

But he couldn't allow it. He pushed himself out of the brocaded chair and grabbed the slip of paper from the footman's hand. "Wait." He shook his head at Brockaway's outraged frown. "We can't do it, my lord. Not yet."

"You barged into my library demanding this very thing, or near it!"

"I know. And it's what I want. But we must wait."

Brockaway waved the footman away. "Wait for what?"

"We must have evidence, admissible and compelling, of Trumbull's guilt. Without it, an innocent woman will hang and four murders — that we know of — will go unpunished. There may be many more. Besides, Angelina undoubtedly has some plan already in hand. If we pull her out before she can fulfill it, she won't be pleased."

"To put it mildly." Brockaway grunted. "Neither would Viola, who must be part of it by this time. The Archer family sticks together."

The two men traded frowns of resignation. Brockaway stared out the window at his topiaries for a moment, then pounded his fist on his desk. "We can at least go shake that Trumbull up a bit."

"I would love nothing better," Moriarty said, "but we can't do that either. If we march into his office breathing fire, he'll burn whatever evidence he's got and flee the country."

Brockaway's face darkened. He looked like a man about to explode from frustration. "Do you mean for us to sit here twiddling our thumbs while our women risk their lives to find some . . .What? Letters? Notebooks? Disgruntled employees willing to speak behind their masters' backs?"

"That's about the size of it."

Brockaway's dark eyebrows furled. He stood staring at the floor, hands on hips, for a long moment. Then he looked up and started shaking his finger so rapidly it made Moriarty a little seasick. "I don't believe it," he said. "About Trumbull, at least. Viola liked the man. She called him a comfortable old fraud and enjoyed the time she spent chatting with him."

"Angelina liked him too," Moriarty said. "But a murderer can be charming, one supposes."

"You're missing the point," Brockaway said. "I don't believe Viola could converse with a man who intended to kill her without catching a whiff of something suspicious. Some undercurrent of threat or contempt. It's inconceivable. Her sense of character is too acute. The other two have the same talent. It comes from their upbringing, you know."

Moriarty didn't know much about Angelina's early years. "You mean their famous intuition. Holmes lectured me about that too. It still seems like a thin basis for belief."

"Not in the least. I rely on Viola's intuition. That's why I like to bring my negotiating adversaries to her salons. She's never been wrong about them, not once." Brockaway snapped his fingers. "But she didn't like that other one, the physician. Gideon Oliver. She wouldn't let him examine her. 'Cold eyes,' she said, thinking he must have fingers just as cold."

"I don't know," Moriarty said, stung by the realization that he seemed to be the only man he knew who lacked faith in women's intuition, or, if he were going to be completely honest, in his wife's. He liked to think of himself as larger than that. "Do you think it would be possible for Oliver and Fairchild to murder half a dozen of Trumbull's patients without his knowledge?"

"'Comfy old fraud,'" Brockaway quoted again. "Yes, I think it's possible."

"Hmm. And now that you raise the suggestion, I remember that Miss Semple said Trumbull never visited

231

Halcyon House at all unless they had a titled guest."
Moriarty didn't know if it was the whiskey wearing off or
the final acceptance of this intuition business, but his
ideas about this murder scheme were turning in a new
direction. "I wish they'd answer my inquiries. Then at
least I'd have a handwriting sample. Something I can
see."

Brockaway chuckled. "I'd bet on Viola's judgment
any day of the week. Besides, I can't sit here and do
nothing. Let's go rattle the old fraud's chains and see
what happens."

* * *

Lord Brockaway dragged James Moriarty into Dr.
Trumbull's consulting room by the collar, ignoring the
well-dressed woman who fled past them with her hat
shielding her face. He shoved his captive onto a sofa and
turned his wrath upon the doctor, bellowing, "Do you
have any idea what this man has accused me of?"

Trumbull jumped up from his armchair and began
edging backward to the relative safety of his desk.
"What's the meaning of this intrusion?"

Moriarty, in his role as accuser of innocent men,
painted a sneer on his face. He sprawled across the silk
brocade in a manner he hoped looked more disdainful
than inebriated. Most of the whiskey had worn off by
now anyway. They had cooked up this ploy for getting
inside the house and up the stairs without resistance. No
one had offered any, but the energy of their performance
had burned away some of their frustrated desires to
pummel someone.

Moriarty regarded the famous alienist, supposed
mastermind of numerous ingenious murders, now
cowering plumply in a corner of his elegant Harley Street
consulting room. Angelina had described him as a sort of

kindly Father Christmas type. Moriarty saw only a trembling, red-faced Scotsman with large white side whiskers and terror watering his eyes.

He caught a whiff of something acrid in the air. Brockaway's lip curled — he'd caught it too. The renowned specialist had evidently wet his trousers. This pathetic individual wasn't cold-blooded enough to commit these cruel murders. He wasn't part of it.

Still, it wouldn't hurt to learn what he knew. After an exchange of resigned shrugs, Brockaway sat in the chair opposite the desk while Moriarty pulled himself up, resting one hand on his thigh. He told Trumbull what they'd learned about the so-called Clennam treatment provided at his private hospital. Once the doctor realized they weren't going to assault him, he gradually recovered his patrician self-possession.

"Your story is absurd, or it would be if it weren't so repellent." he said, shaking his head. "With all due respect, my lord, it simply can't be true. Dr. Gideon Oliver is one of the foremost practicing physicians in London. That's why I accepted his proposal of a partnership to combine my name and my exclusive clientele with his expertise in hospital management. He's a leading proponent of modern treatment regimens, emphasizing healthy diet and regular exercise. He's the farthest thing from a murdering madman that I can imagine!"

Moriarty doubted this man had any imagination. "What about the other one?"

"Alan Fairchild?" Trumbull spoke as if the man's name alone were enough to clear him of suspicion. "He's the rising star of the new science of neurology, as they're calling it. His research has been published in every important journal. He's not the most personable doctor I've ever met, but his technical knowledge is beyond reproach."

"Their public reputations are not in dispute," Moriarty said. "We have enough evidence at this point to be certain that some of the women who stay in Halcyon House go home to meet untimely deaths benefiting impatient heirs."

Brockaway pressed the point. "Don't you know how many women have died under your care?"

"None!" Trumbull's eyes flashed. He'd found something on which to stake a defense. "Not one patient has ever died at Halcyon House nor left in worse condition than when she entered. I'm sure we have the records to prove it. Both Oliver and Fairchild are sticklers for proper documentation."

"What about after they leave?" Brockaway persisted. "Do you follow up on their progress? Do you write to them after they leave to see how they're getting on?"

"I most certainly do not!" Trumbull lifted his chin. "I do not solicit appointments with patients. *They* make appointments with *me*." He spoke with heat, offended to the core. They'd touched a nerve at last, accusing him of a breach of professional etiquette far more insulting than an accusation of murder.

This puffed-up, self-centered charlatan was not their man. Brockaway sneered at him as he stalked out the door. Moriarty echoed the sneer and reached out to snatch a few pages of manuscript from the desk as he passed.

# Chapter Twenty-Three

Angelina trudged down the stairs after her attendant, heading for Dr. Oliver's examination room. Another attendant stalked behind her to prevent any attempt to escape. Knowing what she now knew about the doctor chilled her to the marrow, colder than the treatment she'd received on Tuesday night.

Thank heavens she'd given that notebook to Viola! She'd been left in peace, for an inexplicable mercy, although that in itself seemed ominous. At least now she'd be on her guard.

Angelina shivered, wishing she had another shawl. She felt itchy and edgy this morning. Jenks hadn't given her her morning tea yet. Usually she got a cup before breakfast with her medicine mixed in. She loved the morning one; it made her feel fresh and bright and ready for the day. The night one was nice too, sort of dreamy and detached. Jenks gave her that one in a cup of chocolate. She liked to spend an hour or so on the terrace looking at the stars before bedtime, singing softly to herself, thinking about James and his adorable moustache.

The second attendant stayed outside when Jenks led her into the examination room and closed the door. This room was much nicer than the hydro and electrotherapy rooms, warmed by oak furniture and chintz fabrics. Dr. Oliver stood beside a tall hutch with glass doors. Inside were rows of little brown bottles and boxes with printed labels.

He didn't look up when the door opened, but kept writing on his ever-present clipboard. When he finished, he ignored Angelina, speaking directly to Jenks. "Let's get her vitals first."

Angelina knew the routine. She stepped onto the scale, noting that she'd lost another two pounds. Nothing that couldn't be replaced once she got back to her own cook. She let her pulse be taken and hopped up on the examining table without being told. She braced herself for the doctor's touch and managed to get through his inspection of her eyes, throat, and heart without giving in to a powerful urge to bite off one of his ears.

He made his notes — those endless, evil notes — and said, "Wait outside, Jenks, until I call for you."

When the door closed again, he turned to Angelina with a knowing smile. "I'll bet you're feeling a little irritable this morning, aren't you? It's like ants crawling across your skin, or so I've been told."

Angelina held his gaze as steadily as she could. The effort made her eyes water. "I seem to have caught a cold."

He laughed. "I'll bet you have. Nurse Andrews can be overenthusiastic. She takes infractions personally, you see." He shrugged. "Otherwise, she suits my requirements admirably."

"I ought to be in bed."

"You ought to be tied up and dropped in the river," the doctor said, his tone still mild. "But you've made yourself popular, unfortunately, singing after supper and doing patients' hair. Questions would be asked. Besides, we can't have patients dying in residence, now can we?"

"Your reputation might suffer."

Oliver pursed his lips and regarded her with stony eyes. "The jig is up, Mrs. Moriarty, or whatever your name is. The only remaining question is what to do with you."

Angelina didn't have the strength to spar with him. She wanted to go back to her room, drink her tonic, and crawl under the covers. But wait, hadn't he slipped up there, revealing that he didn't believe her name? That meant Viola was safe — if Nurse Andrews could keep her out of it.

"I may not know your true name," Oliver said, "but I know you were sent here by Sherlock Holmes to spy on me. I'll find that notebook you took from my office. You must have hidden it on the way down to hydro and moved it later." He curled his lip as he shifted his glare to the door. "These endless damned corridors with those damned potted plants everywhere. There must be a thousand places to hide something that small. But we'll find it, don't worry. Your precious Holmes will never see it."

"So many paintings on so many walls," Angelina said. Anything to lead suspicion away from Viola. "Have you checked behind each one?"

Oliver tucked his tongue in his cheek. "I doubt that's a genuine hint. But it's worth a look. It won't leave these grounds with you, at any rate. You'll be thoroughly searched before I let you go."

Angelina couldn't hide the relief that washed over her, even though she knew they didn't kill their victims on the premises. "I'm surprised you'd let me out if you fear me so much."

"I don't fear you in the least. In ten more days, you'll do anything to please me, wherever you are. I'm sure you've noticed a new craving for your morning tea and your evening chocolate."

The word "craving" made Angelina lick her lips. She did want that tea; right at this moment, she wanted it more than she wanted to go home. She swallowed hard, struggling to overcome the desire, but he saw her struggle and understood.

"Yes, you will be taking something home from Halcyon House: a powerful addiction to morphine. And cocaine as well, I hope. I've never tried to create a dual addiction. I can manipulate that in several ways, even after you leave. You'll need your drugs and need them badly, and you won't find the mix you need at the corner apothecary. Even if you should find something similar, I'm smarter than you. I'll have you followed. You'll fall asleep with a window open or let someone get too close as you walk down the street. A substitute bottle, a quick prick in the arm. That's all it takes. Even if Holmes insists on chemical tests in the autopsy, the results will only show that you've been taking opioid drugs for some time. Addicts frequently misjudge their dosage. Every doctor knows it. Holmes won't be able to make a case."

Angelina held her chin high. "I won't take any tonics at all once I leave here."

He puffed at the empty boast. "Yes, you will. You'll want your morphine so badly you'll get up in the middle of the night to go out in search of it. No one is more easily controlled than a drug addict with a craving." Oliver glanced at the shelves of the hutch, which were stocked with different colored bottles and boxes. "I have your special blend right here, as a matter of fact. I'll give you what you want as soon as you answer a few questions."

She stared at the bottles, desire mingled with disgust. "I don't know anything." Her voice held a plaintive whine.

"You knew enough to search my office. Did Holmes tell you to do that?"

"Yes." That lie couldn't do her any harm. And it might keep him from thinking about Viola. "But he didn't tell me anything about his client or what he already knew. He told me to look for little record books, like the one I found. Mainly he said to keep my eyes and ears open, to watch for patients who seemed to be getting different treatment."

"And what have you learned?"

"Nothing. How could I?" Angelina let her genuine frustration show. "You've got Jenks looking over my shoulder everywhere I go, listening in whenever I talk to anyone. Except at dinner with that frivolous chit and that old woman who can't talk about anything but all the famous people she's met at spas. This whole thing was a mistake."

"I could have told Holmes that." Oliver smiled and leaned against the ledge of the hutch, crossing his arms. He smiled in a way she knew well. Angelina nearly groaned out loud.

The man was going to brag about himself. How evil could he get?

"I've been expecting something like this, you know," he said. "You don't plan an operation as bold and innovative as mine without keeping on your toes. I read the obituaries religiously and follow up every inquest concerning my special patients. I've never gotten a verdict stronger than death by misadventure, I'm proud to say."

"Those poor women," Angelina said.

He made a dismissive noise, like a dry spit. "Nobody cares about them; that's why they're selected. Nobody until now. I'll confess I hadn't expected questions from anyone of Sherlock Holmes's caliber. Lucky I read every issue of *The Illustrated Police News*, isn't' it? That's where I spotted his portrait. A rough drawing, but unmistakable." Oliver chuckled. "He does court publicity, doesn't he? If he wants to pass himself off as a fictional husband, he ought to keep that beak out of the papers."

"I'll pass that along."

"If you see him again. Where is he now? He's famous for dashing off in pursuit of his latest quarry."

"How would I know? We're not allowed letters, if you'll recall."

"A necessary precaution and a wise therapeutic policy. Funny how often those things coincide, isn't it?"

Oliver turned his head to study the bottles on the shelves. Angelina's mouth watered as she followed his gaze.

The doctor opened the glass door, watching her, playing with her the way a cat plays with an injured bird. "Who hired him, Angelina?" Now his voice was low, coaxing. "He doesn't work without a client, as far as I can tell."

"He didn't tell me. He's paying me twenty pounds to keep my eyes open, that's all I know. He'll have to pay me twice that when I get out of here. I never agreed to this."

"Hmm." Oliver studied her with a professional eye, then flicked his eyebrows. "Well, we're not quite there yet, are we? Let's increase your dosage another few grains. By this time next week, you'll tell me everything you know about everyone you've ever met."

He opened the cupboard and poured out a small cup. He half filled it from a large green jug, then added several drops from two different bottles, stirring the mixture with a glass rod. He held the cup toward her, then pulled it away as she reached for it. "Unless you don't want it."

She met his eyes briefly, hating what he must see in hers, hating even more the weak-willed woman who grabbed at the cup and gulped down the bitter drink.

\* \* \*

Angelina swung her racket at a shuttlecock and missed. Then again, she might have been swinging at that round little cloud drifting overhead. She swung at the cloud again, laughing. "Come down here, you little puffball!"

It wouldn't come, the cheeky wisp. Oh well. It didn't matter. She swung around and around with her racket extended like the blade of a propeller on one of the flying machines James liked to read about.

That thought sucked the wind out of her sails. She missed James. She missed his broad shoulders and his serious brown eyes. She especially missed those kissable little curls at each end of his moustache.

She sighed and wandered off the court, dragging her racket over toward the wall, where Viola watched the game with her palms resting on her round belly.

Angelina beamed at her little angel. "You're going to be a mummy."

"I am." Viola smiled back, but she didn't seem so very happy. "You're tipsy, Lina."

"Tipsy-wipsy? Or topsy-turvy?" She bent over to see if she could stand on her head and got stuck. "Uh-oh. Help me?"

"Oh, darling." Viola's strong hands grasped her shoulders and pulled her right ways up again. Her sister's shining face filled her vision. Those piercing blue eyes seemed to examine the whole inside of her head.

"What's in there?" Angelina asked, curious.

"A lot of morphine, is my guess. Or whatever it is they're giving you today. They overshot the mark."

A shuttlecock landed at their feet. "Hoopla!" Angelina cried, pointing at it. "That's not real. Is it?"

"Of course it is." Viola grunted as she bent down to pick it up. She turned her back on the badminton game and fiddled with the thing. Then she turned around again and took Angelina's racket.

"That's mine!"

"I'll give it back." She looked past Angelina toward the players and the attendants who watched them. "Listen, Lina. Can you distract everyone for a minute?"

"Where am I want me?"

Viola grabbed her by the shoulders and stared into her eyes again, only wobbling a little bit this time. "Make everyone look toward the house. Can you do that?"

Angelina blew a very wet breath through her very thick lips. "*I* can do *that*." She swaggered right across the grassy court, ignoring the outcry from the players, and stood on the other side, planting her feet squarely on the ground. She pulled herself up straight, filled her lungs, and launched into Mabel's aria from the *Pirates of Penzance*.

Everyone gaped at her, their outrage swiftly changing to delight. They loved her. People always loved her when she sang. She reached a high note and held it, letting it soar out across the grounds, watching Viola bat the shuttlecock over the wall.

Angelina drew in another breath and embarked on a vigorous roulade. Two attendants closed on her with angry faces. She ignored them, continuing to sing at the top of her voice as they grasped her under the arms and hauled her down to the hydrotherapy room.

# Chapter Twenty-Four

Moriarty paced around the dining table, hands clasped behind his back. At the third circuit, he turned and paced the other way. He couldn't sit down — the worry roiling in his chest wouldn't let him — but it wouldn't help to make himself dizzy.

Sandy and Zeke had brought him the first note delivered over the wall by the shuttlecock stratagem, galloping back from Hampstead as fast as they could through the evening traffic. The words on it were written in Viola's hand.

The message was brief. "NOT Badger!!! Have book. Lina bad. Bring home."

Moriarty had read it over and over, cursing the terse style enforced by their inadequate system. They should have used the second shuttlecock to direct the women to the hole in the brick wall. Sandy had suggested that, but Moriarty had quashed the idea, fearing the hole would be monitored. Besides, the instructions wouldn't fit on the scrap of paper that could be fitted inside a shuttlecock. "Thirteen bricks from the bottom, twelve feet from the southeast corner . . ."

They'd agreed it was too complicated. Simple was best; they'd agreed on that too. This slip of paper with its cryptic message was the result.

What could it mean? "Not Badger." Moriarty had already established the viscount's innocence. He wouldn't have believed Viola's bald assertion otherwise.

"Have book." What book? Some kind of evidence, presumably, or why mention it?

The part that had him wearing a path in the Turkey carpet was the disturbingly ambiguous "Lina bad." Had she behaved badly and been punished for it? Was she bad for suspecting Lord Brockaway? Or was she feeling bad, sickening?

Moriarty's greatest fear was that the doctors would initiate one of their insidious methods of slow poisoning, from which she might never fully recover. She would hate that. She hated having so much as a sniffle — anything that muddied her singing voice.

"Bring home" must mean "bring us home." Or it could mean they would bring the book home with them when they were released. The first interpretation suited his urgent need to get Angelina home and safe. But how? And when?

The door knocker resounded through the house. It must be Sandy again, although he couldn't have fresh news this soon. Moriarty bounded into the hall, beating Rolly to the door. If there was news about Angelina, Moriarty couldn't wait so much as half a minute to hear it.

He flung the door wide, but instead of Sandy's ginger moustache, he saw the clean-shaven face of Sherlock Holmes. The unexpected sight left him speechless.

That malady never afflicted his visitor. "I see I have surprised you again, Professor. Forgive me for failing to send warning of my intention to descend —"

"Don't stand there gabbling on the stoop, Holmes. We've a crisis at hand." Moriarty turned around, leaving the door open, and went back to the dining room.

Holmes lost his hat and coat as he followed Moriarty inside. At least he had the sense not to waste time on conventional expressions of dismay. "What's happened?"

Moriarty handed him the cryptic note, explaining their paltry system for exchanging messages.

"Ingenious," Holmes said. "Inadequate, but you had no viable alternative."

Moriarty would never admit how much that judgment reassured him. "I have a friend with influence who could obtain their release this evening. If I knew for certain what this message meant, I'd do it."

Holmes quirked a smile. "Your restraint is commendable, Professor. Not many men could be so calm under these circumstances."

"I am far from calm." Tension hummed in Moriarty's muscles like some primitive, instinctive readiness for battle. Yet brute force would serve no purpose here. His intellect was needed, every ounce of it.

Holmes studied the note. "What about this first phrase: 'Not Badger?' Do you have any idea what that means?"

"Ah! I should have explained. 'Badger' is the nickname of Percy Wilton, Viscount Brockaway, who is Viola's — well, why mince words at this late stage? Protector seems to be the preferred term."

"I understand." Holmes took a cigarette from his case and lit it. "Your initial assumption, or rather that of your wife, was that his lordship was responsible for Miss Archer's presence in that hospital. You speak his name now without a trace of rancor, so you must have cleared him of suspicion. Is he the influential friend of whom you spoke?"

"Yes. Brockaway suspects his wife might be Oliver's client. She has a long-standing loathing for Viola and is a habitué of convalescent resorts. Viola was legitimately unwell. She must be much better if she has taken over — " Moriarty slapped his hand on the dining table, rattling the cups in their saucers. "I'm a gold-plated idiot! Viola would only write that note if Angelina were incapacitated. 'Lina bad' means Angelina is in bad shape, under duress or drugged." He ran both hands over his bald head, tugging at the short fringe of hair behind his ears. "We must get into that hospital, Holmes. We've got to get her out — both of them."

"Once I realized this note was written by your sister-in-law, I understood your wife to be in grave danger. But I must remind you, Professor, that there's more at risk here. We cannot allow these doctors to go free, possibly to start up their murderous enterprise somewhere else."

"What do you propose?"

"That we take stock and form a well-considered plan." Holmes looked at the papers stacked on the unclothed table, his gaze traveling on to assess the cold hearth, the untouched tea, and the odd assortment of pillows and shawls scattered untidily about the room. "I perceive that you've been busy. So have I. Shall we sit down and compare notes?"

Moriarty's pulse quickened. Holmes must have something worthwhile. He wouldn't have come if he didn't think he could win their bet. "Yes, you're right. We must pool our information." He waved a hand vaguely. "Sit wherever you like."

Holmes joined him at the table and pulled over a stack of notes from Mr. Quick's research. He began to read them at speed, his eyes moving rapidly from side to side.

"Tea or whiskey, Perfessor?" Rolly asked.

Moriarty hadn't seen him come in. "Both, I suppose. Holmes?"

"Tea for me, thank you. Whiskey will taste better when we've caught our quarry."

"Tea, then, Rolly. Is that pot cold?"

"'Arf frozen!" Rolly shook his head at his master's absentmindedness and bustled off with the tray.

Moriarty said, "Before we start, Holmes, allow me to concede our little competition. I would gladly treat all of London to dinner at Simpson's if I could get my wife back hale and whole."

"Agreed," Holmes said. "Things have taken a darker turn than we anticipated. But don't lose heart, Professor. Your wife is an ingenious woman, as capable as any I have met. 'Lina bad' might be meant in the way of fashionable young ladies who say a member of their tribe is *too bad* when they mean she is bold or naughty."

"That's true." Moriarty could hear that expression in Viola's sophisticated voice. It comforted him somewhat. "Angelina's ingenuity is why I hesitate to rush in with trumpets blaring. She might have asked Viola to write the note simply because she didn't have a pen handy." He didn't truly believe that, but the sound of it comforted him even more.

Rolly entered with a fresh pot of tea. He put the tray near Moriarty and went back to his post in the hall. Moriarty poured two cups, adding milk and sugar to his. He pushed the amendments toward Holmes to utilize as he saw fit, along with the ashtray Rolly had wisely provided.

Holmes acknowledged the receptacle by stubbing out his cigarette and lighting another one. Leaning back in his chair, he said, "Why don't you start, Professor? Tell me what you've learned, then I'll summarize the results of my investigation. I hope between us we'll have enough to bring charges."

"So do I." Moriarty got up to get his most valuable pieces of evidence, the letters he'd finally received from Oliver and Fairchild, along with the pages he'd snatched off Trumbull's desk. He pushed the other papers aside and laid them out in front of Holmes like a casino dealer laying down cards. "Gideon Oliver wrote the Clennam letters. I obtained these comparison samples by the simple expedient of writing to each doctor with a question relevant to his area of expertise. For example, I asked Oliver about Trumbull's tonics. Was his cough syrup safe for a child?"

247

"A simple ploy, but an effective one, at the cost of only a few stamps. Well done, Professor." Holmes lifted each page in turn, reading with his preternatural focus. It was as if he could inhale the contents with a single glance rather than laboriously reading each word like ordinary mortals. "This casual inspection does appear to support your contention that Oliver wrote the demands for payment."

"It's more than a mere claim. Not trusting my amateur judgment, I had these letters evaluated by —" He caught himself. "By an expert graphologist who prefers to remain anonymous."

Holmes smiled. The glitter in his eyes made it clear he knew perfectly well where Moriarty's expert could be found at this moment. He said, "It may surprise you that I am also a member of the Société Graphologique." He pulled his magnifying glass from his jacket pocket and studied the pages carefully, moving from one sample to the other as he focused on particular details. From time to time, he shot an irritated glance at the mantelpiece, where the clock ticked out of rhythm with the grandfather clock outside the door. Other ticks echoed faintly down the stairs.

After the third scowl, he sprang up to reach for the mahogany clock case. "Allow me to repair this mechanism, Professor. I frankly don't know how you can stand it."

Moriarty bounded out of his chair and gripped Holmes's wrist. "Touch that clock and I'll knock you down." He shocked himself with the intensity of his threat.

He'd managed to surprise the great detective as well. Holmes studied his face with a lifted eyebrow, then shrugged and said, "No matter. I can concentrate under any conditions."

They returned to their chairs and Holmes resumed his analysis. Moriarty poured himself a fresh cup of tea, taking his time adding milk and sugar, moving slowly to still the pounding of his heart. Those clocks had worked their way into the very fabric of his being. He'd reacted to that threat as he would have if Holmes had attempted to strike Angelina.

He sipped tea and watched the sleuth at work. After five minutes or so, Holmes set down his glass and said, "I agree with your expert. The payment notes and the letter in response to the query about cough syrup were written by the same hand, that of Dr. Gideon Oliver."

"There it is, then," Moriarty said, grinning. "That's the proof we need."

"Alas, Professor, it is insufficient. Although I, along with many others, consider graphology a science, there are greater numbers of skeptics. Most people believe handwriting can be easily disguised or imitated. Furthermore, the Clennam letters, as you so aptly term them, are woefully brief."

Moriarty grunted his disappointment. "Well, it's at least another brick in our wall of evidence. I have others." He told Holmes about Mrs. Parsons's murder by means of a box of wasps, summarizing his meetings with August Norton, Beatrice Wrenn, and Flora Semple. This time he succeeded in astonishing his colleague.

"Ingenious!" Holmes cried. "This doctor is a true master of his craft. A pity he could not put his knowledge and imagination to better use."

"I hold no admiration for this man," Moriarty said. "Any competent physician could murder his patients if he were willing to violate his sacred oath to do no harm. To me, this Oliver is merely a vicious serpent to be trapped and extinguished."

Holmes conceded the point with a shrug. "Unfortunately, we have yet to build an adequate trap."

"I can demonstrate the method used to confound the situation by hypnotizing Miss Semple. I conducted that experiment in this room only three days ago."

"I do not doubt the story," Holmes said with a chuckle. "Watson and I have experimented with hypnosis on occasion, though I myself happen to be proof against suggestion. But judges take a dim view of such antics in their courtrooms. You wouldn't be allowed to demonstrate. If the housemaid finds the box with the wasp nest intact, it would help, although a good defense would claim we put it there ourselves."

Moriarty heaved a sigh. "All right, then. The box is out. But all three of these young people are ready and willing to testify. Miss Semple can even confirm our theory about Lady Georgia's cruel treatment while inside the hospital."

"No good, Professor. Your Mr. Norton knows nothing at firsthand. All Miss Wrenn could tell the jury is that a box mysteriously shivered in her hands. You won't find twelve honest Englishmen who would credit that unlikely tale. And poor Flora Semple is accused of the very murder we seek to blame on respected men of medicine. Naturally she would say anything to save her own neck. Her testimony would probably not even be admitted."

"Damn it, Holmes!" Moriarty fairly snarled in frustration. "That's all I've got — unless Mrs. Peacock's friend's son finds something in Mr. Parsons's bank account."

"Even if he did, he couldn't testify since he would have obtained his information through a breach of the bank's confidentiality." Holmes drank off his tea. "Is that all you have?"

In answer, Moriarty held up both empty palms.

Holmes nodded. "Then it's my turn. Unfortunately, I have even less. I did conclude independently that Gideon

Oliver is the mastermind. I spent the better part of a week disguised as an orderly at the lunatic asylum in Colney Hatch."

"I thought I saw you there at the start of all this. It really is a pity about that nose."

"As you say." Holmes's lip curled. Fair enough. A man couldn't help the shape of his nose. "At any rate," he continued, "I learned enough in that place to chill the marrow of judge and jury if we can bring our quarry to trial. Gideon Oliver has served as one of the primary physicians on the women's wing for at least ten years. Some patients told me the most harrowing tales. They said he has used the weakest and most friendless among them to conduct experiments. For example, he has tested how much mercury can be tolerated by women of different sizes and ages."

"Good God, Holmes! The man is a monster!"

"Indeed, Professor. He must be stopped. Unfortunately, my witnesses would be even less convincing than yours. They are pauper lunatics, committed by the courts. I doubt they would even be allowed to testify."

"Surely some other doctor in that hospital must have noticed something."

"Possibly. Possibly not. It's a terrible job. The place is enormous and many of the patients are very sick. They don't keep doctors for long. Men serve their internships and move on as quickly as they can."

"Their memories might improve if jogged," Moriarty said, clutching at straws.

Holmes acknowledged that remote chance with a shrug of his eyebrows. He gestured for the teapot and poured himself another cup. "I developed fairly full biographies of all three doctors, for completeness."

"Anything useful?"

"Not directly. Fairchild and Trumbull are scions of the upper class. They received the conventional training in Scotland, Paris, and London's better hospitals. Oliver has had to climb up the social scale himself with the help of his father's money. Oliver Senior was a very successful apothecary. You may have seen advertisements of his wares. Ollie's Jollies, a full line of pills, ointments, and powders. In spite of the father's money and Oliver's efforts, he never managed to rise beyond the less desirable posts at places like Colney Hatch until two years ago when he formed a partnership with Dr. Trumbull."

"How did he persuade a man of Trumbull's standing to collaborate with him?"

"A very good question, Professor. Trumbull's position was precarious before Oliver came along with his inheritance. A second footman at Trumbull's house in Mayfair told me over a pint of ale that his master had been in deep financial straits until he opened that 'place for loony women up yonder by the heath.'"

Moriarty smiled at the mental image of Holmes eliciting tales from tipsy servants. His disappointment at the demolition of his edifice of proofs was tempered by his satisfaction at having learned more through his scholarly methods, based in archival research, than Holmes had with his vaunted capacity for disguise.

"Is that all you have?" he asked.

"I also sniffed around the neighborhoods of the other victims. As far as I can tell, no one has suggested foul play in any of those cases. I uncovered no relatives as affectionate and watchful as Mr. Wexcombe. Lady Georgia was fortunate in that respect."

Moriarty's stomach growled. He got up and poked his head out the door. "Could you bring us some sandwiches or cake or whatever's handy?"

Rolly saluted him. "Right ho, Perfessor!" He seemed grateful for the task.

Moriarty wished he had more to do himself. He returned to his seat and slumped into it. "I still contend my letters are important pieces of evidence. It would be better, however, if we could supply both ends of each transaction. We need the letters Mr. Parsons and the other heirs wrote requesting the Clennam treatment. Combined, the exchange becomes significant."

"I agree," Holmes said. "We must find those letters, if they still exist. But who would keep them? I would burn mine as soon as the contract was fulfilled."

"I would keep mine," Moriarty said. "If the crime were discovered, I'd want to give the authorities a bigger fish to fry. But it's idle speculation. We'd have to break into their houses to search for them."

"We'll reserve that as a last resort, then," Holmes said drily. He knew Moriarty's confederacy included a gang of experienced burglars, one of whom had just gone downstairs to fetch sandwiches.

Moriarty ignored the hint. "Once we can bring charges, if only on slender grounds, the authorities will be able to pry into bank accounts and personal correspondence. The doctors won't hesitate to spread the blame to their clients and vice versa. Once we get that key —"

"We'll open the door to a flood of evidence." Holmes rubbed his long hands together. "But how do we lay our hands on that key?"

"How indeed?"

Rolly came in with a plate of Antoine's excellent sandwiches — roast beef with horseradish and cheddar cheese with his spicy tomato chutney. The two men ate in silence for a while, thinking while they ate.

Holmes finished his third sandwich and wiped his fingers on his napkin. "We need more than a tale woven out of disparate threads of circumstantial evidence."

"We might already have more," Moriarty said. "Or Angelina might. Viola wrote 'have book.' That must refer to something incriminating, or why mention it?"

"I can think of no reason," Holmes said. "Taken all together, I believe the phrase 'bring home' must mean 'bring us home now.' But how can we accomplish that without flushing our quarry and letting them escape our nets?"

Moriarty smiled grimly. "I have had one idea. It would be neither safe nor lawful, if you're fussy about such things."

Holmes lit a cigarette and blew out a puff of smoke. "I never have been."

"I didn't think so. Then you may recall that August Norton is a fireman with the Hampstead Fire Brigade. He swore he would do anything to help free his fiancée." Moriarty rose and got his map of the metropolitan area. He pushed plates aside and spread it on the table. "Are you familiar with Hampstead?"

"Of course."

"Then you'll know the fire brigade maintains a watch upon the central tower day and night." He pointed at the center of the village.

"Ha!" Holmes laughed. "You're about to propose that we start a fire at or near Halcyon House. An excellent idea, Professor, if a dramatic one. It will give us an excuse to breach the gates so that you and I can enter under cover of the confusion." He tapped a finger on the map. "We'll need considerable confusion to go where we want unchallenged."

"I believe we can arrange it. The place is full of nervous women, remember. We'll have the boys build a good-sized fire outside the wall, big enough to be seen from the watch tower. Norton will raise the alarm. Bells ringing, horses galloping through those steep and narrow streets. Lots of noise and men shouting. That should be quite alarming."

"To which boys do you refer?"

"A motley group of street urchins who follow my friend Gabriel Sandy, the cabman. He's kind to them and they have little else to do. Of course, I will gladly pay for their assistance."

"Street urchins, eh? An excellent idea." Holmes looked thoughtful. "London is full of boys like that, getting into mischief as —"

"Yes, yes, they're everywhere," Moriarty said. He wasn't in the mood for urban demography. "Clever as monkeys, some of them. I'll send Norton a note right away asking him to make sure he's on the tower at the critical time. Then he can raise the alarm and ride with the brigade to the hospital. They can break the gate down if necessary. It's within their purview."

"They won't have to," Holmes said. "Their mere presence will alarm the guards. They'll open up fast enough."

"That would be best. So the truck goes in, firemen rush about shouting and spraying water at Norton's direction." Moriarty faltered. "I'm not sure how that will work. Trained firemen would know at once there wasn't any fire."

"They couldn't be certain. They would search the grounds and any outbuildings to locate the source. They would probably recommend the hospital evacuate the patients to ensure their safety. Fires spread quickly. That is a real risk, you know."

"I'm willing to take it."

Holmes chuckled.

"Not my risk, I know," Moriarty said. "The boys will build their signal fire outside the wall, which is solid brick and nine feet high. But your point is well made, Holmes. The fire should be as far from the gate as possible to justify the maximum intrusion into the grounds. We might want more than one, on different sides."

"That was not my point at all," Holmes said.

Moriarty waved that off. "Under cover of the uproar, you and I will sneak inside. I'll find Angelina and Viola. Unless things have changed recently, they should both be at the far end of the first floor of the new wing. Miss Semple told me that both Mrs. Parsons and Lady Georgia had been lodged on that corridor. A further clue is that the patients' gowns are colored according to the location of their rooms. I need only scout around for women in apple-green dresses."

"I will head straight for the doctors' offices to search for further evidence," Holmes said. "It's a safe bet they'll be on the ground floor of the main building."

"Don't forget about Viola's book."

"Whatever that may be. With all due respect, I have more confidence in my own methods. I prefer to conduct my own search."

"Agreed. We need all the ammunition we can get." Moriarty scratched his head. "I think Lord Brockaway should stay with the fire brigade and manage the situation at the gate. He'll want to come with me, but his authority may be needed if one of our boys is caught by the police or any objection is raised. It will be dark . . ." He lapsed into thought, trying to imagine the scene from the brief glimpses he'd gotten during his brief visit in the guise of an electrotherapeutic devices salesman. That had been only last Monday. It felt like a month had passed.

"The moon was at the half last night," Holmes said. "It will be quite dark on Saturday, apart from the firemen's lanterns."

"Saturday," Moriarty objected. "Why wait? I thought we'd go tomorrow."

"That would not be wise, Professor. It will take a full day to communicate with the principals and ensure that our players are in position at the critical moment. And we need time to construct our disguises."

"What disguises?"

"We can't go into that hospital dressed like this." Holmes gestured at his black coat and gray trousers, nearly identical to Moriarty's attire.

"Why not?" Moriarty shrugged. "Doctors dress this way."

"There are only two doctors at Halcyon House. Probably a few male orderlies. But most of the staff and all of the patients are women. You and I must wear dresses if we want to go unchallenged."

"That's ridiculous!" Moriarty stared at Holmes in disbelief. "We couldn't even fit into women's dresses. It's physiologically impossible."

Holmes laughed, tilting his head back. When his egregious mirth subsided, he said, "Have you never been to a music hall? You, married to an actress? Of course it's possible. It's only cloth. You buy it by the yard. It might be difficult to find gray dresses large enough for us on short notice, however."

Moriarty curled his lip. His knowledge of the theater might be limited, but his resources surpassed those of his rival. "I happen to have a specialist in theatrical costumes on the premises as we speak." Peg would be delighted for a chance to help.

"You do have the most intriguing household, Professor." Holmes leaned back and steepled his fingers again. "There is one more reason to wait until Saturday. We must deliver one last shuttlecock message to warn your wife and sister-in-law. They must be prepared to move quickly when the alarm is raised. We can't risk them running out without that book."

# Chapter Twenty-Five

Viola Archer stood near the vine-covered wall by the badminton court, watching Angelina twirl in circles, her apple-green dress swaying over the emerald grass. She stumbled and giggled, as tipsy as a debutante after her first glass of champagne. She could barely form a coherent sentence today. She wasn't suffering — quite the opposite — but her condition had become alarming.

Angelina had followed her into this silk-lined prison to rescue her, just as she'd risked the other kind of prison to rescue Sebastian last spring. He was well out of it this time, thank goodness. He'd probably insist on disguising himself as a woman and trying to weasel his way inside. Then Viola would have to find a way save him too.

Their elder sister had always done the best she could for them, from the day they'd been born. Only a child herself, she'd taken charge of them — feeding, bathing, pestering senior actresses for advice. She'd fought like a badger to make their father hire tutors for them so they could learn to talk like toffs and have all the advantages a good accent provided.

Lina had given up her own childhood to care for them and they'd repaid her with jabs of guilt and endless wheedling. Now Viola had a child of her own on the way. It changed things; it made a girl think. She wouldn't have to fight the way Angelina had. She'd have Badger supplying all the good things.

It was her turn to do the rescuing now. And she'd be damned six times and twice again on Sunday if she'd let these bastards destroy her sister!

She whistled a light tune, hoping someone on the other side of the wall would hear her. Someone did. A shuttlecock landed almost at her feet. She strolled idly over to hide it with her skirt, then pretended to slap at an insect and bent down to scoop it up.

She held it behind her back and teased out the tightly rolled message, tucking it into her collar. She had to turn her back to push her prepared message into the hollow cork head, so she plucked a fading flower from the vine before turning around. She spotted an attendant looking in her direction. The brutes were as sharp-eyed as gray hawks. She stroked the flower behind her ear and drifted over toward the game, tucking the shuttlecock into her pocket.

She needed a racquet and an excuse to bat her message over the wall. She couldn't ask Lina to provide a distraction again, poor darling. She'd done enough to last a lifetime.

Viola didn't know how long her allies beyond the wall would wait. But if she could get her message to them, they might be home by dinnertime. She must have been too cryptic the first time. She'd tried to be clearer this time, writing in tiny letters, "Have proofs. Tell Badger to bring us home at once."

One of the players cried, "You cheaters! I quit!" and threw down her racquet. Viola sang out, "My turn!" She trotted onto the court and grabbed the racquet, using it to point at the player on the other side of the net. "You won't cheat me, Miss Prancey. I'm too sharp for your tricks."

As she expected, the other player launched into a shrill defense of her virtue, drawing the others into the conflict. Nervous women were so touchy!

Someone shoved someone else and the attendants moved in to sort them out. Viola turned on one foot, lobbed her shuttlecock over the wall, and spun back around again in one smooth motion. Those boring afternoons at Badger's friends' estates had not been wasted after all.

She didn't get to read her note until exercise time was over and they'd been brought back to their rooms to freshen up for supper. Her heart had nearly broken in two when she watched Lina peer eagerly into her vile attendant's flat face as she asked, "Is it tonic time?"

Viola sent her girl to fetch a clean washcloth, snapping her fingers imperiously. When the door closed, she unrolled her slip of hope and nearly sang out loud with relief. They *had* understood her last message. This one said, "Tonight. Watch for fire. Bring book."

* * *

"Hold still, Mr. Holmes," Peg said, gripping the back of his dress.

"I require the full range of motion in both arms," the detective said, raising his limbs to demonstrate.

Peg swatted them down. "I know that, Mr. Swell. That's why I'm putting in these darts. If you'd stop admiring yourself in the mirror for one minute, I could get it done."

Moriarty listened to their bickering with half an ear. He was already garbed in his attendant's uniform. Peg had sized it to fit over his shirt and rolled-up trousers and he found it surprisingly manageable. She'd rigged up a wad of stuff she called a "bum-roll" and tied it around his waist. It provided ample space to work the legs. He'd gone striding around the house to test the affair, up and down the stairs, in and out of every room, ignoring the bursts of laughter gusting behind him.

Peg had done yeoman's work putting these outfits together in only two days. She'd dragooned the mouse maids to sew up hems and sent Rolly off to the shops every other hour. The results spoke for themselves.

"You've outdone yourself, Peg," he said.

She grunted, turning Holmes around to fuss with his scalloped collar. "I've done more with less for worse reasons." She straightened the row of buttons running down his padded chest. "These buttons are held on by the barest thread, mind you. One good tug and you can pull the whole thing right off."

"An admirable feature." Holmes went to the long mirror to inspect his appearance. He'd brought his own wig, made of brown hair to match his eyebrows. It fit like a cap over his own hair, which he'd slicked down flat. The false hair was gathered onto the top of his head in thick coils with a row of stiff curls at the front. Always clean-shaven, he'd made extra sure to leave no dark hollows on his cheeks tonight.

"Well," Peg said, "you ain't pretty, Mr. Holmes. But you'll do."

Holmes chuckled. "My goal is to avoid attention, not attract it." He tried out poses in front of the mirror as if seeking a sort of bodily style. He settled on a stoop-shouldered posture, loosening his knees and reducing his height by a good two inches. The transformation was remarkable. He looked like a dashed unattractive woman — but a woman, not a man.

Moriarty watched him practicing gestures, turning this way and that. He took to the role so easily. Angelina once speculated that Holmes, always clean-shaven and so fond of fancy dress, might be an aesthete along the lines of Oscar Wilde and her brother Sebastian. Moriarty disagreed. He recognized Holmes as one of those rare individuals who was truly *sui generis*: sufficient unto himself.

Rolly appeared in the doorway. "A note from the captain, Professor."

261

"Good." Moriarty read the missive, then summarized for the others. "Lord Brockaway has reserved a private room at the Angel Inn. He'll have supper there to be on hand. We can use it as a base of operations or a retreat, if we need it."

"Always good to have a fallback," Holmes said.

"I wouldn't have thought of it." Moriarty had never been so grateful. All these generous, resourceful people! He didn't deserve them, but Angelina did. "Sandy says he's got two wagons of fuel hidden in the woods on Hampstead Heath ready to roll down at eleven o'clock."

"The rumbling will wake people," Holmes said.

"That can't be helped. We can't leave bonfires stacked against the walls for any length of time or have boys running in and out of those alleys with armloads of wood. Events should progress so quickly there won't be time for the householders to respond."

"An acceptable risk." Holmes folded his arms and inspected Moriarty from head to toe. "Oh no, my good fellow. That won't do at all. You won't get ten feet looking like that."

"What's wrong with me?" Moriarty elbowed him out of the way to stand before the mirror. He looked like a fool, but that was the objective. He didn't have a wig and wouldn't wear one if he had, but Peg had found him an old-fashioned bonnet that tied under the chin. It had a rill of fake curls sewn across the brow. He raised his skirt to show his feet. "I can't do anything about my boots at this late date, but they don't show much."

Peg gave him one of her patent Cockney looks, up from under her eyebrows with a weary-wise expression in her eyes. "It ain't the shoes, Professor. You're going to have to shave off that moustache."

"I will not!"

"Don't be so childish, Moriarty." Holmes smirked. "You don't want to queer the game before it's started, do you?"

# Chapter Twenty-Six

Viola lay in her bed, keeping herself awake by designing the perfect house for her and Baby Badger to live in. Would it really be possible for Badger to divorce his odious wife? Lady Blandford had successfully divorced her husband, the eighth Duke of Marlborough, three years ago and all he did was sleep with a few wives of other men. You'd think attempted murder would count for more than that.

Whenever she felt herself nodding off, she'd imagine herself giving heartrending testimony against Lady Brockaway in the House of Lords. There wouldn't be a dry eye in the audience, including the judge in his big white wig.

When she heard her attendant snoring in soft whistles, she got up to put on her shoes and stockings, moving in exquisite silence. She pulled the precious notebook out from between the mattresses and stuffed it into the pocket of her dressing gown. Then she sat on her bed staring out the window, wondering how she would see the fire they warned her about. Her window looked out onto the wall.

Did they mean for her to bring Lina down to the terrace to watch? She couldn't keep her sister quiet for long, even if she could wake her up and get her downstairs. The men didn't know that, of course. They didn't have any idea what was going on in here. They didn't know that she'd been left in charge, something that had never happened before and never should have been allowed. She was the pretty one. She didn't *do* things.

Clouds scudded past the waning moon, casting long shadows on the wall. Viola gasped as a red flame leapt up, right outside her window. More flames followed the first, each one lashing higher. One leapt like an animal over the wall and onto the vines growing up the side of the house. The drying autumn leaves caught like tinder. Fire spread across the wall with terrifying speed.

Not see it! They'd be lucky to survive it!

She jumped to her feet and shook her attendant. "Fire! Fire! Wake up!"

The groggy woman sat up, took one look at the window, and lunged out the door without a backward glance.

Viola glared after her. "Don't think *that's* not going into my review." She patted her pocket to be sure she had the book and the letters and dashed across the hall to wake her sister.

Lina's attendant lay snoring like a freight train, even though the fire had begun roaring and crackling at the end of the hall. "Fire!" Viola shouted. "Wake up! Wake up!"

She shook Lina awake and dragged her onto her feet. The attendant sat up and opened her eyes. "What are you doing in here?"

"The building's on fire. Get out! Run!"

She sniffed and said, "God preserve us! I'd better wake the others." She stuffed her feet into her shoes and ran out, crying "Fire! Fire! Everybody out!"

"Noisy," Lina whined. She tried to climb back into her snug nest.

"Wake up, darling," Viola said, standing her up and giving her a good shake. "You've got to wake up and walk. I can't carry you."

"I'm not carrying me. You're too big." But she steadied a little, standing on her own.

"That's a good girl."

265

"Shoes," Lina said, pointing at her feet.

"No time for shoes. We've got to hurry." Viola wrapped one arm around her sister and, through a combination of jokes, tugs, and curses, managed to haul her out of the room. The air in the corridor already felt hot, and smoke flowed out of her bedroom.

They made it a few feet down the hall, but as they passed a plump armchair, Lina pulled away. "Sleepy." She yawned and started to curl up on the cushions.

"No, no, no," Viola said. "Not sleepy. Wakey, wakey!"

She scanned the long hallway again, hoping for someone to help her. The smoke had started spreading across the ceiling, like a storm front blowing in. She could see well enough thanks to the lamps attached to the walls at intervals, always turned down low at night. She was grateful not to be in total darkness, but the thought of gas and fire shot spikes of fear up her spine. They had no time to waste!

Someone emerged from the last room on this corridor — Mrs. Northwood, their tablemate, lugging a large valise.

"Thank God!" Viola waved at her. "Help me get her up. She's been drugged."

Mrs. Northwood only sneered. "So should you be. It would speed things up if you would both go back to bed and let yourselves be burned up in this inconvenient fire. We've never tried arson before, but why look a gift horse in the mouth?"

Viola gaped at her, outraged. "You evil, murdering bitch!"

"My, my, such language. Breeding does show in times of crisis." The old witch cast a glance back at her room, where sparks now danced in the smoke. "Better hurry." She chuckled, like a rough cough, as she gripped her overstuffed bag and trotted down the hall.

Viola wanted to run after her and slap her silly, but there wasn't time. It didn't matter anyway. Once they reached the gates, they'd be rescued and that vicious bitch would hang with the rest of her murdering crew. Viola would throw the party of the Season on that happy day.

Smoke now choked her breath, flecked with ashes that clung to her cheeks. Shrieks and shouts sounded from the direction of the yard. Bells clanged everywhere. She was trapped in a nightmare. Her every instinct screamed at her to run, to save herself and her baby.

*Not without my sister! Baby Badger's going to need his auntie.*

Viola grabbed Lina's arm and yanked on it with all her strength. "Up, Lina, up!" She got her arm under her shoulders again, bending awkwardly over her round belly. "Listen! Can't you hear the applause? They're calling for you!"

"What?" That did it. The old war-horse staggered to her feet, straightened herself, and ran a hand through her disastrous hair. She lifted her chin. "I've never missed a cue in my life."

"That's the spirit, ducky. Now, let's show 'em what we've got!" Viola started singing "Ask a Policeman" as she lugged her wobbling sister through the smoke. Lina roused enough to sing along, missing the key but keeping the rhythm.

Not one attendant had stayed behind to help them. Not one! Had fear driven them off to save themselves? Or did they all know the women on this corridor were marked for death anyway?

* * *

James Moriarty and Sherlock Holmes did not ride up to Hampstead clinging to the side of a fire engine with bells clanging and men pouring out of their houses to run along behind them. Captain Sandy had taken one look at

267

their gray cotton dresses, covered his mouth in a short fit of coughing, and changed the plan on the spot. He drove them up in his cab with the curtains drawn and dropped them at a quiet corner of the wall. They found a gap in the opposite hedge where they could watch the road and settled down to wait.

Holmes curled into the posture of a working woman waiting for her husband to collect her after a long shift. Somehow he managed to get his long legs under his skirt in a modest, feminine fashion. Then, to all appearances, he fell asleep. Moriarty knew he was feigning. He had no doubt the sleuth would be fully alert when the time came.

Moriarty couldn't figure out what to do with his legs. They didn't bend like Holmes's did. He ended up stretching them before him, displaying his masculine boots. Well, it was dark, and the game would begin in half an hour.

But it couldn't have been more than fifteen minutes before the racket of alarm bells, horses' hooves, and men's shouts drove up the hill. Holmes sprang to his feet. Moriarty clambered up, shaking his skirt down around his trousered legs.

A crowd of townspeople had gathered behind the fire truck. Able-bodied men had an obligation to assist in these emergencies. Moriarty had forgotten that custom, but he was grateful for it. Their presence made it easy for him and Holmes to work their way right up to the gate.

The guards had apparently not yet noticed that there was an emergency. "What fire?" one of them demanded. "Go practice somewhere else. We've got ladies in here, delicate ones. They're not to be frightened with your antics."

"What do you call that?" August Norton stood in front of the engine, pointing toward the wall beyond the new wing, where smoke billowed up in showers of sparks.

The guards gasped. Without another word, they swung open the tall iron gates.

"Let's go, boys!" Norton ran ahead of the engine, up the road to the main house. Moriarty and Holmes jogged along at the edge of the crowd of townspeople.

When they reached the house, a fireman jumped off the truck, shouting, "Where's your water main?" The driver turned his horses toward the edge of the terrace. The townsmen split into two groups. Some followed the first fireman, unfurling huge canvas hoses as they went. Others grabbed sacks from the back of the truck and ran after Norton.

"This way, Holmes." Moriarty pointed toward the door he'd gone through on his earlier visit. They paused on the threshold. "Angelina and Viola are in the new wing there." He pointed across the terrace, now a chaos of men and hoses, weirdly lit by silver moonlight streaking through shadows.

"You'd better go through the house," Holmes said. "It will probably be faster and a woman seeking to enter that building might be stopped and sent back toward the gate."

That made sense, although it warred with Moriarty's desire to take the shortest path. He followed Holmes inside. The solid oak and thick carpets inside the house muffled the clamor outside as soon as they shut the door.

When they reached the central stairs, he whispered, "Fifteen minutes. No more. We'll meet outside the gate."

Holmes nodded and disappeared into the the dark lobby.

Moriarty ran up the stairs on his toes, propelled by the intensity of his need to find Angelina. He would scoop her up and carry her in his arms all the way back to Kensington. They'd spend the whole of next week in their bedroom —

"That's far enough," a male voice said.

A large hand pressed a cloth soaked in some pungent chemical against Moriarty's face. He gasped and his knees buckled.

\* \* \*

Moriarty's eyes fluttered open. He found himself in a well-appointed library, his arms and legs bound to a hard wooden chair. His stomach churned. The burning sensation in his throat told him he'd been subjected to chloroform. He recognized the smell from his chemistry classes at Cambridge.

He blinked the blurriness from his eyes and saw Alan Fairchild sitting at a desk, withdrawing a needle from his arm. The doctor's eyes rolled back as his body slumped and a crooked smile spread across his face.

The image made no sense. Moriarty shook his head and coughed, trying to rouse himself and return to the real world.

"Ah, you're awake," another voice said. This one came from across the room.

Dr. Oliver stood behind another desk, stuffing papers into an open Gladstone bag. That action seemed familiar to Moriarty, like a distant memory. It didn't bode well.

The door banged open and two men dragged in a groggy Sherlock Holmes. They tied him to another chair, letting his head fall back against the wooden rungs. The detective's eyes fluttered open and he groaned.

"Go get the two women on the green corridor," Oliver told the orderlies. "Might as well deal with the whole gang at once." He clucked his tongue at his captives. "What am I going to do with you gentlemen? You've boxed me into a corner. It's lucky I was working late tonight and luckier still that I decided to add extra guards after we caught your little spy sneaking around at night."

Angelina had been in this room! She must have found the book here, whatever it was. And Oliver had learned she was a spy. How long ago? What had he done to her in reprisal?

Moriarty worked spit into his mouth so he could speak. But Fairchild recovered from whatever he'd given himself. He grinned and said, "Why, it's Professor Moriarty! What are you doing here?"

"That's not Moriarty, you moron," Oliver said. "It's Sherlock Holmes. He signed a false name."

"Of course it's Moriarty. He visited me at Colney Hatch less than a month ago."

Oliver frowned from one man to the other. "Oh, I see. Oh yes. Very clever. I assumed Moriarty was a *nom de guerre*. I never guessed you were working together. Watson, wasn't that the name you gave me? Of course, I noticed you didn't know much about electrotherapy. You could barely distinguish volts from amperes."

Fairchild shook himself like a dog coming out of a pond, arms outstretched. "Ha! Much better."

Holmes spoke, his voice thicker than usual. "A four percent solution?"

"Seven. Four is for the ladies." Fairchild giggled. "Are you another aficionado?"

"I'm familiar with the drug," Holmes said.

Fairchild packed his needle into his valise. "I'd love to stay and chat, gentlemen, but I only stopped by to collect my things. I heard the most appalling story from Trumbull this evening. I could scarcely credit it, but it does explain a few odd decisions you've made, Gideon." He looked at the two men bound to chairs sitting not six feet away from him and clucked his tongue.

"All good things come to an end," Oliver said. "I suggest you leave town for a while. Things could get a trifle awkward until the gossip subsides."

Fairchild nodded. "Trumbull's on the train to Scotland by now. I have a cousin in Chicago who's been begging me to emigrate. Apparently they have a shortage of alienists. And I could use a change of scene." He scouted around his desk, then snapped his valise shut. He tipped his hat at the captives. "*Au revoir*, gentlemen. I do wish you the best of luck." He chuckled at his morbid wit as he walked out the door, shutting it firmly behind him.

Moriarty gaped after him. "Surely he'll alert the police."

"I wouldn't count on it," Holmes said. "But he'll be stopped before he can board a ship."

"I wouldn't count on that either," Oliver said. "He's a sly one, is our Fairchild, with quite the knack for self-preservation. Why do you think I chose him?"

The orderlies burst back into the room. "The new wing's on fire! There's firemen blasting water everywhere. And there's a bloody great toff in a red sash standing in the middle of everything giving orders."

"Where are the women?" Oliver demanded.

"Are you deaf? That wing's on fire. Flames shootin' up, smoke thick as pea soup. We ain't going up there. We didn't sign up for this!" The burly man took the time to shake his fist at the doctor before racing after his fleeing chum.

"Alone at last," Holmes said. He'd recovered his *sangfroid*. "You won't escape, you know, Doctor. There's only one gate and that is being watched by our people."

"I'm disappointed in you, Holmes. Of course there's another gate. The noble rascal who built this house liked to come and go without notice. There's a door behind the ivy, not far from this room." He jerked his chin toward the long drapes on the outside wall.

"Even so," Moriarty said, "we know all about your scheme. We have the names of several of your victims. We have testimony from members of Mrs. Parsons's household. Once we start asking questions of your greedy clients, they'll talk as fast as they can to save their own necks."

"But you won't have your wife, I'm afraid." Oliver didn't seem worried. The man must have the most monumental self-regard. "Burned to a crisp by now, I imagine. I've been keeping her well sedated at night to make sure there isn't any more nocturnal exploring."

A sob escaped Moriarty's throat.

"Bear up, man," Holmes said. "That's an empty boast. He doesn't have full control of his staff. We've seen that here tonight. And your sister-in-law is a capable young woman. I'm sure they've both gotten to safety already."

"God help them." Moriarty's eyes filled with tears. He began to fight his bonds, rocking the sturdy oak chair from side to side.

Oliver watched him for a moment. "Well, that won't do. I can't have you two telling your wild stories to anyone else. And I don't suppose I can count on the fire spreading this far before they put it out."

He pulled a case from a drawer and set it on the desk. He opened it, took out a hypodermic syringe, and filled it from a small brown bottle. He approached Moriarty first. "Now hold still. This will only hurt a little."

Moriarty shouted and struggled but could do nothing to stop the needle from sliding under his skin. He choked out one last, "No," before it all went dark.

\* \* \*

Viola kept on singing, though tears rolled down her sooty cheeks. They'd never make it. She wasn't strong enough.

When they reached the stairwell, Lina sat down on the top step. "Too dark. Don't want to go down."

"Damn it, Lina! Help me save you!" Viola pushed her sister onto her back, grabbed her by the feet, and started dragging her down the stairs. It was bang her head or let her burn!

"Here, I'll get her shoulders." Nurse Andrews appeared out of the murk, climbing past Viola to lift Lina's upper body as easily as she might a child. "You shouldn't be straining yourself, Miss Archer. You'll hurt the baby."

Viola almost fainted with relief, but not quite. She hadn't forgotten the last time she'd seen Nurse Archer have her sister carried away. "My baby is fine. I'm going to save us all and then put you in jail." The words popped out of her mouth before she realized that she ought perhaps to save the threatening until she'd reached Badger's side.

"I know," the nurse said. "That's why I'm helping. You'll put in a good word for me, won't you, Miss Archer? I've done right by you all along, haven't I?"

Viola had to admit the fairness of that. "Get us to the gate and I'll see what I can do."

"Fair enough."

They made it to the landing and awkwardly juggled their burden around the turn.

"Why did you protect me?" Viola asked. "I saw the letter from Lady Brockaway. I'm supposed to be up there too, dead to the world."

"I wouldn't harm an innocent babe," Andrews said, "whatever kind of whore his mother might be. Poor wee thing. It's not his fault, is it?"

Viola bit back a retort. *Later, later.* "You like babies, then, do you? Odd line of work you chose, in that case."

They reached the bottom and began waddling toward the main doors. Not far now.

"My sister has a baby," Andrews said. "Poor little mite. His father wouldn't marry her, you see, nor even admit she was carrying his child. I didn't know. She didn't tell me until they'd both gotten sick." She grunted as she shifted her grip on Angelina. "I've got them both in a nice place now, clean and safe, but not cheap. That's why I need money. These useless women here, they don't deserve half of what they've got. It's only fair for them to pass it on."

"That's it? That's your excuse?" Viola goggled at her in sheer disbelief. "These women are past their prime and enjoy a little well-earned luxury, so you murder them?"

"They'll die soon enough anyway," the nurse said.

Viola found herself at a loss for a smart retort for the first time in her life. "You're lucky I keep my promises."

She lowered Lina's legs to the floor to open the terrace doors, then helped her murdering savior lug her intended victim out into the night.

"Look, James! Look!" Lina cried, waking up now the hard work was done. She pointed at the burning roof of the new wing, laughing as red and gold sparks burst into the air. "Fireworks! Hooray! Long live the queen!"

* * *

Moriarty snuggled his wife to his chest, luxuriating in her warm — very warm — embrace. He bent his head for another languorous kiss when she shook him, hard.

"Wake up!"

"Angelina?"

"No. Holmes. Wake up! Damn it, man, shake it off!"

Moriarty swam back to the present. He was still in Oliver's study, still tied to a chair. He shook his head and groaned.

The narrow face of Sherlock Holmes loomed into his view, dark eyes probing. "We must make our exit posthaste, Professor, before the fire spreads to this

275

building." He knelt behind the chair and started tugging at the ropes.

Moriarty cleared his throat and worked his jaw. As the ropes fell away, he stretched his arms and rolled his shoulders. "How did you get free? How did you recover from the drugs?"

"To answer the second question, I have by nature a phenomenal metabolism. Also, I have been incrementally making myself proof against such an attack. In my line of work, I expose myself to enemies of the most nefarious kind and must be prepared for anything."

Moriarty heard the word "phenomenal" and let the rest flow past in a stream of Holmes-babble. "I'm in your debt. We could have died here tonight."

Holmes accepted the thanks with a raised eyebrow. "I'm not sure we would have. I'm not half as groggy as I would expect to be. Either the doctor did not intend to kill us, but only to delay us, or he miscalculated the dosage. He's used to treating women, remember."

"And in a hurry, I suppose." Moriarty got to his feet and tested his legs. They worked. "And the ropes?"

Holmes flashed a grin. "Practice, Professor. I've had Watson tie me to a variety of chairs. The secret is to fill the lungs and flex the muscles as the ropes are being tightened. Then when you relax, you have enough play to work the knot under your fingers. The rest is mere dexterity."

"Good gad, Holmes. What an odd life you lead." Moriarty sniffed at the air. "Is that smoke?"

"I believe that's what roused me. Some deep instinctive sense of survival."

"Thank God for it," Moriarty said. "Shall we go?"

They helped each other through the cluttered room, neither yet quite steady on his feet. They found a thin layer of smoke rolling across the ceiling in the corridor.

"No heat yet," Holmes said, pausing to study the scene.

"Well, let's not wait for it." Moriarty tugged at his sleeve and started moving toward the door to the outside.

Holmes turned too fast and stumbled on the edge of the carpet. He caught his foot in the hem of his dress, tearing it with a loud rip, and fell headlong to the floor. "Damnation!"

Moriarty helped him up. "Watch your feet. I'd forgotten we were wearing these awkward things."

They tore off their dresses and tossed them aside. James threw his floppy bonnet after them. Then each wrapped an arm around the other for support as they hobbled the length of the corridor, wary of further traps. They gained the outer door at last and stumbled onto the drive.

They were met by a scene of controlled excitement, with one group of men chasing sparks to beat them out with burlap sacks while others manned the giant hose leading out of the basement of the main house, spraying water on the few flames still shooting out of the east wing. Attendants herded a few stragglers toward the cluster of women beside the gate.

The two men picked up their pace, forcing strength back into their drug-weakened limbs. When they'd cut the distance in half, Holmes stopped. "I say, Moriarty. About that stumble back there with the dress. And letting ourselves be chloroformed, and the minor fact that we seem to have panicked and forgotten to search —"

Moriarty cut him off with a wave of his hand. "Let us never speak of it again, not any of it. Not to Angelina. Not even to Watson."

Holmes snorted. "Especially not Watson."

# Chapter Twenty-Seven

Angelina slurped hot tea from the bottle Gabriel Sandy kept wrapped in rags in his cab, feeling more like herself with every well-sugared sip. A good cup of tea could fix practically anything — except her dread for James, who had gone into that maelstrom in a valiant, misguided attempt to save her.

She struggled to see through the throng of men crowding her view, all dark-clothed and purposeful, striding here and there. Tall men, short men, men in hats. None of them were James. Smoke hung over the whole scene, eerie in the weak moonlight. "Where did all these people come from?" she asked Sandy.

He explained the ingenious plan James had devised to rescue her and Viola. She assumed James had a plan for arresting the doctors before they could escape the country. They might have heard about the fire already. It must be visible for miles. Nurse Andrews had come out with them and had been handed over to a local constable.

"There they are!" Zeke shouted. He'd been standing on top of the cab watching the road to the main house.

She saw them too now, the tall, familiar figure of her husband beside a man of equal height who must be Holmes. Both appeared to be in one piece, if a little wobbly.

She thrust her mug at Sandy and stumbled up the drive, not too steady on her pins yet herself. "James! James!"

"Angelina!" A few more strides and his strong arms were wrapped around her, holding her tightly against his chest. Tears sprang into her eyes as her heart regained its proper rhythm now that it had its mate again. They stood like that for an uncountable span, then drew in deep breaths. Together again. And safe.

They walked arm in arm to join the others. James nodded at Badger, who stood with his arms wrapped around Viola, his wide hands protecting her belly.

"Viola," James said. "Thank goodness. You appear to be unharmed."

"She saved me, James," Angelina said. "She was so brave. I didn't know she had it in her."

Viola shrugged off the compliment. "I have a few surprises left."

Angelina beamed at her, then tilted her face up to wink at her husband. "You'll never believe this, darling. Badger was so relieved to get her back he actually almost smiled."

"Now I am shocked," James said, winking back.

Badger, bless his stolid heart, frowned. Perhaps he feared any display of emotion would open the flood gates.

Holmes strolled over to join their group. He must have been talking to the firemen, indulging his insatiable curiosity. He acknowledged the women with a nod and a correct, "Ladies." Then he said, "Viscount Brockaway, I presume. I hope you'll forgive the informality and allow me to introduce myself. I am Sherlock Holmes."

The well-bred viscount managed to keep his eyes on Holmes's face while the rest of them gaped at the top of his head. He was wearing a brown wig styled in a high French pompadour. He seemed unaware of the accoutrement, standing with his usual erect posture and speaking in his usual crisp public-school tones.

James cleared his throat to catch Holmes's attention, tapping his own head. Holmes pulled off the irregular headgear with a rueful smile. "A well-fitted wig is more comfortable than one might imagine."

"You should keep it," Viola advised, ever practical in such matters.

"You need no introduction, Mr. Holmes," Badger said, extending a hand for a hearty shake. "I'm forever in your debt. If your well-honed instincts hadn't prompted you to take Mr. Wexcombe's story seriously, I might have lost my dearest treasure."

James said, "We all owe Holmes a great debt. Without his insuffer — I mean, his persistent prodding, the worst might have befallen us. As it is, I'm glad to see we've all made it through without a loss."

"Loss!" Angelina cried. "I knew there was something missing. What on earth has happened to your moustache?"

"Oh yes." James rubbed his upper lip. "No sacrifice too great, my dear. It'll grow back."

"My lord?" August Norton appeared, pulling off his crested helmet. "The fire's out. The men are making sure they haven't missed any embers."

"Good work," Badger said. "I'll see that you all receive special commendation."

"That'd be right decent of you, my lord. They're good men." Norton shot a grin at Captain Sandy, who had been standing at the edge of the group listening to their banter with half an ear while he continued to receive reports from his boys. "We also caught a sly-looking fellow sneaking out of a little gate in the ivy. The captain here warned us to keep an eye on it."

"Dr. Oliver, no doubt," James said with a significant glance at Holmes. "I'm glad you caught him."

"Nothing gets past my boys." Sandy turned a wry frown at the smoking mess inside the grounds. "Although they do get carried away at times."

Holmes followed his gaze. "Is it safe to go inside the main building, Mr. Norton?"

"I wouldn't recommend it. There's gas pipes in every corridor, up and down. Until we're absolutely certain, it's best to keep a distance. The women are being taken across the street into private houses for the time being."

"I need fifteen minutes in that office," Holmes said. "We still need proof if we want a conviction."

"Proof, did you say?" Viola reached into the pocket of her bedraggled robe and pulled out the notebook with the bundle of letters. "Something like this, perhaps?"

Holmes accepted the materials. "Miss Archer, I stand amazed." He bowed his head to her. He opened the notebook, squinting at the pages in the faint light. "It's too dark to read, but I believe this should serve our purposes handily." He fingered the bundle of envelopes. "Are these the letters from other clients?"

"Yes," Angelina said.

"Excellent." Holmes handed it all to Badger. "My lord, perhaps you should keep these until we can deliver them to an officer of the court."

Badger accepted the packet and tucked it into his coat pocket, then he wrapped both arms around Viola again. Watching them made Angelina long to go home. She wanted a bath. She wanted to see Peg. She wanted more tea. And oddly she wanted a dish of plain scrambled eggs and toast.

Mr. Norton had one more task for them that night. "Forgive me for asking, Mr. Moriarty, but what about my Flora? When will we get her out of jail?"

"We'll go at once," Badger said. "I owe both of you a debt as well. My coach is just around the corner. We'll go down and shake up a judge at the Old Bailey."

The group broke up. Sandy said, "I'd better collect my boys. That deserted hospital is too great a temptation."

"Take them all out for a feast," James said. "On me." He dug into his pocket and handed over a fistful of coins.

Holmes followed Sandy, saying, "How do you choose your boys, Captain? Or do you let them choose you?"

Angelina and James were left alone in the shadow of the iron gates. Firemen still roved about shouting, but most of the townsfolk seemed to have drifted off. She looked a proper mess in her dirty nightgown with a rough blanket around her shoulders and a pair of Sandy's extra socks on her feet. Heaven only knew what state her hair was in!

These weren't exactly the most romantic conditions, but a girl had to work with what she had. She faced her husband, lacing her arms through his to clasp them behind his back. She looked up at him and smiled into his eyes.

"James, darling, there are things I have to tell you. Things about me. My past. I wasn't ready before, but now — well, now I think it's time."

James smoothed a hair from her brow, smiling at her as if discovering her all over again. "Whatever you wish, my angel, whenever you wish. And I promise you, this time I'll be ready to listen."

# Chapter Twenty-Eight

James Moriarty sat on the terrace of the Beaumont Hotel in Torquay reading the London papers. This would be their last morning at the seaside. After three weeks, the doctor had declared them fully restored and ready to return to their normal lives. The sea air and healthy diet had removed all traces of drugs from their systems. Memories of the peril they'd come through would linger in their minds, but not, thank goodness, in their bodies.

They'd get home just in time to enjoy front-row seats at the trial of the century. The papers rumored that Lady Brockaway herself might be haled into court to explain the letter in her writing requesting the "Clennam treatment" for her husband's long-standing and very pregnant mistress.

The past three weeks had been blissful. He and Angelina had indulged themselves in the best suite of rooms, taking meals on their private terrace as often as not. No temperamental servants to placate, no noisy workmen to avoid. No harrowing nights alone and sleepless, worrying that they'd never have a chance to get past their messy beginnings and build a life together.

The one blemish on their healing respite had come when a middle-aged man wearing a gold watch chain and several expensive rings had approached Moriarty in the smoking room after overhearing a conversation with another fellow about the health of their wives.

"I have a tip for you," he said. "A way to take care of those Mrs. Clennams once and for all."

Moriarty had knocked him to the floor with one well-placed blow. Then he'd grasped the varlet by the collar and the seat of his tailored pants, hauled him through the French doors, and thrown him into the fountain.

That incident inspired him to have a word with the hotel's director, who had been so horrified by what he heard that he'd sent for the police to have the varlet arrested. He'd treated the old tabbies to a week of full services at no charge and begged the Moriartys to consider themselves his guests whenever they chose to visit.

The letters Angelina had found in Oliver's study had led the authorities to a dozen other deaths, which were being reexamined in the light of the new evidence. The whole murder-for-hire operation had been perpetrated by only three persons. Robert Trumbull, the old fraud, had convinced the grand jury of his innocence and escaped to his family home in Scotland. At least his career on Harley Street was over. Alan Fairchild had not been seen since the night of the fire at Halcyon House.

Mrs. Northwood, who had been picked up at her home near Regent's Park, confessed that she and Gideon Oliver had cooked up the scheme together at a benefit dinner for the asylum at Colney Hatch. She hadn't administered any drugs or electric shocks herself, which might save her from hanging, but she would spend the rest of her life in jail.

Dr. Oliver faced certain execution. His notebook had appalled the whole civilized world. Everything in it had been corroborated by Nurse Andrews, who was talking as fast as she could to save her own neck. Her current address was Newgate Prison. Moriarty hoped she had been locked into Flora Semple's cell. He had an appreciation for symmetry.

\* \* \*

Angelina did a terrible job of concealing her excitement as they drew closer to home. James quirked a smile at her. "What's all this giggling in aid of?"

"I have a confession to make, darling."

"What, another one?" They'd told each other their whole life histories, from birth forward, snuggled into the downy bed in the hotel. Each had been astonished to learn that the other had known their marriage wasn't legal and even more astonished to learn that neither one of them very much cared. Even so, they planned to rectify that minor error as soon as they could reach an agreement on the size of the wedding party.

"One last secret," she said. "You'll like it, I hope."

Rolly flung wide the door, grinning from ear to ear, resplendent in blue livery. He greeted them in a near approximation of the English language. Someone had been giving him lessons in their absence.

Everyone crowded into the hall to welcome them home: Peg, Antoine, the mouse maids, and Rolly. Handshakes were exchanged all around. The crisis of the past month had turned this chilly house full of secrets into a warm home filled with friends.

Angelina pulled Moriarty into the dining room, whose walls had been newly papered in a sedate pattern of brown and russet foliage, echoed in the tawny brocade draperies. A fire glowed in the hearth, with the smoke flowing cleanly up the flue.

The room beyond it had enjoyed the same expert rehabilitation. The sober wallpaper had been carried through, avoiding the jarring mismatch of the previous arrangement, but here it was lightened by a stained-glass window set into the far wall. A writing desk and chair had been placed in the nook beneath the window. Too small for Moriarty's purposes, but a pleasant place for Angelina to manage her morning correspondence. A comfortable armchair sat by the hearth with a good lamp on the table beside it.

"What do you think?" Angelina asked. "It's a morning room. Look, you can read the newspapers there while I write my letters."

"It's an island of peace where once all was storm."

She bit her lip, pleased. "I hired Viola's decorating firm to do everything. It's cost a fortune, but —"

Moriarty stopped her with a kiss. "We'll go back to Vichy after Christmas and refill our coffers."

So that's what all the telegrams had been about! He'd assumed it was baby business and kept his nose out. He wouldn't mind becoming an uncle, though he'd been relieved to learn he would never have to share his wife with any children of their own. Rescuing strays and well-meaning criminals strained his paternal capacity to the limit. "Shall we see what's been done upstairs?" he asked, holding out his elbow.

More of the same in lighter colors, befitting the feminine character of a drawing room. The rococo chairs had vanished, replaced by sturdier, yet stylish, seats in various styles. The back windows had also been replaced with stained glass, admitting a soft light that reflected off the small grand piano. Both fires had been lit in honor of their homecoming. The room felt warm and inviting.

"Perfect," Moriarty said. Then he held up a hand. "But wait." He cocked his head, listening, then let out a sigh of relief. The household clocks still ticked out of rhythm. As they began to chime the quarter hour in their unruly round, he tilted his head back and laughed. "Your decorators missed that small detail."

"No, they didn't. They brought a man in to fix the clocks, but the housemaids stopped him. Peg wrote me about it. She said poor Rolly nearly fainted with astonishment when the little dears blocked the man's way and spoke to him directly. They said Master had gotten very fierce about them clocks and wouldn't let nobody touch 'em." Angelina laughed. "I must say it surprised me too."

"Bless those girls," Moriarty said fervently. "Bless them all. Give everyone a raise, as much as you like. I could never have gotten through . . ." Tears clogged his throat until he remembered that all was well. He kissed his wife again — something that couldn't be done often enough. "Well, my dear, it appears we have a home at last."

"There's more. Something for you on the top floor."

"Really?" He gave her a puzzled look but climbed the stairs to the fourth floor. He hadn't been up here since they'd bought the place, when it had been cold and stuffy, half full of moth-eaten castoffs and dusty crates.

He didn't recognize it as the same space. The ceiling had been removed and the rafters painted white. The windows had been repaired and fitted with shutters. A small fireplace he hadn't noticed before was lined with blue-and-white tiles, the mantel built up into a set of glass-fronted shelves, already loaded with reference books and scientific instruments. More shelves ran around the room just above head-height. Moriarty spotted his own collection, ordered by topic, the way he liked them.

A large oak table dominated the long room. They must have assembled it in place. It was big enough to unroll a map of the whole metropolitan area, which he knew because such a map was now spread across its surface. Stools had been placed around the table and a pair of comfortable reading chairs sat before the hearth. A telescope stood at the foot of a spiral staircase leading up to a trapdoor in the roof.

A man could accomplish all sorts of things in this enviable workplace. His workplace. He could write monographs or analyze demographic trends. He could practice tying himself to a chair, if he felt so inclined. He could invent his own career, perhaps giving London's only consulting detective a run for his money.

"Do you like it?" Angelina asked. He hadn't heard her come up.

"It's a paradise. My dearest, darling wife! How on earth did you know?"

She shrugged, all innocence. "I had a little help. Viola told the decorators to consult with Sherlock Holmes."

Laughter bubbled up in Moriarty's belly, growing into a hearty peal, echoing from the rafters of his new sanctuary.

# Historical Notes

### Real people and places

I fashioned everyone in this book out of whole cloth, except for Sir Arthur Conan Doyle's immortals: Sherlock Holmes, John Watson, and James Moriarty. I reshaped them, obviously, for my own narrative purposes. This is one of the risks of fame — that your works will outlive you and become the playthings of lesser minds.

The Middlesex County Pauper Lunatic Asylum at Colney Hatch was absolutely real, operating from 1851 to 1993. I've blogged about it (www.annacastle.com/blog/), if you want to read a little more. Look under the categories 'Medicine' or 'Places of Interest.'

I cheerfully appropriated the beautiful Linley Sambourne House in South Kensington, London as the model for the Moriartys' new house. It's open to the public, managed by The Royal Borough of Kensington and Chelsea, and well worth a visit. You can find pictures of this on my blog as well.

I chose Hampstead because I've been there and it's lovely and because it once enjoyed some renown as the source of iron-bearing waters once regarded as medicinal. The wall around Halcyon House is much like the wall around Fenton House on Hampstead Grove; otherwise, the place is pure invention.

# About the Author

Anna Castle holds an eclectic set of degrees: BA in the Classics, MS in Computer Science, and a Ph.D. in Linguistics. She has had a correspondingly eclectic series of careers: waitressing, software engineering, grammar-writing, a short stint as an associate professor, and managing a digital archive. Historical fiction combines her lifelong love of stories and learning. She physically resides in Austin, Texas, but mentally counts herself a queen of infinite space.

# Books by Anna Castle

Keep up with all my books and short stories with my newsletter: www.annacastle.com

## The Francis Bacon Series

### Book 1, *Murder by Misrule*

Francis Bacon is charged with investigating the murder of a fellow barrister at Gray's Inn. He recruits his unwanted protégé Thomas Clarady to do the tiresome legwork. The son of a privateer, Clarady will do anything to climb the Elizabethan social ladder. Bacon's powerful uncle Lord Burghley suspects Catholic conspirators of the crime, but other motives quickly emerge. Rival barristers contend for the murdered man's legal honors and wealthy clients. Highly-placed courtiers are implicated as the investigation reaches from Whitehall to the London streets. Bacon does the thinking; Clarady does the fencing. Everyone has something up his pinked and padded sleeve. Even the brilliant Francis Bacon is at a loss — and in danger — until he sees through the disguises of the season of Misrule.

### Book 2, *Death by Disputation*

Thomas Clarady is recruited to spy on the increasingly rebellious Puritans at Cambridge University. Francis Bacon is his spymaster; his tutor in both tradecraft and religious politics. Their commission gets off to a deadly start when Tom finds his chief informant hanging from the roof beams. Now he must catch a murderer as well as a seditioner. His first suspect is volatile poet Christopher Marlowe, who keeps turning up in the wrong places.

Dogged by unreliable assistants, chased by three lusty women, and harangued daily by the exacting Bacon, Tom risks his very soul to catch the villains and win his reward.

## Book 3, *The Widows Guild*

In the summer of 1588, Europe waits with bated breath for King Philip of Spain to launch his mighty armada against England. Everyone except Lady Alice Trumpington, whose father wants her wed to the highest bidder. She doesn't want to be a wife, she wants to be widow; a rich one, and the sooner, the better. So she marries an elderly viscount, gives him a sleeping draught, and spends her wedding night with Thomas Clarady, her best friend and Francis Bacon's assistant. The next morning, they find the viscount murdered in his bed and they're both locked into the Tower.

Lady Alice appeals to the Andromache Society, the widows' guild led by Francis Bacon's formidable aunt, Lady Russell. They charge Bacon with getting the new widow out of prison and identifying the real murderer. He soon learns the viscount wasn't an isolated case. Someone is murdering Catholics in London and taking advantage of armada fever to mask the crimes. The killer seems to have privy information — from someone close to the Privy Council?

The investigation takes Francis from the mansions along the Strand to the rack room under the Tower. Pulled and pecked by a coven of demanding widows, Francis struggles to maintain his reason and his courage to see through the fog of war and catch the killer.